Genny could feel Tristen's heart beating swiftly against her own breast and as he trailed hot kisses down the curve of her neck, she sighed with the pure pleasure of it.

"Why are we always quarreling?" she murmured.

"I do not know. But I think we have found a place for peace. Perhaps we should stay in bed all the time."

" 'Tis morning, milord," she protested mildly.

"Art thou shy, Lady Genevieve?"

"They await our arrival downstairs."

"Let them wait," he replied as his busy hands continued to roam freely over her body.

"But they will think . . ."

"And they will be absolutely right," he rasped as he rolled her over, pinning her body beneath his, letting her feel how much he wanted her.

PASSIONATE SURRENDER

SHERYL SAGE

AVON BOOKS ◆ NEW YORK

PASSIONATE SURRENDER is an original publication of Avon Books. This work has never before appeared in book form. This work is a novel. Any similarity to actual persons or events is purely coincidental.

AVON BOOKS
A division of
The Hearst Corporation
1350 Avenue of the Americas
New York, New York 10019

First Avon Books Printing: September 1993

AVON TRADEMARK REG. U.S. PAT. OFF. AND IN OTHER COUNTRIES, MARCA REGISTRADA, HECHO EN U.S.A.

Printed in the U.S.A.

RA 10 9 8 7 6 5 4 3 2 1

This book is dedicated to Joe and Mike who believe, encourage, and support us in all things. We love you guys! And to Pamela, Shayla, and Phillip (the computer orphans), thanks for understanding our dream. Without all of you we could never have done it.

A special thanks to Ellen Edwards and Christine Zika of Avon Books for all their help and support.

And to Mom and Dad who think there's nothing I can't do. I love you both.

—SM

Prologue

England, 1278

The warm breeze drifting across the lush green hillside did little to soften the hearts or countenances of the two men silhouetted against the blinding sun.

Devoid of any true remorse, the black-clad priest hurried through the liturgy, his flushed, heavy jowls fluttering with each intonement. His brow furrowed as his gaze shifted to the countenance of the large man facing him. The man's square jaw was tightly clenched, his blue eyes icy and unresponsive. The granite expression prompted the holy man to hasten his benediction. Then, snapping closed his prayer book, he tugged nervously at the sweat-soaked collar of his robe.

The other man's black hair took on highlights of blue as he stepped forward. Reaching down, he grabbed a handful of the cool, freshly turned earth heaped beside the deep hole. As he raised himself, his immense form seemed to eclipse the sun and fill the cavity with murky shadows.

1

His movements were slow, glacial, as though time itself were suspended. He turned his hand, releasing its contents, allowing them to spill mutely into the dark depression. His words, although spoken quietly and calmly, could not disguise the unbridled anger in his voice.

"May you live in hell, Kathryn, as I do now."

As the remaining soil blew away from the man's hand, the priest raised his eyes to the stony visage.

By tacit consent, they turned and walked away, leaving the grave-diggers to their task of covering the coffin.

Chapter 1

Westminster Palace, 1282

When the two knights rode through the castle gates, their bedraggled appearance hinted at the long and tiring journey they had endured. As they dismounted from their horses, Lord Tristen Sinclair, Earl of Ravenswood, handed his reins to the stable boy who had come to tend them.

"Take care, son; 'tis the finest piece of flesh this side of heaven."

"Aye, milord," answered the lad, addressing the large, imposing, dark-haired knight who, even in his dusty attire, exuded power and authority. And he reverently grasped the reins of the enormous, awe-inspiring, coal-black stallion to lead it and the other animal away.

"Most men would refer to their mistress as such, not their mount," said Alexander with a low chuckle.

"Nay, Demon is far easier to handle than a mistress, and not nearly as demanding," replied Tristen, his full lips quirked wryly.

3

"Mayhap, but I would still rather bed a wench than my horse."

Both men chuckled as they ascended the massive stone stairs into the castle. They had barely entered through the archway leading to the great hall when a plump, saucy wench approached them. She was beyond the bloom of youth, but her face still showed signs of the beauty she must have been at one time. Her clothes were made to display her more-than-ample figure, leaving her shoulders bare and her breasts nearly so.

Her voice was a honeyed caress when she spoke. "We thought you would never get here!" She brushed her large bosom enticingly against Alexander's arm.

"And miss seeing you, Jane? Perish the thought," said Alexander in a familiar, jesting tone.

"Follow me, milord, and I be showing you to your room," she said, respectfully addressing the Earl of Ravenswood. "And if you wait here for my return," she added, running her fingers down Alexander's chest, "I might be willing to see to some entertainment for you later." She winked up at the handsome warrior, giving promise to the night's activities.

"You'll get no argument from me, Jane," said Alexander. "However, Lord Tristen may choose to sleep in the stable tonight." He laughed heartily while Tristen scowled in his direction.

"Just make sure you are fit to ride out in the morning," replied Tristen, command in his voice. "As soon as this meeting is over, we will be heading back to the camp."

Alexander knew it was so. Of late Tristen took little time for himself or physical pleasures. He was an excellent leader, always thinking of his men, but sometimes Alexander wished he would wear his mantle of responsibility a little more loosely.

It had been twelve years since they had met, both young and fearless knights then. Friendship had flourished naturally between them. That was before Tristen's marriage to Kathryn Aldred. Before he had become the Earl of Ravenswood. Before so many circumstances had changed his friend forever.

Alexander knew that beneath all of Tristen's gruffness lay a man with a warm heart. He was also one of the few who knew the pain that underlay the iron-clad exterior his friend displayed. Long had he hoped for some occurrence to bring back to life the inner man Tristen had buried so deeply.

"Offer the king my respects, Tristen, and should you have need of me, I will be no farther than my bed." With that Alexander playfully patted Jane's backside before she preceded the earl up the stone staircase from the great hall to the sleeping chambers reserved for visiting nobility.

As Tristen sat soaking in the bath Jane had drawn for him, the tepid water washing away his fatigue, he wondered again why he had been summoned here from his tour at the northern border. Perhaps King Edward required only a report on his progress. But if he had wanted merely that, would he not have sent a runner? No, Tristen suspected that his monarch wanted more than a report. But what?

Rising wearily but somewhat refreshed from his lengthy soak, he concluded that the only way to find out was to see Edward himself.

Edward, King of England, leaned back in his ornate chair. He had just finished a splendid meal, and two goblets of fine sweet wine had lent a mellowness to his disposition.

"You have word of the Earl of Ravenswood?" he asked, looking to his devoted secretary, Robert Burnell.

"Aye, sire. He has arrived."

"Good. We are most anxious to hasten this matter, as is our loyal friend, the Earl of Montburough."

The king stared past Burnell, thinking of Richard Warren, Earl of Montburough. The man not only stood steadfastly for the crown but also had shown himself over the years to be a true friend to Edward. Alas, even being a trusted ally of the king did not shield a warrior from the atrocities of battle. Edward closed his eyes, reliving his friend's unfortunate accident of five years ago as if it were yesterday.

Richard had felt that to guard Edward's back in battle was both a duty and an honor. On that particular day the fighting had been exceptionally brutal, with heavy casualties on both sides. Richard's horse, though battle-trained, had become frantic and unmanageable under the relentless clash and fury and the cloying smell of blood that filled the air. Even in remembrance Edward physically shuddered, as once again he saw Richard thrown from his mount, trampled in a wild frenzy by the animal's powerful hooves.

Richard had survived but had never walked again, his lower limbs rendered tragically useless. And now this man, to whom the king had on more than one occasion willingly entrusted his very life, was entreating him to ensure his daughter's future. A small enough favor to ask, yet one of consequence to both Montburough and the king.

Edward was all too aware of the unscrupulous adventurers who preyed on heiresses, hoping to steal their property, and Montburough was one of the crown's holdings that he had no intention of letting fall into the wrong hands. It was his strongest fortification along the strategically important west coast near Bristol. The earl's declining health and the unmarried state of his named heir, Lady Genevieve Warren, gave the king adequate cause for concern.

Edward's mouth twitched in amusement as he reflected on Lady Genevieve. Over the years he'd heard a great deal about Richard Warren's daughter, not the least of which was her expertise with weapons, including his own favorite, the longbow. He had seen her once as a very young maiden. At that time few could have rivaled her beauty, and Edward had no reason to doubt she would still outshine many a female subject.

In his latest missive Richard had praised not only her favorable appearance but also her expert ability to administrate the estate and its people. Edward knew that, had it not been for the accident that had left Richard bedridden, the man would have seen his daughter married years ago. But many a time his friend had written of his selfishness in keeping her close, Lady Genevieve being such a comfort to him in his otherwise barren life. Edward doubted that Richard would even now have written asking him to arrange a marriage were it not for the threat imposed by Richard's nephew, Philip Aldred, with his persistent supplications of late for Lady Genevieve's hand. His objections to his nephew made clear, Richard had relinquished the ultimate decision regarding a suitable husband for his daughter to the king's sole discretion.

The king now rose to his considerable height, which was head and shoulders above ordinary men.

"Tell me, Burnell, what think you of Philip Aldred?"

Clearing his throat, Burnell ventured, "He seems most favored by the women of the court, sire."

"He is favorable to look at, I grant you that. But what of his character?" he asked rhetorically. Burnell remained silent. "From what I have gleaned, he is weak and indolent, as was his father," Edward mused.

Walter Aldred, too, had been considered

handsome by the females of the court, Edward
remembered. Unfortunately, his pleasing physical features were his only attributes. Still, they
had been enough to lure Beatrice Warren into a
secret marriage, against the wishes of her older
brother. Walter had smugly informed Richard
Warren of the union only after he had gotten
Beatrice with child. Confident that the honorable Earl of Montburough would provide for his
sister and her family—including himself—the
slothful laggard had squandered his property in
foolhardy wagers. Walter Aldred's reckless
management of his holdings and shiftless neglect of his responsibilities had caused the
crown to strip him of his title. Upon his death,
he had left only a meager parcel of land as an
inheritance to his infant son, Philip, and a pal-
try dowry for Philip's older sister, Kathryn.

Edward picked up the curled parchment
Richard Warren had sent and unrolled it before
handing it to Burnell.

Robert quickly perused its contents. "The
Earl of Montburough appears most distressed
at leaving an heiress daughter for young Aldred
to prey upon," he commented.

Edward settled his gaze on Burnell, flashing
the charming smile that induced all in his service to gladly do his bidding. "My friend Richard Warren no longer need worry. We have
seen to that, have we not, Burnell?"

"Aye, sire."

The king rubbed his hands together, well
pleased. "Have Sinclair sent to me."

"Aye, sire. Immediately," replied Burnell.

* * *

With the word *marriage* ringing in his ears, Tristen was glad all his years as a knight had taught him to stay steady on his feet even when his knees could barely support him.

The king continued speaking, having taken slight notice of Tristen's altered composure.

"You are one of my most trusted and loyal knights, as was your father before you. It is my wish that this marriage take place with all possible speed. I hear she is a most comely woman, Sinclair, and comes to you fully dowered with land and a prosperous estate."

Having finally recovered enough to address the king, Tristen stepped forward, determined to persuade Edward to reassess his decision.

"Sire, is there not another more worthy of the maiden's hand?"

An ardent advocate of the holy state of matrimony since his marriage to Eleanor of Castile, the king quickly dismissed Sinclair's reluctance. He was not to be dissuaded from his promise to his friend Richard Warren, especially when he was convinced of the rightness of the union.

"Nay, Sinclair, you are most worthy of the match. I would want no less. The woman comes with the highest of recommendations from my advisors, and her father is a loyal and admirable man as well as a friend to the crown." Stroking the short dark beard covering his lean jaw, the king paused before revealing the identity of the bride.

"The Earl of Montburough has long and

faithfully served this crown. Now his declining health has prompted him to petition my aid in obtaining a suitable husband for his only child.''

Tristen's face contorted under the impact of Edward's disclosure. The Earl of Montburough's daughter! Kathryn Aldred's cousin! Was this the king's idea of some obscene joke? If so, the humor was lost on Tristen.

Sinclair was certain that the king, with his customary thoroughness, was acquainted with his knight's disastrous marriage to Kathryn Aldred. So this proposal that he marry a blood relation of Kathryn's fairly reeked of perversion.

''Sire, you cannot mean for me to marry—'' Tristen began, only to be interrupted by Edward.

''You have been alone for too long, Tristen. It is time to see you married again. And if it pleases the throne also, so be it,'' he added, making a dismissive movement with his hand.

To his horrified chagrin, Tristen realized that no amount of persuasion would alter the king's decision. Edward was always steadfast in his resolutions. Straightening himself, he replied in the only acceptable manner.

''Aye, sire.''

''Married!'' The word burst forth from Alexander amid great and hearty laughter. Tristen was sure that, even though they were in his private chamber above the great hall, everyone in the castle must have heard Alexander's mirthful outcry.

"I would that my predicament not be known to all within these walls," he said in a tone that sobered Alexander quickly.

"When is the blessed event to take place?" asked Alexander in a more subdued but still mildly taunting manner.

"I will sign the marriage contract tomorrow."

"Tomorrow! Edward wastes no time."

"Aye. Then we leave to rejoin our men and continue the campaign. Edward has already dispatched a messenger to the Earl of Montburough, and I'll send my brother in my stead. Christopher can wed the wench for me by proxy."

Alexander knew this situation was most unsettling for his friend; however, he couldn't help but find it quite amusing. Tristen, always so self-contained, was completely beside himself with agitation. If nothing else, this turn of events had stirred some emotion in the man, albeit only anger and frustration at the moment.

"I would not have my wife know nothing of the pleasures of marriage for such a long time," said Alexander in his casual, jesting way.

"I would that she never know," replied Tristen, bitterness hardening his features.

"My friend, there are advantages to having a woman at your beck and call," Alexander pointed out.

"There were few enough advantages the first time," Tristen responded tersely, thinking of his previous marriage.

Kathryn had been beautiful and he young and

naively in love. So enamored of her was he that
even her modest dowry had not affected his decision to wed her. Unfortunately, it was not until after their marriage that Tristen had
discovered Kathryn's inability to love anyone
other than herself. The memory of her vanity
evoked a loathing in him that had not dimin-
ished even though she'd been dead for more
than four years.

Tristen rose from his chair. Walking to the
fireplace, he leaned one large hand on the mantel and stared into the flames, his whole being
engulfed in fatigue and despair.

"I am most sure that a woman who waits till
the age of one and twenty to be married is either
as cold as a winter wind or as wanton as one of
Jane's chambermaids," he said with disgust as
he pressed both hands to his eyes, fighting the
stinging weariness in them.

"Mayhap you misjudge the lady. Warren is
an honorable man. He would not offer what is
not fit for having."

"Nay?" Tristen said with caustic insinuation.

"Mayhap you would do better to go see for
yourself before we rejoin the men," said Alexander as he handed his distressed friend a
brimming goblet of ale.

"Nay. She can wait till our tour is complete,"
Tristen replied, knowing that, with only a
month left in his annual obligation to the king,
he would scarcely delay the inevitable. "When
I return, she will soon find out that my loyalties
are to the crown and not to some wretched

wench. I will not play husband to Warren's
daughter, be she virgin or slut.''

Alexander winced at the harsh words. He
knew Tristen would not have been receptive to
any matrimonial alliance. But for the prospec-
tive bride to have the misfortune of being a close
relation of Kathryn's clearly trebled Tristen's
ire.

''Perhaps you shall change your mind once
you see her,'' Alexander offered lamely.

''Doubtful, my optimistic friend. Or has it escaped your attention that the king may have
deliberately chosen not to show the wife before
marriage for fear she might displease?'' Tristen
drained the remaining contents of the goblet
before banging it down on the mantel. Scowling, he muttered, ''Edward may be content to
be bound by the shackles of marriage. I, however, am not!''

Chapter 2

Montburough Castle

Genevieve Warren pulled back the tapestries shrouding her bedchamber window and looked below to the gardens. The brilliance of the blossoms was breathtaking, even from this distance. The blooms were all the luminous colors of the rainbow, and although they had lost some of their magnificence in the past two weeks, they were still captivating. She turned slightly toward the immense trees silhouetted against the pale morning sky. They always reminded her of brave sentinels ready to defend the garden against all intruders. The fanciful notion brought a smile to her lips, but it soon gave way to a somber expression as she realized that even the dusty green leaves were showing signs that summer was coming to an end. That thought, and the nip in the air, made her shiver slightly.

Lost to all else, she jumped at the familiar voice.

"Will you be standing there all day with the wind whipping at your face?"

"Maggie, you startled me," Genevieve said, placing a hand to her heart.

" 'Tis no wonder, with your mind being so far away," chided the woman who had been her nursemaid nigh from the cradle.

Genevieve smiled, remembering all the lectures Maggie had given her throughout the years on letting her imaginings run away with her.

"My father is well this morning?" she inquired while Maggie weaved her hair into a thick golden braid that fell to her waist.

"Aye. He is well and requests your presence after you break your fast."

Maggie busied herself helping Genevieve dress, sighing in dismay.

"Maggie, your sighs betray your thoughts," said Genevieve as she raised her arms above her head to allow the older woman to pull the gown around her.

"And how would you be knowing what I am thinking?"

"You are thinking as you are always thinking, about me," she replied with gentle laughter.

"Aye, I was thinking, 'tis a pity your dear mother departed this earth so young, never seeing you grow to womanhood." Maggie sighed again. "Or seeing to your fate. You should be having babies yourself by now," she said, lacing up the sides of Genevieve's soft blue kirtle.

"I believe that one must first have a husband," Genevieve replied softly with an odd inner twinge.

"Aye," agreed Maggie, turning the girl around to fasten the belt about her slim waist.

The topic had been a favorite of Maggie's for the past five years. As ever, though, her arguments were futile.

Genevieve had been promised in marriage at birth, but her betrothed, the heir of Chadwick, had always been sickly and had succumbed to ill health while Genevieve was still very young.

Lord Richard, having lost his wife to fever the same year, gave little thought to securing another alliance for his daughter. Instead, he spent months at a time away from Montburough in service to the king. It was not until his injury five years ago that he had come home to stay, choosing to keep his only child close to his side.

"Do not be so upset, Maggie. I have all the love I need right here with you and Father."

"Nay, child. You need a man, a strong man, to protect you and Montburough. 'Tis my hope your father will see to the task soon."

Her morning ministrations completed, Maggie turned and left the room. "Perhaps," Genevieve whispered to the unanswering chamber, "it is my fate never to know a man's touch."

After her morning repast, Genevieve walked the length of the hall to her father's bedchamber, pausing a moment to smooth the skirt of

her kirtle before pushing open the heavy, ornate wooden doors.

Richard Warren lay in bed, struggling vainly
to adjust the cushions that supported his upper
body.

Knowing that her proud, silver-haired father
would never ask for help, Genevieve hurried to
his side to accommodate his efforts. Though he
had no patience with anyone fussing over him,
Lord Richard's regard for his daughter allowed
her to perform ministrations he would have
found demeaning at another's hands.

He smiled indulgently at his only child as she
perched on the edge of his bed, her gold-flecked
green eyes regarding him warmly. He was always delighted to see her and seemed enliv-
ened by her radiant good health and sparkling
vitality, which were in such stark contrast to his
own deterioration.

"Ah, Genny," he said, receiving her with his
customary enthusiasm as he enfolded her hands
in his.

Genny smiled at the greeting, recalling how
he had always insisted that "Genevieve" was
too large a name for one so small.

"You are looking well, Father," she said.

"I thank you for your kind words, my dear,
but it is not so." He gazed at her with unexpected solemnity, yet when he spoke again,
his tone was gentle. "There is much I wish to
discuss with you," he said.

Her brow furrowed with concern at the seri-
ousness in his voice.

"Genny, I had so wanted to talk to you before now, but prudence dictated that I wait."

Genny could tell that her father was having great difficulty with whatever he was trying to say. She could feel the uncharacteristic trembling of his hands as he clasped hers more tightly. During the past few months his health had been declining rapidly, until it was difficult for her to reconcile the robust warrior he had once been with the man who now lay upon the bed. Genny was grateful that at least his sharp mind and keen wit had remained intact even if his body could no longer obey his commands. She felt a great wave of sorrow and love as she reflected that she drew much of the strength that was required of her in her daily maintenance of their holdings from this man.

"Pray, Father, what troubles you so that you are entertaining such dark thoughts on this splendid morning?" Genny asked gently, hoping to allay whatever worries he might have.

"I know this is sudden," he said brusquely, "but Lord Sinclair is an honorable man. King Edward assures me of his suitability."

Puzzled, Genny echoed, "His suitability?"

"As a husband," her father said abruptly.

Genny paled. Had she not been sitting, her legs would never have supported her. *Husband?*

Her voice was shaky, and she faltered for words.

"I . . . I . . . am to marry Lord Sinclair?"

"Yes, my dear. I have petitioned King Edward on your behalf, and he has been most indulgent. With the decision now made, the king feels it best to expedite the union, and I agree.''

Genny was suddenly light-headed, trying to absorb what her father was saying. *She was to wed Tristen Sinclair, Earl of Ravenswood?*

An air of mystery always seemed to accompany whispered discussions of her late cousin's husband, and an aura of secrecy clung to stories of Kathryn Aldred's premature death.

Images of her cousin, her dark hair painstakingly arranged to accentuate the flawless, alabaster skin and piercing blue eyes that had captivated so many, filtered into Genny's mind. Kathryn's petulance as a child had given way to a practiced charm that had ensnared more than a few prominent suitors, yet she had chosen Lord Sinclair above them all.

''Lord Sinclair agrees to this?'' Genny asked, apprehension knotting inside her as she emerged from her momentary reveries.

''Aye,'' her father replied, taking in her struggle to recapture her composure. ''My child, you must know that this decision was not reached easily, but that it is sound. I would not give you to any man unless I was confident he would bring you no harm.''

Genny looked into her father's eyes. She knew he loved her above all else and would never ask her to do anything that he thought might bring her unhappiness.

''Genny, I have had you to myself for too long,'' he said, cupping her chin lovingly in his hand, his eyes tenderly searching her face. ''Never has a father had such a loyal and loving

daughter as I. But I have been selfish in not
securing your future for when I am gone. You
will need a proven man to keep Montburough
strong and prosperous. Lord Sinclair is such a
man. King Edward assures me of his mettle and
his allegiance. It is my wish, my daughter, that
you reconcile yourself to this marriage. It will
not only unite two strong holdings, but, with
Montburough as your dowry, it will guarantee
its continuance.''

Realizing that losing her would cause her father great pain, yet knowing that securing her
future would do much to ease that pain, Genny
knew she could not deny him. Squaring her
shoulders, she swallowed hard.

''Will you honor your poor father's request?''
Richard prompted.

''I shall,'' she replied finally in a soft but
steady voice.

Gently Richard gathered his petite daughter
tightly to his chest, valiantly fighting the tears
that brimmed in his eyes.

Three days later, in what seemed like breathless haste to Genny, she and Christopher Sinclair stood in the presence of those at
Montburough and repeated the vows required
of them.

Lord Richard sat in what had been his favorite chair, wearing a look of contentment that
Genny had not seen for some time. In order to
spare him any indignity, she and Maggie had
conspired to carry him downstairs before anyone assembled in the hall. Even with the blan-

ket shrouding his legs, his firm features and
broad shoulders today appeared to be those of
a strong and vital man. Genny winced, however, as she noticed his hands gripping the arms
of his chair. She knew the pain he was enduring to be there, and she resolved to be strong
for him, no matter her own inner turmoil.

When the vows were completed, she lifted
her gaze to Sir Christopher. He was a handsome man with raven-black hair. The fine lines
about his eyes and mouth added interest to his
amiable features. He inclined his head toward
her, meeting her eyes. Embarrassed that she
had been caught studying him, Genny blushed
deeply.

Noticing her discomfort, Christopher smiled
reassuringly, and the warmth of his smile was
reflected in his gentle blue eyes.

At that moment documents were set before
her so that she might write her name next to
that of her husband. Pausing, tremulous in the
face of the inevitable, she slowly ran her finger
over the signature already present. *Lord Tristen
Blakely Sinclair, Earl of Ravenswood.* The writing
was large and bold, and Genny's mind suddenly reeled with speculation about her new
spouse, the stranger with whom she was to
mate and remain all the rest of her days.

What manner of man was he? she wondered,
with a shiver.

With no answer, and with trembling hand,
she lifted the quill and inscribed her name next
to his.

Chapter 3

Genny sat in her bedchamber amid many packed trunks. Slowly drawing a silver brush through her hair, she let each of the golden strands slip softly to her waist.

On the morrow, she was to leave all that she had known since birth to go to an unknown land, wed to a faceless man. Oddly, despite a measure of natural trepidation, she found the thought somehow exciting. Her adventurous nature was clearly coming to the fore.

Setting the brush aside, Genny gazed out the window, watching, for perhaps the last time, the waning sun cast its muted rays into her chamber as dusk settled over Montburough.

A distinctive knock sounded at the door.

"Come in, Maggie," Genny called.

Maggie's cheeks were flushed from her ascent up the long staircase. "I must admit you do look the radiant bride," she said, taking note of Genny's sparkling eyes and flowing tresses. "Philip has just arrived."

"Philip!"

In all the confusion, Genny had not given her

cousin a thought. It had been weeks since she had seen him, and everything had happened so fast. Why, she was now a married woman! Philip was always so full of gossip from court when he visited that Genny was eager now to share her own with him.

"Does he know yet of my news?" she inquired.

"It would seem likely. 'Tis not every day the Earl of Montburough's daughter gets married. He has asked that you meet with him in the garden."

Genny grabbed her cloak and hastily sought him out, sure he would want to be first to congratulate her. After all, they were more than just cousins; they had been friends for most of their lives. As a young boy whose father had died, Philip had been sent to live at Montburough so that he might benefit from the scholars Lord Richard had, in his unorthodox way of raising his daughter, commissioned to educate Genny. Philip had remained at the estate until Aunt Beatrice had taken both Kathryn and him to court to attempt to secure their fortunes through marriage.

Fate was a strange thing, Genny reflected. Kathryn Aldred *had* made a good marriage—to the stranger Genny had just wed—while Philip remained unattached.

As Genny approached the garden now, she saw that Philip's back was to her, but he stood so tall and straight, she would have known by his stance that it was he.

Hearing her approaching steps, he turned to face her, revealing features so perfect, so symmetrical, that any more delicacy would have made him too beautiful for a man. Today, however, his handsome face was reserved, unsmiling.

"Philip, dear, when did you arrive?" she asked gaily.

"Late this afternoon," he replied in an oddly flat tone.

"Then you have heard of my news?" A smile curved her full lips, and she knew her unwarranted excitement must sparkle from her eyes.

"Aye." But there was a cold edge of irony in his voice as he looked upon his cousin, whose fair complexion, delicate features, and golden curls he customarily regarded with pleasure.

"I wish you could have been here," Genny said sincerely, assuming his shared regret at the lapse accounted for his lack of spirit.

"I, too, wish I had been here," he muttered tersely, turning away from her. But his reasons differed widely from hers. His jaw clenched as he recalled his mother's tirade upon his return to Aldred Keep earlier that day. He had feared displeasing his forceful mother, and he had known well that the king's denial of his petition for Genny's hand would be unwelcome news. He had, however, been spared the task of informing her.

"Don't cower there in the doorway," Beatrice Aldred had commanded her son by way of greeting. "While you were off begging the

indulgence of the crown, the king and my dear
brother conspired to rob us of everything!''

Philip attempted a defense of himself. ''We
agreed that Uncle Richard would never break
down and consent to my offer of marriage to
Genevieve. I had to seek a higher authority.''

''We agreed to nothing. I told you to bed the
pampered girl and be done with it. Then Richard would have had no say in the matter, and
you would have had Montburough,'' Beatrice
said, berating her bewildered son.

For it was not the loss of Montburough that
pained him so much as the loss of his beautiful
cousin. For years he had pictured the petite en-
chantress as his wife, bearing him handsome,
healthy sons who would one day inherit the
great wealth of Montburough.

''Instead, you failed to do anything, and now
Lady Genevieve is to be married to your poor
sister's husband,'' Beatrice concluded, grimac-
ing as though the very thought was nauseating.

''The Earl of Ravenswood?'' Philip questioned when he finally found his voice. He had
been quite young when Kathryn married the
earl, and he did not recall Tristen Sinclair very
well. He knew only what his mother had told
him in the years following his sister's untimely
death—that Sinclair had sorely abused Kathryn,
beating her, ridiculing her in public, and bedding castle wenches in their own bed. Rather
than endure life with this man, Kathryn had
chosen to embrace death, finally finding the
peace that had eluded her on this earth.

Philip shuddered at the thought of his precious, golden Genny being subjected to the same ill treatment. "How could this happen?" he asked in disbelief.

"It happened because you lacked the courage to act. They are to be married by proxy today. Bah! The earl couldn't even be bothered to do the deed himself. He sent his brother in his stead." Beatrice paced the floor, her devious mind evidently churning. "Perhaps there is still time," she muttered. "Philip, you may yet be able to stop this injustice. You will ride to Montburough."

"But, Mother . . ." he began.

His protest was promptly severed by his mother's sharp tongue. "This time you will do as I say. You wouldn't want your cousin to suffer Kathryn's fate at the hands of the earl, would you?" she said slyly.

Beatrice paused briefly, as if to assure herself that her arrow had hit its mark. Philip's pained expression clearly told her that it had.

"Go to Montburough," she commanded. "Find Genny. You know what you must do."

But upon arriving at Montburough, Philip had learned he was too late. Genny was already married. And now, standing with her in the garden, he didn't know what to do.

"Are you not happy for me?" Genny asked, placing her hand lightly upon his arm to coax him from his unusual silence.

"Nay!" Philip replied, turning back to face her. "How could I find pleasure in losing my heart's desire?"

"Philip, whatever do you mean?"

"I assumed you knew how I felt," he said, impulsively placing his hands on her shoulders. "I love you. I have always loved you. Did we not talk of marriage?"

"Aye. But we were children, Philip." Even in the dim light Genny could see the hurt in his pale blue eyes, and she was stunned by the look of despair on his face.

"I have always loved you, too . . . as a sister loves a brother."

"You would have grown to love me as a woman loves a man," he declared.

"Nay, Philip. We are but dear friends."

Genny stiffened as she felt his grip on her shoulders tighten.

"What could your father be thinking to marry you off to the Earl of Ravenswood? Has he lost his wits?"

"Philip Aldred, you mind your tongue. My father is not addled, and well you know it."

"I can think of no other reason he would give you to that contemptible miscreant!"

"My father assures me that I have married an honorable man," Genny replied angrily.

"And I assure you he is not," Philip growled, his refined features distorted with anger.

His sudden harshness took Genny off guard, and she stepped away from him, unnerved at this unfamiliar and vaguely threatening aspect of her childhood friend.

"I can assume from your words, Philip, that you did not come to congratulate me or bid me a fond farewell. I would not have wanted us to part in this manner, but, I think 'tis best I bid you good night.''

Turning to leave, Genny was halted as Philip gripped her arm.

''You mustn't do this, Genny. I cannot let you go to him. He cannot care for you as I do.''

''Philip, you are hurting me,'' she said as she attempted to free the arm trapped in his iron fingers. He continued to apply the cruel pressure, as if he heard not her plea nor felt her struggles.

''You must listen to me! He will bring you nothing but harm. He is a cruel and vicious man!''

''Philip, let me go!'' she demanded, trying vainly to break free of his hold, growing more frightened by the moment by her cousin's intemperate behavior.

''Release the lady,'' came the quiet but firm command.

Philip's face grew rigid as Christopher Sinclair entered the garden, and he quickly relinquished his hold on Genny's arm.

''Aldred. It would be best you bid Lady Sinclair a good-night and be on your way,'' Christopher said, warning implicit in his soft voice.

Philip squared his shoulders as if to challenge the other man's authority, but then he visibly wilted, simply watching mutely as Christopher took Genny's arm and led her away.

Genny lowered her head to her pillow. Exhausted from the events of the day, she was sure that sleep would come easily. But the lon-

ger she lay there, the more she realized it was
not to be. Climbing from the bed, she wrapped
her robe around herself. Retrieving a candle-
stick from the mantel, she proceeded downstairs to the great hall.

Having reassured himself that Philip Aldred
had departed the castle, Christopher had seated
himself at a table in a shadowed corner of the
great hall to finish his ale. He had nearly drifted
off to sleep when he caught a faint flicker of
light out of the corner of his eye.

Blinking, he gazed at the golden-haired vision moving slowly into the room. *Jesu, she is
small*, he thought, *and beautiful*. Indeed, Lady
Genevieve was not at all what he had expected
to find when his brother had sent the message
for him to come here. Rarely had he encoun-
tered a maiden who possessed such natural
grace. As she moved across the room, it seemed
as though her feet scarcely touched the floor,
her robe flowing smoothly behind her, her hair
cascading freely down her back.

He should speak, he knew, and alert her to
his presence, but for the moment he decided
simply to watch her. Then he would quietly slip
out unnoticed, not wishing to intrude upon her
solitude.

Genny crossed to the roaring hearth. She remembered many a night spent in this very
room, seated upon her father's knee while he
told her tales of far-off lands and gallant
knights.

Suddenly she sensed the presence of someone moving stealthily behind her, and without

hesitation she instinctively whirled around, grabbing the large man by the shoulders and wrenching him backward while taking his legs from beneath him. His body landed with a heavy thud. She quickly straddled him, placing her dagger to his throat.

"Lady Genevieve, 'tis I, Christopher Sinclair!"

With the blood roaring in her ears, Genny paused to take a deep, calming breath. "I almost killed you! What were you doing stealing about in the darkness?" she demanded.

"Had I known you hid weapons under your bedgown, I would not have been so foolish, milady," he replied wryly.

He was still short of breath, partly due to the fall and partly because she was atop his chest.

"Please call me Genny. We are family now, Christopher," she said matter-of-factly.

"Indeed! And are we to expect you to topple all the men of the family and sit astride their chests? Dressed in your bedclothes?" he asked, grinning mischievously.

Genny paled, only to blush bright crimson when she realized her indelicate position. She quickly raised herself from Christopher and straightened her robe, finally allowing him to sit upright.

"Pray, Genny, what did you think you were doing? Had I been a robber or murderer, I could have taken that thing and used it on *you*," he reproached her, pointing at the dagger.

"I think not," she replied pertly.

A soft laugh began rolling through Christopher's chest. Only moments earlier he had thought this woman to be helpless and fragile.

"I shall have to warn my brother that his wife keeps a dagger beneath her sleeping gown. A husband would want to know that." He was nearly overcome with laughter at the thought. As his breath returned, he was finding the whole incident impossibly amusing.

"That is ridiculous. When I am in bed, it is beneath the pillow," she said primly.

Her comment only served to make him laugh all the harder, irritating Genny and rankling her tattered pride.

"Stop that howling and let me look at your head," she chided. As she parted his hair and felt around with her fingers, she came across a bump and the dampness of blood.

"Ouch!"

"I thought I heard your head hit when you fell. Do not move," she commanded. "I shall return." With a springy bounce, she was gone.

Christopher's mouth curved into an unwilling smile as he watched her leave the room. He could not believe that little slip of a woman had sent him tumbling to the ground. *This was no ordinary lady!* he reflected as he stiffly raised himself to the nearby bench.

Genny returned carrying dressings, water, and salve, placing them on the table next to Christopher. Wringing one of the clean cloths in the basin of water, she proceeded to cleanse his wound.

"Where did you learn to fell a man twice your size?"

"Rory taught me."

"Oof!" he exclaimed, jerking away from her touch. "Take care, woman. 'Tis the only head I have."

Genny giggled, remembering how often Maggie, complaining of Richard Warren's obstinate pride, had told her that men could bear up under anything but doctoring.

"And who, pray tell, is Rory?" Christopher asked with suspicion.

"Rory was the captain of the guard here at Montburough while I was growing up."

"And he taught a girl a warrior's skills?" he asked in disbelief.

"Oh," she said airily, "that wasn't the only defense he taught me. I am also skilled with the longbow and the spear. And although I can use a sword, it is difficult for me due to my size," she added with evident pride.

"Hmm. Perhaps you should have a smaller sword fashioned for you. One that is lighter in weight and more manageable for a woman." Suddenly he rolled his eyes upward. "Ach! What am I saying?"

"Do you really think it is possible, Christopher?" she asked excitedly, seizing on his idea and ignoring his dismay.

Oh, God, he thought, *I shall pay dearly for this if Tristen finds out.* "Perhaps we should speak with my brother first. He may not take kindly to the idea of his wife carrying her own sword."

"Whyever not?" she asked, puzzled. "I would think he would want me to be able to protect myself," she added, her dignity slightly ruffled at the notion of her husband objecting to her behavior.

Christopher took her small hands into his own as he leaned forward on the bench. "Genny, I think you will be just what my brother has needed for a long time. And if I don't miss my guess, it will be Tristen who will need to protect himself."

She raised her eyebrows in a questioning manner as Christopher continued.

"He has guarded himself well thus far, but you will be a formidable foe."

"Christopher, I am not his enemy. I am his wife," she replied, rejecting his idea as absurd.

Christopher gazed into her eyes. "We shall see, Genny. We shall see."

Chapter 4

Ravenswood Castle

When she entered the great hall, Genny readily assessed that the wondrously thick outer walls of this magnificent castle did not even begin to do justice to what lay within.

Her first glimpse of the fortress had come earlier that morning—from a half-day's ride away. Ravenswood lay strategically inland off the western coast of England near the Bristol Channel, which had boasted a thriving seaport since the days of William the Conqueror. The three-day journey from Montburough had been tiring, but the grandeur awaiting rallied Genny's curiosity and energy. Although weary, she graciously accepted the warm greetings of all the servants lining the length of the great hall to welcome their new mistress, and she was mindful to make individual comments as Christopher presented each loyal subject to her.

Nearing the end of what had seemed to be an endless queue, Genny looked up into the face of an older woman with plump pink cheeks and an infectiously friendly smile. Her hair gleamed like polished pewter, her pale blue eyes aglow with genuine warmth.

"And this dear woman is Matilda," said Christopher in a voice laden with significance. "The curse of Ravenswood."

"Fie, don't you go scaring the mistress, Christopher," replied the woman, her beaming smile multiplying the tiny lines edging her soft blue eyes.

"Tilly has been here with us since Tristen and I were knee-high," Christopher explained fondly. "More than once through the years we have felt her assaults on our backsides."

"Only when your behavior warranted it," she replied tartly before turning her full attention to Genny. "I speak for all at Ravenswood when I say we are most pleased to welcome you to your new home, Lady Sinclair. We hope you will be happy here."

"Thank you, Tilly."

"Mary, take your mistress to her chambers and see to her bath," Tilly commanded the young girl standing next to her.

"Thank you for your most able escort, milord," Genny said to her brother-in-law.

"The pleasure was all mine, Genny. We shall sup with Mother and Elizabeth after you are rested. They will be eager to meet the newest member of the Sinclair family."

After following Mary up the long, winding stairway to the sleeping chambers, Genny came to a halt as the maid paused in front of a large, elaborately carved wooden door.

"This is his lordship's chamber," the girl said.

The steady rhythm of her heart suddenly erratic, Genny slowly stepped into the room and began to scan the unfamiliar surroundings. Exquisite tapestries nearly covered the great gray stone walls. The fireplace was large enough that it would be sure to supply ample warmth to the vast chamber in the coldest of weather. Above the hearth hung an ornate jeweled replica of the Sinclair family crest. On a rich, forest-green background, a large black raven, its wings tipped with precious emeralds and black onyx, loomed ominously as if poised for flight.

Genny's eyes shifted to the immense bed, and her heart hastened a beat. *Come now, Genny,* she chided herself, *you are not a child unaware of the relationship between a man and wife.* She gingerly approached the commanding bedstead and placed her hand on one of the four wooden posts that stretched nigh to the ceiling. The carving was ornate and smooth beneath her fingers, and the imposing panels adorning the head and foot were crafted to match.

Her trunks had been moved into the chamber while she was greeting the servants, and they now sat in the middle of the room, looking stranded and out of place. Oddly uneasy at the sight, Genny moved to the three small windows on the far wall.

The view was one of great beauty. Like everything else she had seen thus far at Ravenswood, the grounds appeared endless, and from this vantage she could see what must be the formal gardens, their late-summer flowers still in glorious bloom.

Beyond the gardens were the stables. Indeed, as Christopher had mentioned to her on their journey, they were sizable. Genny intended to have a closer look at them as soon as possible.

But now Mary had finished preparing her bath, and after three full days of traveling, Genny welcomed the opportunity to bathe properly in the warm, perfumed water.

While she soaked, Mary began unpacking her belongings, and when she rose, refreshed, from the tub, the girl helped her dress for the evening meal, then left her to await Christopher, who would escort her into the great hall . . . and her future.

"Mother, I present Lady Genevieve."

Genny curtsied low before the older woman. Then, raising her head, she met the same sky-blue eyes that adorned Christopher's visage. Lady Eleanor was fair and slight but evinced a look of quiet strength. Her hair was now a shimmery silver, but Genny imagined it had once been dark and rich. She was a most decorous woman, and when she spoke, her gentle voice was in keeping with her countenance.

"Lady Genevieve," she said, extending her hand to bid Genny rise. "Please, *you* are mistress of this keep now."

"And this, Lady Genevieve, is Elizabeth, my wife," Christopher said proudly.

Although Elizabeth was not an exquisite beauty, Genny could easily see how her shining brown tresses, her sparkling aqua eyes, and her immediately evident abundance of energy had attracted Christopher. When he had informed her that his wife had already birthed two children and was expecting yet another, Genny had certainly not thought to encounter such a young, vibrant woman as this.

"My husband has told me so much about you, Lady Genevieve!" Elizabeth's voice fairly radiated excitement.

"Then I am sure he has told you that I would wish to be addressed simply as Genny," she said with a smile, instantly at ease with Christopher's engaging wife.

"Genny 'tis, then," Elizabeth bubbled gaily.

The remainder of Genny's nervousness was quickly put to rest as they progressed through dinner. The Sinclairs made her feel entirely welcome, and the conversation flowed merrily.

"I do wish my son had been here to greet you, Genny," Lady Eleanor said wistfully.

"I am not unaware of the duties one has as a loyal servant to the king. I am confident he will return as soon as possible," replied Genny.

"Oh, he returns. It is persuading him to stay for any length of time that proves difficult," said Elizabeth dryly.

"Mayhap he will have more reason to stay home now, Elizabeth," quipped Christopher, grinning at Genny.

Genny blushed at the inference as Elizabeth giggled lightly.

"Genny, I trust you find Ravenswood to your liking," said Lady Eleanor.

"Oh, aye, milady. And if it is convenient, I would very much like to see the rest of it tomorrow."

"I am sure Christopher can arrange that, my dear," the woman offered warmly.

"Christopher, I would like to assess the breeding stables first, if you do not mind."

Elizabeth gasped. "Whatever for?"

"Genny is an expert in horseflesh, dear," Christopher blithely explained. "She intends to breed the Arabian she brought with her from Montburough, and when I boasted of Tristen's stallion, she wondered at mating Demon to some of our mares."

"Oh, not just any mares, Christopher. They must be suitable—good bloodlines, even temperament, strong muscles, and agreeable to the breeding."

"Are we talking of horses . . . or of wives?" Christopher asked with teasing laughter in his eyes.

"Christopher!" cried Elizabeth in embarrassment.

Genny blushed, and Lady Eleanor, though her elegant eyebrows had arched at Genny's expert horse talk, now gave a light chuckle.

"Genny, my dear, you may go anywhere you wish. Even the stables. This is now your home," said her mother-in-law.

"Thank you, Lady Eleanor," Genny said sincerely, relieved by the woman's reassuring welcome.

After dinner, Eleanor retired to her chambers, leaving the young people conversing well into the late hours. At long last Christopher enticed Elizabeth to bed with gentle admonitions concerning her delicate condition. Always the chivalrous knight, before he and Elizabeth retired, he escorted Genny to her own empty—and oddly lonely—chambers.

Upon learning to her dismay that Lord Sinclair would not be returning to Ravenswood for at least a month, thus delaying still further her acquaintance with the stranger who was to be her husband—and heightening her trepidation—Genny had summoned forth her usual resilience, taking the opportunity to learn all she could of her new home.

She had spent much of her time exploring the stables and examining the stock, heaping compliments upon Edmund, the young but efficient stablemaster, for his able and excellent management. Though dubious at the outset, he gradually came to welcome her avid attention to his domain. Even if she was a woman, he valued her knowledge and soon reveled in their discussions of the intricacies of breeding.

The small group of men-at-arms that remained at Ravenswood to protect it in the absence of the earl had quickly learned that the new Lady Sinclair was no ordinary lady. Her daily jaunts to the exercise field to practice with

the longbow had at first earned her many a
stare. The men had been ill at ease in her presence, and their disapproval of her strenuous activities, though wisely unspoken, was clear.
Nonetheless, they had soon discovered that she
was not only persistent but also accomplished,
and over time they lost some of their discomfi-
ture. She had painstakingly earned the grudg-
ing respect of each and every one of them,
including Sir Marcus, the captain of the guard
and one of Tristen's oldest and most trusted
men. Ultimately, after a long and silent battle
of wills, all had vowed their loyalty to Lady
Genevieve not only as the Countess of Ravenswood but also as one who could be depended
upon to stand firm in defense of Ravenswood.

Now Genny found herself pacing her chamber nervously, pondering how the month that
had seemed such a long time to wait had
dwindled to, at most, a precious few days.
During the past week the men who had been
campaigning with Lord Sinclair had begun
returning in small groups to Ravenswood,
heralding that soon the earl himself would return.

Despite the vastness of the bedchamber,
Genny felt restless and confined, and she decided a walk in the cool night air might calm
her inner distraction. Donning her woolen
mantle, she made for the stairs.

The night air was pleasant but brisk, and
Genny was finding her stroll more invigorating
than soothing. Wandering through the de-

serted courtyard, she heard the faint sound of
music and singing, and she let herself be drawn
toward the source of the merriment.

"Milady!"

Startled, Genny turned to see Sir Marcus,
barely discernible in the darkness.

"Sir Marcus, you startled me."

"Begging your pardon, milady, but 'tis awfully late for you to be out of doors unescorted."

"I could not sleep and thought to take a stroll.
Sir Marcus, I hear music, singing. Where is it
coming from?" she inquired.

"The knights' hall, milady. The men are celebrating Lord Tristen's successful campaign and
the arrival of the rest of the men."

"Oh, splendid!" she cried excitedly. "I
should like to meet these valiant warriors, Sir
Marcus."

"Milady, you . . . cannot," he stammered.
"They have been . . . celebrating mightily, and
. . . it would not be fitting."

"Sir Marcus, I was virtually raised by my
father's knights and squires. I do not fear a man
full of drink. Come now and take me. Or shall
I go on my own?"

Looking extremely uncomfortable, but having no choice save to do the mistress's bidding,
he reluctantly led the way to the hall.

The men had started singing another bawdy
tune as the pair entered.

Come hither my maiden and tend to my need
Due to the battle my sword's not been sheathed

Bring what you have to relieve this great pain
We'll do it not once but again and again. . . .

The rumble filling the hall abruptly began to fade as, one by one, the men became aware of the intruders. All eyes widened and mouths fell agape as Genny moved into the room with Sir Marcus at her side. One of the men vaulted from his seat.

"I am sorry, milady. We did not realize you were present," he offered nervously. "We meant no offense."

"It is no matter . . . ?"

"Thomas, milady." The pockmarked soldier bowed low, though his gaze remained steady and appreciative on the beautiful face of the new Countess of Ravenswood.

"Thomas," she repeated, smiling warmly at the man. "I did not come to disrupt your celebration. Indeed, I would be honored to join you. I wish to meet each and every one of you," she declared, gesturing expansively. "After all, a castle is only as strong as those who protect it."

The great room had fallen deathly silent during the exchange, but now shouts of approval rang out, and one of her devoted subjects respectfully offered the countess a brimming tankard of ale. To the amazement and renewed cheers of the newest arrivals at Ravenswood, Genny drank heartily, and soon the festive music resumed.

Genny contrived to greet each man, and her grace, her fervor, and the obvious respect accorded her by those who had already come to know her soon enamored even the most reserved newcomer.

Tankard after tankard of ale was depleted, and many of the men engaged in boisterous traditional dance. In no time at all, Genny had mastered the unfamiliar steps and was soon in the thick of the men's merriment.

Chapter 5

The journey had been long and tiresome, and when Tristen arrived at Ravenswood, he and Alexander were more than ready for a rest. As they rode into the courtyard, they both smiled at the familiar figure who emerged from the castle.

"Tristen, a sorrier sight I have not seen in a long time!" Christopher cried.

"I have missed you, too, Christopher," replied Tristen dryly. But upon dismounting, he clasped his brother in a manly embrace.

"Alexander, how good to see you," Christopher said, extending his hand in greeting. "Although now we shall have to lock up all the maidens, else they swoon at your feet," he jested. Christopher knew that the winsome Alexander had only to flash a suggestive grin and women hied to do his every bidding.

"As long as you do not lock up your dear wife, Christopher."

"Just see you remember that she *is* my wife," Christopher retorted slightly uneasily. The man had, after all, once courted Elizabeth.

"How could I forget? You are ever reminding me." Alexander chuckled. "Speaking of wives," he added mischievously, "where is Tristen's?"

Tristen glared at him, but before he could make a reply, Lady Eleanor entered the courtyard. Tristen strode to embrace her.

"Mother, you are looking well," he said, placing a kiss upon her cheek.

"I am so glad you are home. It has been too long, my son," she said, returning his embrace. "I am, however, vexed that you did not inform us of which day you would be arriving."

Tristen made no reply. He had been certain that, had his mother known the day of his arrival, she would have contrived an elaborate wedding feast, and that was exactly the reason he hadn't informed her.

"It is good to see you, too, Mother," he said instead before releasing her.

Lady Eleanor turned to Alexander. "Welcome to you, too, Alexander."

" 'Tis good to be back at Ravenswood, Lady Eleanor."

"We are most glad you will be here to share in the festivities."

"I would not on my life miss Tristen's marriage celebration," he replied, casting a wink at his glaring friend before bending to kiss Lady Eleanor's hand.

"I would prefer to dispense with a celebration, Mother," Tristen asserted, remembering the lavish entertainment Ravenswood had hosted in honor of his marriage to Kathryn

Aldred. Kathryn had flourished amidst all the
attention, and he had thought the wedding
feast to be but the first of many happy occasions
he would share with his new wife. Now, however, he shuddered to recall how he had confused her hunger for flattery with love for him
and a zest for life.

"Surely you would not deny Genny a wedding feast. I am certain she would welcome the
celebration," Lady Eleanor said, patting his arm
reprovingly.

"Genny?"

"Lady Genevieve prefers to be called Genny.
It is a pet name her father gave her," answered
his mother, smiling.

"It better suits her anyway," said Christopher.

"Well, I for one am most eager to meet Lady
. . . Genny," said Alexander with good humor.

"I'm sure you are," replied Tristen dryly.

"I *am* always enthralled with the Sinclair
women," Alexander admitted with an unre-
pentant grin.

"We've noticed," muttered Christopher.

Eleanor watched the exchange with amusement.
Looking at the man, she could understand how
a husband could worry. Alexander was tall, even
taller than Tristen, and most considered her son
a big man. He had broad shoulders framing an
immense chest that tapered to a narrow waist,
slim hips, and long, muscular legs. And if his
physique alone was not enough to attract the ladies, his face was.

Handsome was not the word to describe him;

breathtaking was closer. His skin was fair, and the sandy blond locks that framed his face came to rest well below his collar, as was the current fashion. His jaw was firm, interrupted only by a pleasing cleft in his chin. His nose, long and sleek, was a formidable peer for his other dramatic features, by far the most intoxicating of which was the moss-green eyes accented by the thick, dark lashes that belied his fairness.

"Mother, will you see to Alexander's comfort while I check on the men who have returned before us?" asked Tristen.

"Certainly, dear. Come, Alexander, we must clean you up and make you presentable for your audience." And her gentle laughter rippled through the air as she led him into the castle.

Exuberance filled the hall, as Genny was lifted onto one of the long trestle tables to do a dance full of dips and turns. The hall came alive with cheering and clapping as she demonstrated her agility in the particularly intricate steps.

Tristen had entered the hall unheeded and stood watching the woman on the tabletop twirling and swaying gracefully to the music. Her gown swirled, revealing slim, well-shaped ankles. His eyes raked boldly over the loose-fitting gown that, belted at her slender waist, clung to her body with her movements, conforming to the contours of her uptilted breasts and curved hips. Her golden hair tumbled carelessly down her back, and her lilting laughter pealed.

Nearing Sir Marcus's side, Tristen raised his voice to be heard over the merrymaking. "The men have wasted no time in procuring entertainment, I see," he commented, gesturing toward the graceful wanton. At that moment, just as he drew near the table, she lost her footing and almost tumbled off. His grasp was swift and sure around her tiny waist.

Breathless and startled, Genny found herself staring into the eyes of her rescuer. The eyes of a stranger. They were a mesmerizing blue, very dark, like hypnotic twin pools you could dive into and drown in before becoming aware of the danger.

Moving her gaze upward, she noticed hair as black as a raven's wing, unkempt and longer than was common, with one wave that dared slip down to brush his forehead. His complexion was hard to discern through the dark beard that obscured his face, but what was visible was deeply bronzed, indicative of time spent in the wind and the sun. His nose was thin and straight, aquiline.

Lowering her gaze, she took in his dusty tunic and soiled hauberk, which bore the distinctive emblem of Ravenswood. It covered his broad shoulders and an intimidating chest that tapered down to narrow hips and powerful, agile-looking legs.

A sensuous spark flew through her breast as he set her on the floor, his hands still around her waist. But when he made no move to release her, she became angry—both at him for his effrontery . . . and at herself for the unwelcome surge of excitement she felt beneath his touch. "Please unhand me, sir," she said in an oddly quavering voice.

"Come, wench, surely you would not deny me what so many have already sampled," he said with the certainty of a man unaccustomed to refusal. With the same certainty he lowered his mouth to her lips.

His kiss was firm, hungry, and demanding, his hold around her waist tightening, his fingers pressing into her flesh as if to assert his claim upon her. Forced to endure the punishing kiss, Genny felt her knees weaken in the face of his overpowering lust. Belatedly fighting to regain control over her body and her mind, she struggled to free herself of his grasp.

Tristen felt her writhe within his embrace, heard the small cries that emanated from her throat, and her spirited response struck him as a creditable reflection of his own desire. Well pleased with her ready arousal, he lifted his mouth from hers to gaze down at her.

Already livid, Genny was shocked and incensed to see the lustful arrogance emblazoned upon the stranger's face. The swiftness and vigor with which she slapped his cheek took him off guard and plunged the room into ominous silence as the men watched the earl's expression change from one of victory to one of rage.

Sir Marcus swallowed hard, knowing he need

tell his lord—and quickly—that this capricious creature was his wife. But Lady Genevieve spoke first.

"Sir Marcus," she said icily, "please make this man aware of whom he has thus accosted before you arrange him an escort from Ravenswood."

Nearly gasping for breath, Sir Marcus managed weakly to form a reply. "Milord," he fairly squeaked, "may I present Lady Sinclair, the Countess of Ravenswood."

As the woman looked outraged at Sir Marcus's respectful address to her attacker, the man's words hit Tristen like a blow to his middle. But his shock yielded quickly to renewed fury, and without warning he reached out to grab her arm, his fingers hard and bruising as he yanked her forward, causing her to stumble.

"Unhand me!" Genny demanded. "You are making a grievous mistake!"

"As are you, *milady*," hissed Tristen as he dragged her toward the door, mindful of the solemn faces of his men as they parted to let him pass and stinging under the chagrin he had experienced in their view.

"Sir Marcus!" Genny cried into the suddenly oppressive silence surrounding her, frantically wondering, why no one was stopping this varlet from abducting her. The man opened the door, pulling her roughly behind him. Sir Marcus briefly met her eyes with a troubled expression but made no move to help her.

The door shut behind them with a resounding thud, leaving Genny alone and helpless with this ominous stranger in the cold, dark stillness of the night.

"My lord will hear of this atrocity," she blustered. "Those men may be afraid of you, whoever you are, but I am not. I will not submit to you, and you shall die in the trying." Genny spat the words into the man's face as with her free hand she withdrew the dagger from beneath her gown.

Sharp pain radiated up Tristen's arm, and in his surprise he released his hold on the woman. A small weapon had cut a deep slash in his right forearm, and his blood was quickly soaking into his tunic.

Taking advantage of his surprise, Genny moved away from him and stood, weapon poised, ready for battle.

Tristen glanced up from his arm and faced his diminutive opponent.

"Put down that puny weapon before you hurt yourself," he growled, and began advancing upon her.

" 'Tis not I who will be hurt," she warned.

However, eyeing the size of her oppressor and assessing his intensity, she debated the soundness of confronting him. Deciding on wisdom before valor, she turned to flee—only to be stopped by the two strong arms that encircled her from behind. The stranger fitted her tightly to his chest and wrapped his powerful fingers around her wrist, increasing the pressure until her hand reflexively released her weapon.

Genny watched helplessly while her dagger

fell to the ground, stunned at the ease and skill with which the man had disarmed her. But when, obviously thinking he had the advantage, he released his hold on her hand, she quickly seized the moment to spin and nimbly knee him in the buttocks as he bent to retrieve the weapon.

His cry of surprise echoed in the courtyard when he landed unceremoniously face-first in the dirt.

Wasting no time in exulting, Genny picked up her skirts and held them high while she ran across the bailey to the great hall. Even as she dashed up the stairs she heard heavy, pounding footsteps in hot pursuit. Running into the hall, she was relieved to see Christopher seated at the long table, amicably sharing an ale with another soldier.

Both men glanced up at the visibly shaken and disheveled woman who had burst into the room, her chest heaving as she tried to catch her breath. Concern etched upon his face, Christopher swiftly rose to come to her aid.

"Genny—" he began, only to be interrupted by a crash when the great doors were thrust forcefully open.

As her attacker charged into the room, Genny reasoned that surely this madman was not so far gone as to attack her in his lord's castle. It seemed she had misjudged the extent of his insanity, however, for he lost no time in continuing his pursuit of her. Instinctively, she ran around the table to evade her assailant. He followed, a look of outrage on his bearded face.

Although the man was quick, Genny was lithe, and she was able to remain out of his reach. Rounding the table for the second time, she panicked when the man, instead of following her, leaped *onto* the table and prepared to lunge at her.

Stepping behind the seated stranger, Genny took notice of the sword affixed to his belt. Swiftly and without forethought, she grabbed the sword and raised it in defense against the assailant now only a hairbreadth away from her.

"It would appear that the damsel is not taken with your charms, Tristen," a freshly bathed Alexander said, trying valiantly to hold in his laughter.

"Tr—Tristen?" Genny echoed in confused disbelief, still holding him at bay with the out-stretched sword.

"Alexander, 'tis true my charms seem not to hold the appeal others have for the lady," said Tristen, ignoring Genny's gasp.

Christopher took in the scene before him. There upon the table, feet planted firmly amid mugs of ale and platters of food, stood his brother. Genny stood below, arms raised, hands clenched tightly around the purloined sword, its sharp point strategically aimed at the juncture of Tristen's thighs.

"Lady Genevieve," said the seated stranger, breaking the silence, "I am Sir Alexander, knight and, for reasons unknowable, friend of Lord Tristen." He rose to bow. "Allow me, milady," he entreated smoothly as he cautiously reached to regain possession of his sword.

Taking Genny's hand, Alexander placed a chaste kiss upon the back, not failing to miss Tristen's dark-eyed glare.

"You . . . are . . . most welcome to Ravenswood, Sir Alexander," Genny replied haltingly, struggling to recapture her shattered composure and scattered wits and to make sense of the confounding circumstances.

"Alexander, I believe our presence is no longer required," Christopher suggested diplomatically, nodding to Genny and Tristen. "Good night, Genny, Brother."

"I have not yet finished my repast," objected Alexander, clearly unwilling to miss what promised to be an interesting exchange.

Finally bounding down off the table, Tristen gruffly addressed Alexander. "I am gratified that this untoward intrusion has not affected your appetite. You haven't any need to curtail your meal, my friend. The *lady* and I are taking our leave."

Clasping Genny's hand, he murmured for her ears only, "You will come with me quietly now, for if you refuse, I will drag you out of here by your golden locks."

Genny flinched at the harshness of the words, but, determined to allow him to humiliate her no further, she straightened her shoulders and spoke with poise.

"Good night, Sir Alexander, Christopher."

"Milady," Alexander replied as he bowed

gracefully yet again, a devilish inflection in his tone.

"Good night, Genny," bade Christopher, then placed a chaste kiss upon her cheek. "Be not afraid, Genny," he whispered quietly in her ear.

Unable to reply, Genny simply nodded as her new husband led her from the room.

Chapter 6

Ascending the stairs, Genny was not sure how her feet managed to move, for they felt heavy, weighted. Tristen opened the door to his bedchamber, bidding her enter before him. His belongings having been moved in upon his arrival, the room now smelled of leather and spice, much like the man himself.

"Sit, Lady Genevieve," commanded Tristen, motioning to one of the chairs in front of the fireplace.

Despite his arrogant tone, Genny was thankful for the suggestion, for her knees were knocking in rhythm with her heart and threatening to give way beneath her. She sank quietly into a chair as she watched her new husband push her dagger into his belt and pour himself a goblet of wine from the decanter.

After pacing for a few moments, he turned to face her, his back to the fire.

Even in her agitation, Genny could not take her eyes off him. His glossy black hair gleamed with highlights from the flames dancing behind him, and the play of light and shadow made his bearded face even more striking and mysterious. His broad shoulders, dramatically silhouetted, appeared as if they could easily bear the burdens of the entire world.

He was the most handsome man she had ever seen, Genny thought. Handsome and terrifying.

"I think you would quite agree that this is not the best of situations we have been thrust into," he said now with deceptive mildness.

"We—we have not enjoyed the most . . . auspicious of beginnings, milord," Genny stammered.

"Do not tell me, Lady Genevieve, that you had no objections to this marriage even *before* it began," he scoffed.

"I . . . I did not," Genny replied with candor. "True, I knew naught of you. But I was assured you were a good man, milord," she replied softly.

"There are many good men. That does not necessarily mean you would wish to wed them," he said harshly.

Genny tried to collect her turbulent thoughts. Obviously, he was ill-pleased with their union.

"I was told you had agreed to this marriage. Was I misinformed, milord?"

"Agreed? It was *decreed!*" he answered cruelly.

Genny closed her eyes, hoping to still the nausea suddenly churning in the pit of her stomach. She took a deep breath. "Are you . . . are you telling me that you do not wish to be married to me?" All her dreams and fears, the anxieties and anticipation that had assailed her tremulous heart over the past month, now seemed petty and foolish in the face of harsh reality.

"Whether I *wish* to be or not, we are wed," he said unpleasantly. "However, I do not intend to carry this farce any further than need be."

Genny was remorsefully certain that her behavior toward him that evening had done nothing to further the cause of a happy marriage.

"I had not meant to harm or humiliate you, milord," she said urgently, seeking the words that would undo her deeds. "I beg your indulgence of my earlier actions. I knew not, milord, it was you."

"Rest assured, 'twas not I who was humiliated. Your earlier *actions* are of little significance," he growled. "Save for helping to confirm my decision."

"Your decision? I do not understand, milord."

"Lady Genevieve," he said slowly, as if she were addle-minded and only through precision could he make his intentions understood. "Any union between us is a farce. I am sure you agree."

Agree? After years of waiting to be a wife and mother? Genny was not sure why rejection by a man she had known naught of as little as an hour ago should pierce so deeply, and yet it did. She bore no love for this stranger, though his swift dismissal of her and any potential she might have to make him a faithful wife, a mother to his children, pained her.

She searched his chill blue eyes but found nothing to encourage even the faintest of hopes or dreams. "Aye," she answered softly, lowering her gaze to hide the hurt she felt. " 'Twas a mistake."

"I am pleased you agree, then, that this mockery of a marriage shall remain in name only."

The ringing in Genny's ears was so loud it was deafening. *A marriage in name only?* She supposed she should feel relieved that she would not be made to bed a stranger. Yet to have her fate so coldly sealed, with such rancorous finality, stung her pride and made her feel oddly humiliated. She did not care to examine the other inchoate feelings stirring in her breast as she raised her head to regard the man before her.

Oh, Father, what have you done to me? she lamented silently. But, no, she would not feel pity for herself. If this man found her undesirable—loathsome, even—that did not mean she would cease to exist. She would hold her head high. It was he, after all, who chose to make a mockery of the marriage. So be it.

Thus controlling her anguish, she answered in a steady voice that belied her inner turmoil.

"Very good, milord." She rose to her feet. "Now, if you will pardon me, it has been a long and tiring day, and I wish to retire."

He smiled strangely at her response, evincing, Genny thought, pleasure that she did not want this marriage either, but something else as well.

"Not quite yet, milady. There is the matter of consummation. Our people will expect proof that the king's bidding has been happily accomplished."

Genny's eyes widened, and her heart nearly pounded out of her breast.

"You needn't act the quivering virgin," he said cruelly. But when she remained in frightened silence, he said, "Bah! I have no intention of attacking you. There are ways of getting around this."

With that he strode to the bed and tore the coverings from it, exposing the sheets. Pulling her dagger from his belt, he yanked up his sleeve and pressed the point of the blade into his forearm, reopening the wound she had inflicted earlier as Genny watched in stunned silence, a small trickle of blood ran down his arm, and he let three or four drops fall to the sheets.

Genny stared mutely at the crimson blossoms on the white linen.

"That should satisfy our well-wishers. Now you may retire, milady," said Tristen, pulling his sleeve back down. "You may sleep here tonight. Tomorrow I will have your things removed to another chamber. Good night, Lady Genevieve."

"Good-good night, milord."

Tristen felt an odd twinge of disappointment as he left the room. Silently chastising himself for such foolishness and attempting to congrat-

ulate himself on successfully evading a future
filled with pain, he went down to the great
hall, where he sat in lonely silence, holding his
wife's small jeweled dagger in one hand, his
strong wine in the other. But his thoughts continued to roil.

Genevieve. His pulse quickened uncontrollably as he remembered his first glimpse of her,
her golden mane falling about her exquisite
form, her petite body swaying gracefully to the
music. Against his wishes he found himself extremely cognizant of his new wife's seductive
beauty. And one could not help but be captivated by her vitality. Even during their alter-
cation he had admired her spirit and bravery.
Never before had he beheld a woman so unpredictable, and her vivacious spontaneity sparked
unbidden yearnings deep within him.

Shaking his head to clear away such
thoughts, he chided himself for even fleetingly
acknowledging a perilous attraction.

Tristen awoke early, groaning when he raised
himself from the bench. "Lord of the castle and
I'm sleeping in the damned hall," he muttered
as, still drowsy, he stretched to relieve the ache
in his back. Then, as a procession of images
from the night before began to slowly march
through his mind, creating a heavy throbbing
in his loins, he blinked away any remnants of
sleep.

Damn! How could one woman have evoked
so many different emotions within him? He
could not remember ever being so aroused,

amused, excited, and enraged all at the same time. She had even invaded his dreams, he realized, robbing him of much-needed rest.

Frowning deeply, he rose and walked up the stairs, remembering the words he and Lady Genevieve had exchanged. She had reacted exactly as he had thought she would. After all, women of her kind did not really need the marriage bed. So why did he now wonder if he had made a mistake in so hastily demanding that they keep separate chambers? Had he somehow forfeited an advantage—other than the obvious convenience of slaking his lust whenever he chose—to his petite adversary? Nay, that was nonsense. Yet he was at a loss to explain his odd sense of unease.

Like a tremulous virgin, the wench in question had already fled his chamber when he entered to dress. Shaking his head at his earlier fancies, he prepared to return to the hall for the morning repast.

When he arrived, he noticed everyone was there but Genevieve.

As her maid descended the stairs, Tristen called out, "Mary, find your mistress and tell her we await our meal for her."

Before the maid had a chance to reply, Elizabeth spoke. "Oh, Tristen, Genny ate some time ago. I am sure she is already at the stables."

"She is *where?*" Tristen demanded.

Elizabeth paled, realizing she had evidently said the wrong thing. "At the stables. She is always there this time of the morning," she answered meekly.

"I for one think she works too hard," said Christopher. "But she tells me there is much to be done before breeding season and the birthing of the foals." He could tell by Tristen's glare that Genny would need whatever defense he could summon. "She has been such a help to Edmund. They get along quite famously."

"Indeed, Brother. And how is it that my stablemaster is now in need of help from a woman?"

"He welcomes her interest, my dear," said Eleanor in her quiet but masterful way. "Edmund tells me he has learned much from Genny. He quite admires your wife."

"And this is meant to recommend my new wife to me?" Tristen said dangerously.

"Come now, Tristen, you cannot mean to tell me you fail to see that Genny is unlike other women," Christopher remonstrated. "Especially after last night," he said with a manly wink. Sobering quickly, he added, "Edmund, like the rest of us, is simply quite fond of Genny."

The thought of his wife spending hours with the handsome young man somehow enraged Tristen, causing him to lash out at his brother.

"It seems you are quite enamored of my wife, dear brother. Perhaps you would do well to remember you have a wife of your own," he growled, ignoring the gasp Elizabeth gave at his inference.

"Perhaps you should listen to your own advice, Brother," retorted Christopher.

Looking like a thunderhead about to burst, Tristen muttered an oath and rose, striding from the room and hurrying down the steps of the hall, headed for the stables.

After a sleepless night Genny had sought the solace of the stables especially early that morning. She had quietly slipped through the hall, not wishing to disturb the slumbering man who had been the cause of those many restless hours, yet determined to maintain the routine that had sustained her prior to his disruptive arrival.

Her joy now at finding the handsome steed pawing restlessly at the earth of the stable floor was genuine. "Oh, Edmund, he is magnificent!" she exclaimed, walking around the stallion and gently stroking his coal-black coat. "I can hardly wait till *his* foal is born this spring." Genny continued to assess the stallion's qualities.

"Aye, milady. Demon is the best stud ever brought to Ravenswood," Edmund replied enthusiastically. "He's a fine beast—a gift to the earl from King Edward himself."

"Really?" Genny said, picking up a brush to groom Demon's splendid mane. "I had no idea Lord Sinclair was so esteemed by the king."

"Your husband's valor makes him revered by many, including His Majesty."

Genny turned at the voice, and a smile lit her face when she saw Sir Alexander standing there. She could not help but think that his golden locks and charming smile had probably disarmed the fairest of maidens.

"I would presume you to be adorned greatly with keepsakes from *your* many admirers," Genny said with a twinkle of amusement in her eyes.

"You flatter me, Lady Genevieve. But, alas, a vast number of women have overlooked me for lesser spoils," he mischievously replied.

"Your problem is you are too pretty, sir," replied Edmund. "A woman wants a man who won't be taking away from her own beauty."

"I quite agree, Edmund." Genny laughed lightly. "Very few women I know could rise above your fairness, Sir Alexander."

"That is quite a compliment from one who possesses such rare and enchanting beauty as you, milady," replied Alexander in his customary flirtatious manner.

"Oh! Please desist, my brave knight, for I grow faint at your lavish tribute," exclaimed Genny, crossing her hands over her heart in a playful gesture.

They all three laughed heartily, and Genny moved to continue tending Demon. But as she did so, her gown became tangled around her ankles. She lurched forward, and only Alexander's strong hands clasped tightly at her waist prevented her from falling.

Tristen marched angrily toward the stables. "What is wrong with everyone around here?" he growled. "They behave as though the wench were a saint. She has been here but a month, and she has managed to turn everything inside out and upside down. Can they not see her for what she is? A conniving, flirtatious vixen!''

The longer his strides, the angrier Tristen became. Once again his mind replayed the events of the previous night. He'd seen the hungry looks on the enchanted faces of his men—looks Lady Genevieve had no doubt returned in kind. The kind of looks Kathryn had shared with many a man.

Then, too, Lady Genevieve certainly raised no objections to a bedless marriage.

Ha! Why should she? She already had a castle of men at her beck and call, he inwardly fumed.

The sound of laughter brought him up short as he entered the stables. Then every muscle in his body tensed as his eyes fixed on Alexander holding his wife around her waist. His chest heaved, and his hands balled into fists at his sides.

''Lady Genevieve.'' The venom in his voice instantly silenced the laughter.

Genny spun around to face her husband, and Alexander's hands slipped down to his sides. She could see Lord Tristen's eyes, dark with anger, darting first to her, then to Alexander.

''Is this how you spend all your mornings, milady?'' he questioned dangerously.

She stared boldly back at him and thrust her chin upward in defiance. ''Aye, milord.''

'' 'Tis no wonder, then, my brother thinks

you work too hard out here. Rolling in the hay can be exhausting.''

He heard Genny's gasp as he narrowed his eyes at his friend.

''Tristen, I think you misconstrue the circumstance,'' said Alexander.

''I misconstrue nothing. On the contrary, I understand *Lady* Genevieve quite well,'' he retorted.

Each breath Genny took was harsher than the one before. Again he implied that she was less than virtuous! How dare he? His conduct was intolerable, completely uncivilized. Perhaps this was the way he characteristically treated women, but she did not intend to become accustomed to it.

''Do not waste your breath, Alexander,'' Genny said, guessing that the familiar use of the man's name would further infuriate her husband. ''Milord perceives only what he wishes to perceive.''

''Tristen, you cannot mean to soil your lady's reputation in this manner!'' Alexander objected. ''Or mine, for that matter. Well you know I have no need to seduce another man's wife,'' he added.

''I soil nothing that has not already been soiled by the lady herself,'' Tristen replied.

A second time in less than two days Genny's hand flew through the air to deliver a stinging slap to her husband's face.

''You . . . you bastard!'' she fumed. And she turned on her heel and exited the stables.

Tristen rubbed his cheek.

"If she had not done it, I would have," said Alexander through clenched teeth. "I was hoping your temperament would be much improved over last night, but it appears only to have worsened."

"Tread lightly, Alexander. There are some boundaries that even friends should not attempt to cross," Tristen snapped. He turned to follow Genny. "She is my wife. I will deal with her as I see fit."

Genny ran, not knowing where she was going, her vision blurred and her eyes stinging with tears. Each breath became an effort as she continued to run. The blood pounded so loudly in her ears that she did not even hear Tristen's approach. He lurched forward, grabbed her arm, and jerked her against him.

"Let go of me!" she shouted, gasping.

He looked down at her. Her breasts heaved upward with each breath, and tears stained her fair skin. Some of his anger mysteriously drained away at the sight. But why? Never before had a woman's tears touched him. Why now?

"Do not ever run from me again," he said quietly.

Her breathing hitched as she slowly raised her eyes to look at him. Was she only imagining a softening in his countenance?

"I have done naught to deserve your anger," she said softly.

How easy it would be to give in to her. That soft skin, that fair face. She possessed such an innocent quality that he was tempted to believe in her purity. But, nay, surely her tempting visage merely masked her true craven nature. She, innocent? Ha! Any number of his men could probably tell him otherwise.

"That was quite good, milady," he said, such sneering sarcasm back in his voice that the words made her flinch. "Lies flow so easily from your pretty mouth. Such a pity you did not choose to wed a man gullible enough to believe them."

Renewed anger flowed through her veins, and she thrust her chin forward. "I had no choice! I did not *choose* to marry any man. Certainly not you!"

Staring down at her, he twisted his lips into a snarl. "Listen well, *wife*. I will not tolerate being made the fool. Have you not even wit enough to hide your carnal intentions toward other men in your husband's presence?"

Genny could only stare at him. He obviously believed she desired Sir Alexander—or had already made him her lover. It was ridiculous, laughable.

And was it not he who just last night had demanded that theirs be a marriage in name only? He did not want her, but he did not want any other man to have her either. Perhaps he was not as indifferent about their union as he would have her believe? Well, it mattered not. He'd made the decision for separate chambers. Now he could live with the consequences.

"Am I no longer even to smile at another man, milord?" Genny replied sharply.

"You will cease all vulgar flirtations," he confirmed harshly.

Slowly he moved his hands down her arms, his dark eyes never leaving her face.

"You will never lie with another man again," he pronounced, his voice calm, his intent clear.

"No man touches me unless I allow it. And *you* shall certainly never lie with me!" she spat in contempt.

Tristen let out a growl of outrage and jerked her against him. Genny raised her hands against his massive chest in futile protest. His fingers wound into her golden tresses to hold her still as he lowered his mouth to meet hers. "In this, too, you have no choice," he murmured, crushing her lips with his, claiming her.

At the urgent press of his lips to hers, at the feel of his now clean-shaven face caressing her cheek, a ripple of fear coursed through Genny's body. Then an unfamiliar heat began to rise within her belly as his tongue slid across her lips, demanding entrance. Genny gasped at the unusual pleasure of it, and as her lips parted, his tongue entered and probed. With a tiny whimper at the confusing stimulation, she ceased her struggles and went limp in his fierce embrace, with the result that her breasts molded to his chest.

In a frustrating mix of anger and pleasure at her response, Tristen abruptly released her mouth. Then, drawing a deep breath, he resumed his mocking taunts. "Well, wife, despite your objections, I find you both yielding and

passionate. Tell me, which of your many lovers
were you thinking of while I kissed you?''

So confused and angered was Genny that she
could not think to defend herself. He was her
husband, and her body had responded as he
had bidden it to. Yet for this response, he
thought her wanton.

So be it, then. She would never respond to
him again. She jerked away from him. ''I hate
you!'' she whispered through clenched teeth.
Turning on her heel, she hastened to the refuge
of the castle.

Tristen cursed as he ran his fingers through
his hair. Well, what had he expected? he fumed.
Indeed, at first she had acted innocently
enough, but then . . . yes, then she had responded as an experienced wench would, one
who knew exactly what to do, exactly how to
wield her sensual power to entrap a man. Yes,
she was precisely what he had judged her to
be. He was certain of it.

Sobbing, Genny flung herself across her husband's huge bed, vaguely noting that fresh lin-
ens now replaced the soiled ones that had
served to relieve her husband of his conjugal
responsibility.

A soft knock sounded at the door. Quickly
wiping the tears from her eyes, Genny bade the
intruder enter.

''Genny, are you all right?'' asked Christopher's wife solicitously.

''I am fine, Elizabeth.''

"I am so sorry, Genny," Elizabeth said, clearly not believing her. "It is all my fault."

"What do you speak of? I know of no misfortune that could be your doing," Genny said.

Elizabeth wrung her hands. "I told him where you were."

Taking a deep, steadying breath, Genny pushed herself to a sitting position.

"It was not where I was that angered Lord Tristen, Elizabeth. It was what I was doing. Or, rather, what he thought I was doing," Genny said wryly.

"I do not understand."

"Neither do I," Genny replied. She rose and walked to the window. "Except that I am not at all what Lord Tristen wanted in a wife—of that alone am I sure."

"Oh, Genny, you are everything that any man could want. You are beautiful, and so full of life," countered Elizabeth.

"Nay. For one thing, I am past my youthful years. We both know that, Elizabeth, as does Lord Tristen."

"Genny, mayhap he simply needs time to adjust. He was hurt very badly before, and I fear it has left him with a less-than-favorable opinion of women."

"But what could make him hate me so?" asked Genny. "My mere presence seems to anger him. Everything I do is wrong. What is this past hurt you speak of, Elizabeth?"

"I am not sure I should be the one to tell you, Genny," the young woman replied nervously.

"I cannot do battle with an unseen foe,"

Genny protested. "You must help me. I beg of you, what makes my husband hate me so? Please, Elizabeth!"

"Genny, I cannot speak of it," said Elizabeth, biting her lower lip in agitation. "Please do not ask this of me," she pleaded.

Seeing her friend's distress, Genny knew she could not pursue the burning question of her husband's ill treatment of her. Indeed, she supposed that truly it was her husband's responsibility to explain his own actions.

"Thank you for coming, Elizabeth. I think I shall rest now for a bit," she said gently.

"I understand. I shall see you at supper," Elizabeth said softly. She clasped her hand briefly before leaving the room, closing the door quietly behind her.

The great hall was alight with the soft glow of the oil lamps that lined the walls as Genny, refusing to be intimidated by her husband's presence, entered for the evening meal.

After greeting the family, she took her place to the right of Tristen and awaited his signal for the meal to be served. She sat stiffly in her chair, tasting little of the food, for she had no appetite, and contributing not at all to the conversation around her. Tristen, too, seemed rather solemn, she noted.

"Tristen, did you have the opportunity to look over the changes Genny has made in the stables?" asked Lady Eleanor in an attempt to involve him in the discussion.

"I was at the stables this morning," he answered tersely, glancing at Genny briefly before returning his gaze to his food.

"Genny, have you told Tristen of your breeding plans for this spring?" Christopher inquired.

"You have plans for breeding, Lady Genevieve?" asked Tristen icily, his voice laden with innuendo.

Genny nearly choked on her food, but she composed herself to answer in a straightforward way. "Aye, I plan to breed both Apollo and Demon. Edmund and I have purchased six very suitable mares. I think we will produce most desirable offspring, and I am sure they will do you honor in battle, milord."

"Indeed, I anxiously await the arrival of Demon's foal," replied Tristen, responding to her simple candor in kind.

"Is not the topic of breeding inappropriate to table?" Elizabeth asked somewhat prudishly.

"My dear sister-in-law, I would think in your present condition that the idea of breeding is never amiss," Tristen replied with surprising mischief.

A blush spread over Elizabeth's cheeks.

"Tristen, I hardly think my wife's blessed condition bears comparison to your wife's breeding horses," Christopher protested loyally.

Tristen laughed. "Mayhap, then, Lady Genevieve will enlighten me away from the table about the details of her endeavors. However, such enlightenment will have to await my return to the castle," he concluded.

"I was not aware you were leaving so soon, my son," said Lady Eleanor.

I was not aware he was leaving at all, thought Genny.

"My time away from Ravenswood has been lengthy, Mother. I desire to inspect the villages and outlands, to assess their progress in my absence," Tristen responded, giving voice to only a small part of the reason for his hasty departure.

"Do you consider this the best time to embark on such a journey? After all, you have had such a short time with us . . . and Genny," Lady Eleanor added significantly.

"I am confident my wife is most understanding of my situation," replied Tristen. He turned to look at her, and the blush on her cheeks and her averted gaze made him wonder if she was aware that *she* was the reason he was leaving.

Lady Genevieve was not at all what he had imagined she would be. He had anticipated neither her beauty nor her spirit, and both were proving threatening to his plans for a celibate marriage. Thus, he had decided to put as much distance as possible between himself and temptation, determined to squelch the unbidden desires her presence evoked.

"You have just arrived. What would you have Genny do in your absence?" asked Elizabeth.

Genny, however, reflecting on all that had passed between her and Tristen since his arrival, had no objection to his hasty departure. In truth, she found the notion favorable.

"I will do as I have done for these past weeks, Elizabeth. I have numerous tasks with which to occupy my time in milord's absence. Indeed, I would not restrain him from fulfilling his obligations," she pronounced, avoiding Tristen's eyes. She realized that an even greater barrier was being erected between them thusly, but could she truly protest it?

"I shall depart on the morrow, at dawn's light. But first, Christopher, let us take our leave to review our holdings," said Tristen. "I trust you ladies will excuse us," he added as he rose from the table, abruptly quitting the room with Christopher.

Chapter 7

The days gave way to weeks as Genny resumed her customary activities in the absence of her husband. And on this, the day of his return, she saw no reason to alter her routine.

Mounting Apollo for her ride to the village, Genny contemplated her new family. Although she had come to dearly love her husband's relatives, she still missed her father greatly. And even with the general acceptance she had found here at Ravenswood, she missed the ready approval and love she had known at Montburough.

Riding at a slow but pleasant pace, she glanced at Sir Marcus riding beside her, and her mind wandered back to weeks ago when she had finally succeeded in convincing him to allow her to participate in weaponry training with the men. Most of them had gradually accepted her presence and her abilities on the fields of practice, but some still had not.

"It don't seem proper, her being a lady . . ." one such man had growled as he had watched the Countess of Ravenswood in a longbow competition with one of the younger squires.

"It appears to me the lady handles herself quite well," Sir Marcus had replied.

" 'Tis only a boy she opposes. Let us see how she fares with a man," the hard-drinking Daniel had sneered in a voice loud enough for all to hear.

"I do not think Lord Tristen would approve," Sir Marcus had objected.

Genny had approached the two men, meeting Daniel's antagonistic stare. "I am my own woman, sir, and I accept the challenge."

The practice ground had fallen silent as the two opponents readied themselves for the match. Day after day Daniel had watched with open disapproval the demonstration of Lady Genevieve's skills. Now, it seemed, he would have the chance to physically challenge her presence.

Genny held tightly to the immense longbow, pulling back hard on the cord before releasing it, sending the feathered arrow swiftly and surely to its mark, hitting the target dead center.

Next Daniel stepped up and sent an arrow flying. It landed next to Genny's, and his grin held more than a hint of arrogance.

The men cheered as arrow after arrow was released, each opponent proving a worthy adversary for the other.

One of the young squires removed the dispensed arrows as Daniel ostentatiously stepped back well beyond the mark usually used for longbow practice. While he prepared to expend his final arrow, he cast Genny a look of ridicule meant to unsettle her. Then, taking careful aim, he released the cord so fiercely that the arrow shook violently after embedding itself in the center of the target, feathers floating on the air.

Undaunted by his maneuver, Genny stepped back to the spot from which Daniel had delivered his shot. The men grew silent in anticipation. Taking a steadying breath, Genny sighted down her arm at the target precisely as Rory had taught her years ago. She released the cord smoothly, sending the arrow faithfully to its goal, where it struck Daniel's embedded arrow, splicing it in half lengthwise.

Shouts of approval and adoration sounded throughout the practice field. Genny turned to her opponent.

"Well done, Daniel," she said, expressing sincere admiration for his skill.

Her overture of friendship had been met with only a terse nod as Daniel abruptly turned and left the gathering, and in the ensuing weeks the man had avoided the training fields during the squires' practice time. Genny wondered if he was still upset by his perceived humiliation.

Sir Marcus's voice now intruded into her musings. "Mistress Sarah will be delighted to see you."

A smile formed on her lips. "I surmise it is not my visit but Edmund's presence that will delight her," Genny said, glancing over her shoulder at the young man who rode behind them.

Edmund was the grandson of Thisbe, the old woman who had long tended to the health of Ravenswood's villagers. If one were to believe village lore, she had been doing so since the beginning of time. Edmund, orphaned at a tender age, had lived with Thisbe and accompanied her wherever she went. Having learned many of her healing skills, he had early on discovered that many of the same principles could also be applied to animals. When Lord Sinclair had learned of the young man's ability with beasts, he had brought him to Ravenswood and made him stablemaster.

Genny smiled now at the blush that crept onto Edmund's face at the mention of Sarah.

Genny had met the widow Sarah on her third day at Ravenswood, when she had visited the village for the first time.

She had not understood Christopher's insistence on her having an escort, since she had never required one at Montburough, but not wishing to defy the kind Sinclair family, she had reluctantly agreed.

Then as now, Sir Marcus and Edmund had flanked her as she rode Apollo into the village.

Curious faces had peeked out from behind shuttered windows, and those outside had paused in their labors to steal glances at the new Countess of Ravenswood atop her enormous steed.

Genny had soon dismounted to proceed on foot.

From the few whispered complaints she had heard of Lord Tristen from her Aunt Beatrice after Kathryn's death, she had wondered if she might find a disgruntled group of ruffians. She knew that some lords treated their vassals with disdain, solely concerned with the silver their serfs could provide to line the castle coffers. She was relieved to find evidence to the contrary in the clean streets and well-kept cottages of her husband's holdings, pleased to see for herself that her new family was not guilty of the mistreatment of those placed under their care.

Continuing on her way through the hamlet, Genny had stopped in front of a cottage where a small boy was chopping wood, the strain of the task evident on his young face and in the frail arms that quivered each time he raised the large axe.

"Such a mighty task for one so young," said Genny, approaching the boy. "Have you chopped all this wood yourself?" she asked, gesturing to the logs stacked neatly in a pile taller than the boy himself.

"Aye, milady," he replied with pride. "We will be needing more than this to keep us warm this winter," he said, struggling to place another log upon the chopping block.

"What is your name, lad?" she asked kindly.

"Lionel, milady."

"How old are you, Lionel?"

"Five, milady," he answered, puffing out his chest with dignity.

"Five! Lionel, has your father set you to this task?" Genny asked with consternation.

"Nay, milady. My ma. She can no longer wield the axe. I do all the chopping now," he added with a mature solemnity beyond his years.

"Lionel, would you put down the axe and come to me?" Genny asked.

Though he did not understand the reason for the request, the boy set down the axe and walked slowly toward the lady, a frown creasing his unlined face.

Genny gently took his hands into hers, turning them to examine the palms. As she suspected, the small hands were rough and callused, and fresh blisters were developing from the handle of the mighty axe. Although it was not unusual that peasants required their children to do many chores, most did not expect a boy this young to handle a task this large. Anger seethed within her as she released the small hands.

"I would speak with your mother, Lionel," she commanded.

The words were hardly spoken when a young woman bearing a large basket of wet garments rounded the corner of the small cottage.

"Ma . . ."

"Lionel, what be the meaning of this?" the woman asked as she lowered the basket to the ground, revealing her advanced state of pregnancy. "I apologize, milady, if he has disturbed you," she said, brushing a stray lock of hair from her sweat-covered brow.

Genny's vexation dissipated as she took in the fragile appearance of the woman who stood before her. The woman was small of stature, not much larger than Genny herself, and appeared to be about the same age. Her friendly smile radiated to her large, chestnut-brown eyes, belying the weariness that only moments before had been so evident. Such a woman could not possibly be held responsible for the hardships borne upon this child.

"Mistress, I would speak to your man," demanded Genny.

Lionel looked up at his mother with compassion, and Edmund approached Genny to whisper, "Milady, her husband was killed five months past."

Genny blushed, ashamed at her hasty judgment of the situation. "Mistress, I regret my untoward thoughts. It is obvious that we at Ravenswood have been remiss in not aiding you with your burdens."

"Oh, nay, milady. All at Ravenswood have been most helpful when they are able," the woman replied with warmth.

"It is most kind of you to say so, but I would not agree. Sir Marcus, see to it that Mistress . . ." Genny paused, realizing she knew not the woman's name.

"Sarah, milady," supplied Lionel's mother graciously.

"See to it that Mistress Sarah has help to prepare her household for the winter."

"I would be most honored to take the task upon myself, milady," interjected Edmund, gazing tenderly upon the woman.

"I think that is most admirable, Edmund. I applaud your chivalry," Genny commended,

concealing her smile as she took in the young
man's obvious regard for the widow.

"Thank you, milady. You are most kind,"
said Sarah, releasing her gaze from the handsome young stablemaster.

"Sarah, I would that you address me as my
friends do. Please call me Genny."

"Milady, that would be improper!" responded Sarah.

"Oh, Sarah, you shall soon find out that I do
not esteem overrigid behavior," Genny said
easily.

In the weeks that followed, Genny had visited often with Sarah, and, like today, Edmund
had made a point of escorting her whenever
possible.

As Genny, Sir Marcus, and Edmund approached Sarah's cottage, they heard the excited cries of young Lionel.

"Lady Genny, Lady Genny!"

"Lionel, I would swear you have grown since
I last saw you! Soon you will be a man," said
Genny, watching his youthful pride blossom as
he squared his shoulders. "How fares your
mother?"

"She is well, but much bigger, milady," declared the boy, holding his hands far in front of
him.

Genny laughed at his depiction of his mother's advancing pregnancy. "I had better examine for myself the accuracy of your description,"
she said, holding Lionel's hand as they entered
the cottage.

True to Lionel's word, Sarah sat in a chair,

her abdomen large, the end of her pregnancy nearing. Her serene countenance lent testimony to her pleasure at the prospect of another child.

"Sarah, please do not attempt to rise," implored Genny as the woman struggled to stand.

"Thank you, Lady Genny. I am not sure I would have accomplished the feat," lamented Sarah, settling back once again in the chair.

"It will not be long now, Sarah."

"Aye. I fear this babe will not wait till Thisbe is healed," Sarah said with worry.

Thisbe had fallen days ago, wrenching her ankle, her advanced age hampering the healing process. With Edmund's help, Genny had taken it upon herself to administer aid to the village people during Thisbe's convalescence.

"Do not worry, Sarah. I promise you that I shall be here," Genny decreed. "Are you resting comfortably these days?"

"As well as can be expected," said Sarah, shifting her position awkwardly.

"Oh, but, Sarah, you shall soon hold a small babe for all your inconvenience. I can think of no other gift so worth the trials of suffering," said Genny, her own heart heavy with the realization that she would never hold a baby of her own. Since her husband refused to share the marriage bed, she would have to be content in caring for other women's children. The awareness left a deep, yearning sorrow within her breast.

"Aye," answered Sarah, "nothing compares to the innocence and sweetness of a babe."

A light knock at the door ended the women's exchange. Edmund, having finished repairing the roof of the cottage, entered to reluctantly hasten their departure, reminding Genny that today would bring the arrival of her husband.

Chapter 8

G enny soaked in the lavender-scented water for so long she was sure the puckers in her skin would be permanent. Then Mary brushed, dried, and styled her hair, arranging it atop her head with soft wisps that fell about her temples and the nape of her neck. Although Genny preferred to wear her hair loose, she had to admire how lovely it looked with the strings of pearls and satin ribbons interwoven among the tawny curls.

With that painstaking task completed, Mary proceeded to dress her in a gown Genny herself had designed and the castle seamstresses had just completed.

The undergarment was a white linen-and-lace chainse, its long, flowing sleeves banded tightly at her wrists. The kirtle itself was of emerald-green velvet, the sides slit low to her waist. The gown was belted with a wide golden girdle that rested low on her slim hips.

Mary was carefully fastening the golden circlet and veil to Genny's meticulously arranged hair when Elizabeth entered the chamber.

"Oh, Genny, you look absolutely breathtaking!" Elizabeth said, walking around her to view the full effect.

"Do you really think so?"

"Oh, yes. And I have something very special for you to add. Lady Eleanor asked me to give you these to wear." Elizabeth extended her hand, producing the most exquisite pearl necklace Genny had ever seen.

Genny gently lifted the long strand from Elizabeth's hand. Every pearl matched exactly in size and color.

"Elizabeth, these are beautiful!" she exclaimed as she held the necklace up to admire it more closely.

"And they will look beautiful on you," Elizabeth said, taking the strand from Genny. "Now turn around and let me fasten them for you." Genny stood very still while Elizabeth draped the pearls around her neck. "There." She turned Genny around to look at her. "Tristen will be very pleased," she pronounced.

"If he ever arrives," Genny replied dryly.

"Oh, he is here already. Has he not been to see you?" Elizabeth asked in surprise.

Genny fought off anger and disappointment, wondering just how long her husband had been back but not willing to humiliate herself by asking.

Elizabeth quickly added, "I'm sure he wanted to bathe and dress properly before seeing you. After a man has been gone for so long, he sometimes looks dreadful when he returns."

"Aye," Genny replied, not hiding her annoyance very well.

A knock on the door ended the awkward moment. Mary answered it, admitting a young boy who stood breathlessly just inside the bed-chamber, his nervousness at being in Lady Sinclair's private chamber evidently robbing him of speech.

"Yes?" Genny prompted him.

Slowly regaining his faculties, the lad finally found his voice. "Milady, the stablemaster has sent me to tell you that Mistress Sarah's babe is coming," he said anxiously. "He awaits your reply belowstairs," he finished, shifting his feet awkwardly.

"What be your name, young man?" inquired Genny.

"John, milady," the boy said, bowing in an impressive show of chivalry.

"John, return to Edmund and ask him to have Apollo readied and to meet me in the bailey immediately," Genny commanded.

"Aye, milady." John bowed again swiftly and hurried from the room to do her bidding.

"Where are my slippers?" Genny urgently asked her maid.

"Genny, whatever is going on?" questioned Elizabeth.

Busy putting on the green satin slippers Mary had promptly produced, Genny answered vaguely, "I have to go."

"Go? Go where?"

"To the village," she answered, moving quickly past Elizabeth to the other side of the room to retrieve the surcoat resting over the back of a chair.

"To the village! Why?"

"You heard the lad. Sarah is having her babe," she replied, attempting to rush past Elizabeth again. But Elizabeth grabbed her arm, halting her steps.

"Genny, what are you doing? Thisbe will deliver the babe."

"Nay, Thisbe has taken a fall and injured her ankle. I must go," she said, squirming out of Elizabeth's grasp.

"You are supposed to be at the feast honoring your marriage. Whatever will Tristen say?"

"He need not be told," she replied, quickly gathering her medicines into a cloth bag.

"I think your absence will be rather obvious!" Elizabeth pointed out, clearly distressed.

"Elizabeth, please calm down. The celebration is still a few hours away. I should be back before it even starts. If I am not, you'll simply conceal my absence till I return."

"Oh, I couldn't!" Elizabeth's voice quavered. "They would know, Genny. I am terrible at deception."

"Elizabeth, you must do this for me," Genny said sternly.

"I am afraid, and if Tristen finds out . . . Genny, he will be furious if you are not here."

Genny's own anger surfaced at the husband who had not even chosen to see her upon his return.

"He has waited this long with ease," she said darkly. "A few hours will hardly make much difference. Besides, if all goes well, he need never know." Genny pulled her surcoat over her gown.

"Now I really must go, Elizabeth. I am sure Edmund is anxious. Do not worry so. Everything will be fine," she said, placing a kiss on Elizabeth's cheek before swiftly leaving the room.

Riding into the village, Genny and Edmund saw a crowd gathered outside Sarah's cottage. Dismounting, they hurried to the door, and the townspeople cleared a path for them.

Upon stepping inside, Genny moved quickly through the outer room to the curtained doorway and through it to the bed where Sarah lay.

Sarah was pale and covered in perspiration. Her breathing was labored, and a low moan escaped her lips as an intense contraction took hold, her body writhing in pain.

Lionel was sitting at the foot of his mother's bed, sobbing into his hands.

"Milady, we're so glad you're here," said one of the women standing beside the bed. "She's having a hard time of it. It's not natural with a second babe."

After taking off her surcoat and laying it on the chair, Genny went to Lionel and gently raised him to his feet.

"What is all this crying?" she asked softly.

"She's going to die, Lady Genny. Just like my pa." His words were barely discernible through his choking sobs.

"She is not going to die, Lionel. You will soon have a baby brother or sister. Now come, this is no place for you," she said, taking the boy's hand and leading him to the outer room, where Edmund was nervously waiting.

"You two would do well to keep one another company," she said. "And, both of you, cease your fretting."

At Genny's severe look, Edmund collected himself and rallied a calm facade for the benefit of the frightened little boy, who, like Sarah, had come to mean much to him over the past several months. He even managed a smile, though Genny saw his nearly imperceptible wince as another anguished cry reverberated through the cottage.

Genny hurried back to Sarah, and from her examination, she could tell they still had a while to go yet. Having determined this, she sent the village women to collect from Thisbe the things for which she would soon enough have need. Awaiting their return, Genny gently wiped Sarah's forehead and face with cool, damp cloths.

"Lady Genny, thank you for coming," Sarah rasped.

"I promised I would be here. We will do this together," Genny said reassuringly, clasping Sarah's hand in hers.

"It is taking too long. Something is wrong, I know it." Between her labored breaths, Sarah's voice sounded frail and frightened.

"Nay, 'tis just a stubborn babe. Now try to rest a bit while I get things ready."

Not wishing to alarm Sarah, Genny, like Edmund, maintained a calm exterior. But inwardly she worried. For inwardly she had her own misgivings about this birth.

Chapter 9

Tristen entered the great hall to the sounds of music and laughter. The food and wine were abundant, and the inhabitants of the keep were having a merry time. Walking to the head table, he proceeded without notice until he stood directly behind Elizabeth.

"Oh!" Elizabeth jumped, sending her goblet tumbling across the table as Tristen's light kiss landed just below her ear.

"Is it me or having Alexander so near that makes you jittery?" he asked with a laugh.

"Neither. You startled me, Tristen," she replied curtly.

"Let me take a look at you," he said, raising her gently by her hands. "You are my favorite sister-in-law, you know."

"I am your only sister-in-law."

"That is what makes you my favorite." He turned to his younger brother. "Are you never going to give this poor woman a rest, Christopher?" he chided, winking at her obviously increased girth.

Elizabeth blushed warmly, but Tristen could

not help noticing that her hands were cold and trembling.

"I really frightened you, Elizabeth. You are yet atremble."

"I am simply tired. Genny and I have been very busy getting ready for the celebration," she quickly replied. Then her hands began to tremble even more, and her knees grew wobbly.

"You had better sit down, Elizabeth. You are looking awfully pale," Tristen said anxiously. "Perhaps I shall have to remind Lady Genevieve of your delicate condition," he added sternly.

"I would not presume to do that," said Christopher. "Genny is very practiced in herbs and healing. Actually, she is quite accomplished in medicinal matters."

"Oh, really? And where did my wife acquire this knowledge?"

"From what I understand, she helped the healing woman at her father's village," Lady Eleanor inserted.

"Indeed, another unusual practice for a *lady*, do you not agree?" asked Tristen.

"Not for our Genny," Christopher refuted with a smile.

Tristen scowled at his brother before returning his attention to Elizabeth, who really was not looking well at all.

"Where is my wife, by the way?" he asked, scanning the crowded room.

"She has yet to come down," said Lady Eleanor. "She is probably putting on the finishing touches, dear."

"Or getting up the courage," added Alexander under his breath.

Catching the muttered words, Tristen glared at his friend but declined to comment.

"Elizabeth, dear, were you not with Genny earlier?" asked Lady Eleanor.

Elizabeth choked on the wine she had just tasted, and Christopher had to gently pat her back. After several deep gulps of air, she replied faintly in a small, frightened voice, "Aye."

All eyes at the table were turned to her, awaiting more detail. Elizabeth, in the prolonged silence, shifted uncomfortably but said nothing, and Tristen became aware that something was amiss.

"Is there something you would like to tell me, Elizabeth?" he asked, his voice low and demanding, his gaze fierce and stony.

Elizabeth paled and leaned on Christopher's arm for support.

"I am waiting, Elizabeth," Tristen said darkly.

"I am feeling faint, Christopher," Elizabeth murmured. And her sudden pallor lent credence to the declaration.

Christopher's concern for his wife vied with his outrage at Tristen's disregard for Elizabeth's delicate condition.

"Alexander, summon Genny," he entreated in his anxiety for his wife.

"Nay, all I need is a little air," Elizabeth beseeched. To no avail. Alexander hastened out of the hall. "Oh, no," she muttered in confused consternation.

"Behold what your surliness has done," Christopher rebuked Tristen in indignation.

"I had not meant to distress Elizabeth," Tristen replied with sincere remorse.

"Christopher, please do not be angry with Tristen," Elizabeth implored her husband. "You do not understand. This is not Tristen's doing. 'Tis my own fault."

The brothers watched as the color quickly returned to Elizabeth's cheeks.

"I . . . That is, Genny . . ." Elizabeth stalled, only to be interrupted by Alexander, who had returned to the hall alone.

"Lady Genevieve is not in her chambers," he reported.

At the disclosure, all at the table turned again to Elizabeth, whose pallor had returned.

"I told Genny I would be unable to do this!" she suddenly wailed, and yielded to convulsive sobs.

"Unable to do what?" Tristen inquired in bewilderment.

"D-Diversion," she whimpered.

"Whatever are you talking about, my dear?" asked Christopher, solicitously patting her hand.

"I had hoped she would have returned by now. I told her Tristen would be vexed," she added in her own defense.

"Returned?" Tristen questioned. "Returned from where?"

"The village."

"The village! What is she doing there at this time of night?"

No answer was forthcoming.

"Answer him, Elizabeth," Christopher said with ominous authority.

"She is delivering a babe!" Elizabeth shouted back at her husband.

"Oh, dear," said Lady Eleanor under her breath, clearly surprised at Elizabeth's strong response.

Alexander, who was standing next to the older woman, heard her, and the corners of his mouth twitched as he fought to suppress a smile.

"Marcus!" Tristen shouted, beckoning his captain of the guard. The roar silenced the entire hall. "Have my horse readied immediately!"

"Yes, milord," replied Sir Marcus, and he hurriedly left the hall.

Turning back to his family, Tristen placed both hands upon the table, leaning halfway across its immense expanse to address those seated. "And as for you, my dear family. I do not know what liberties you have allowed Lady Genevieve in my absence, but I am home now, and this preposterous behavior will promptly cease!" And he spun around and stormed from the hall.

"Alexander," said Lady Eleanor, placing her hand upon his arm, "perhaps you should go with my son. I think he is about to make a fool of himself, and he very well may need you.''

"As you wish, milady,'' replied Alexander, grinning. "But I doubt he will need my assistance for that.''

Chapter 10

The scream pierced the night as Sarah's body heaved in another contraction.

Genny stripped off her green kirtle in the stifling heat and tension of the small room. The dainty circlet that had held her hair in place had long since been dislodged, and her thick waves now spilled loosely down her back to her waist.

"Hold her still, Anna," Genny commanded.

She had sent the other village women away after they had returned with Thisbe's medicine bag, requesting that Anna stay, knowing she had often aided Thisbe in many of the village birthings.

"I am going to check her progress," she said.

Placing one hand on Sarah's abdomen, Genny probed delicately with the other. Sarah screamed at the pressure, and Genny quickly withdrew her hand. Wiping her fingers on a cloth, she motioned with her head for Anna to follow her. They passed through the curtain into the outer room, where Edmund and Lionel sat waiting apprehensively.

" 'Tis over, Lady Genny?" asked Lionel anxiously.

"Nearly," Genny replied, smiling sweetly at the fearful young boy. "Will you fetch me more wood and fresh water? We are in need of them," she said, handing him the empty wooden bucket.

She waited until Lionel had left the room before she spoke to Anna and Edmund. "The babe is turned. It cannot be born the way it is now positioned."

"Do you know how to turn it, milady?" asked Anna.

"I have turned foals for birthing, but never a babe," Genny answered nervously.

"What will happen if it is not turned?" asked Edmund in alarm.

There was a moment of silence before Anna quietly answered, "She and the babe could die."

Placing her hand upon Edmund's arm, Genny looked into his anguish-filled eyes. "I shall do all within my power not to let that happen, Edmund. I promise," she pledged.

Genny led Anna back into the room and instructed her to help move Sarah so she lay across the bed with her knees bent high. Grabbing a stool from the corner, Genny placed it so she could sit directly in front of Sarah's raised legs.

"Hold on to her tightly, Anna. She needs to be still so I do not harm the babe."

Sarah screamed in agony as Genny gently inserted her hands into the birth canal, encircling the unborn babe within. Genny made attempt after futile attempt to secure a firm grasp, but Sarah's thrashing made it impossible.

"I cannot hold her still, milady. She is too strong for me," Anna said as she vainly struggled to hold Sarah down.

"You must keep trying, Anna. You must!"

Not one word was spoken by either man as Tristen and Alexander rode through the village. Nearing Mistress Sarah's cottage, they heard a bloodcurdling scream that penetrated the tranquility of the night. It sent a shiver up Tristen's spine, making the hairs on the back of his neck stand on end.

"I would assume that is the one," said Alexander, pointing to the small domicile from which the scream had emanated.

"Pure instinct, I suppose," replied Tristen dryly.

Entering the cottage, they found Edmund pacing worriedly in a useless attempt to relieve his anxiety.

"Milord!" he cried, his jaw hanging open at the unexpected arrivals from the castle.

"Edmund," replied Tristen, folding his arms across his massive chest.

"Edmund!" cried Genny from the room concealed behind the curtain.

The young stablemaster looked questioningly to his lord, who nodded that he should answer the summons. Edmund parted the curtain and hurried into the tiny bedchamber.

"Edmund, do you love this woman?" Genny

asked him, nodding toward Sarah, who writhed under the coverlet loosely draping her.

"Aye, milady."

"Is it your intent to marry her?"

"If she will have me."

"Will you?" Genny asked of Sarah.

"Aye," she replied through her pain.

"Splendid! With that settled, Edmund, I am in need of your assistance, and since you will soon be marrying Sarah, there is naught you will see now that you will not behold later."

Tristen could hardly believe he was hearing correctly as he listened to his wife's conversation through the curtain. He turned to Alexander, but Alexander was pushing aside the drape a fraction and staring into the room, wide-eyed in amazement.

"Sweet Jesu," he murmured.

Tristen peered in, too, totally unprepared for the sight that greeted him.

His wife was stooped over the bed, wearing only a linen chainse that exposed an enticing amount of bosom in a most provocative way. Hers were small breasts, but plump enough that a man would want to get his hands on them, thought Tristen. Her hair hung about her shoulders in tawny waves, some strands clinging to her face, which was slick with tiny beads of perspiration.

Another agonizing scream rent the air.

"Hold tightly to her, Edmund, and as soon as I get the babe turned, help her push." Genny's velvet voice rang with command but that did not lessen her femininity in the least.

As she labored for what seemed an eternity to right the unborn infant's position, sweat began to roll down her throat and onto her breasts. As the shiny droplets tumbled into the cleavage exposed by the neckline of her undergarment, Tristen watched, mesmerized, feeling a tightening in his loins.

"A bit more, Sarah. Hold on," said Genny, trying to comfort the terrified, pain-racked woman. Struggling a while longer, she was finally rewarded when she felt the babe shift to the proper position. "Push, Sarah!" she cried.

Sarah, near to collapse from exhaustion, tried to push, pulling hard against Edmund's strong arms, then gasping as she lay back weakly. Due to the long hours of labor, she had little strength remaining for the final delivery of her child.

"Push, Sarah," pleaded Edmund tenderly.

"I cannot. I am too tired," Sarah rasped.

"You must," he cajoled, gently stroking her damp hair and face.

"Come, Sarah, push!" Genny prodded.

"I can't . . . I can't."

"Push, damn you!" Genny shouted, the enormous roar from such a petite creature making both Tristen and Alexander jump.

Sarah gathered what little strength she had remaining and pushed with all her might till the babe's head crowned.

" 'Tis coming, Sarah! Keep pushing! Come now, keep pushing!" cried Genny, urging her on.

With one final push, the infant came, and Sarah collapsed in fatigue.

Pulling to ease the child out, Genny gasped at what followed. The newborn was almost totally blue, the tiny form still and lifeless.

Quickly Genny tied the cord with a leather strap and, taking a knife, severed it. The babe had not yet moved, and she knew she had little time to render aid.

Cradling the tiny form, she went to the clean bucket of cool water and gently immersed him up to his chest.

"Live, damn it," she pleaded softly. She raised the man-child, then lowered him again, this time all the way up to his tiny chin. "Breathe," she whispered, her eyes filling with tears.

The awful tension in the room was broken as the infant suddenly gasped for air and began choking. Genny quickly lifted him out of the water and cleaned his mouth and nose. He began to cry lustily.

"Saints be praised!" exclaimed Anna as she handed Genny a dry cloth with which to wrap the babe.

Tristen had not realized he had been holding his breath as he watched his wife feverishly battle for the newborn's life. He had felt the anguish expressed in her eyes, felt her sheer determination to will the babe to live. Only when the cry rent the silence did he breathe deeply in relief.

Genny set the swaddled infant in the crook of Sarah's arm. "A finer lad I have never seen, Sarah," she said softly.

"Thank you, Lady Genny," replied Sarah through her tears.

Genny looked up into Edmund's eyes, which were filled with tears of joy.

"You are quite a lady, milady," he said most respectfully.

"Thank you." Her voice was barely above a whisper.

Anna placed her hands on Genny's trembling shoulders. "You need rest, milady. You are shaking like a leaf."

"I quite agree," concurred a deep voice from the curtained doorway.

"Lord Tristen!" gasped Anna. She quickly curtsied.

Genny stared, not trusting herself to speak over the lump in her throat.

"If you are finished, Lady Genevieve, we will take our leave. Attempt to make yourself presentable," said Tristen curtly as his eyes roved critically over her dishevelment. "I will await you outside." He turned away without waiting for a response.

Genny stood riveted to the spot long after he had left. Finally she felt a light touch on her shoulder.

"I am sorry, milady. I had not meant to have Lord Tristen angered with you." Edmund's voice was as caring and gentle as his touch.

"Do not distress yourself. I am sure he will be more understanding when he calms down," Genny said. And she hastened to make sure all was in order for her to leave Sarah and Lionel in Anna's care.

* * *

Alexander watched with amusement as Tristen paced back and forth in front of the cottage while waiting impatiently for Genny to obey his command. Then both men's heads snapped up as Genny finally emerged from the cottage, on her face an almost childlike grin of satisfied exhaustion.

Tristen found himself momentarily disarmed by her beauty, and the fact that her seductive body was now hidden from his gaze by her kirtle and surcoat did little to alter his unbidden physical response to her. Angered at his lack of control, he addressed her more sharply than he had intended.

"Perhaps you have forgotten that a feast is being held in our honor, milady. Surely you of all people would not wish to miss the revelry."

Genny tensed at his open hostility and mocking tone. "Nay, milord, I have not forgotten. However, I see little cause for celebration," she said boldly, despite Sir Alexander's presence.

"Come, wife," Tristen said darkly. "The hour grows late. I have expended much time in fetching you."

Genny was still rankled enough to defy him. "Indeed, milord, why did you ride out here to fetch me? I would have returned as soon as possible. Did not Elizabeth tell you so?" she asked.

Tristen stared at her, his eyes flashing, his jaw tensing in reaction to her audacity. "Mayhap I misunderstood amidst her sobs," he answered angrily.

Genny approached to stand directly in front of him, unafraid to challenge his lofty height with her own petite stature. "You did not upset her, did you? She had naught to do with this, milord, and I will not have her upset in her condition."

Tristen's eyes narrowed in rage at her open defiance, but even in his anger he did not fail to notice that her overwhelming beauty was somehow enhanced by her agitation. He shook his head to try to clear his thinking, but all he could manage to conjure was the image of how her creamy white breasts had looked only moments ago, straining against her white chainse, glistening damply in the candlelight.

Taking advantage of the moment of silence, Alexander sought to reassure her. "Worry not, Lady Genevieve, Elizabeth is quite all right."

"Thank you for your concern, Sir Alexander. Elizabeth is so young, and already she is to birth her third babe."

"I would not worry, milady. Christopher is a most caring husband," Alexander replied, pointedly glancing at Tristen.

"Aye," Genny agreed, also sliding her gaze to Tristen. "He loves his wife greatly."

Tristen grew restless. "If you two have concluded your sentimental discourse on Elizabeth's welfare, we will take our leave."

Genny turned to mount Apollo, unaware that Tristen followed closely behind to render her aid. Firmly grasping the pommel with one hand, she gathered up her skirts with the other and smoothly mounted.

The maneuver revealed her legs from ankle to mid-thigh, and Tristen, standing close by, was both shocked at her wanton disregard for propriety and momentarily breathless at the proximity of her slender white legs. His heart beat rapidly, and he was unable to tear his eyes away. His gaze traveled the length of her well-shaped calves to her firm thighs clasping the animal's flanks.

Belatedly aware of Tristen's scrutiny, Genny attempted to arrange her gown to cover her bare legs, but her efforts were futile. At Edmund's urgent alarm about Sarah's plight, she'd had no time to change into one of the specially designed gowns she usually wore that allowed her to ride astride without immodesty.

Tristen was slow to notice that Alexander had moved his mount to Genny's other side, but the realization that his friend now beheld the same compromising view of his wife jolted Tristen into action. He dragged Genny from the saddle and into his arms, then strode purposefully across the yard and set her unceremoniously atop Demon.

"Milord," Genny exclaimed, "I have my own mount!"

" 'Tis dark, and I will not have you ride on your own through the woods," Tristen replied curtly, unwilling to divulge the real reasoning behind his actions. He quickly mounted behind the sideways-sitting Genny, inadvertently causing her to lose her precarious balance. His arm snaked out to capture her, lest she slide completely off the saddle.

"And you wanted to ride yourself? You can't even stay on a horse!" Tristen mocked.

Genny's anger flared. "I am quite accomplished at riding, milord."

"I have seen how you ride," Tristen growled, the vision of her exposed flesh still fresh in his mind. "However, tonight you will ride as a proper lady." And after securing Apollo's reins with his own, he spurred Demon forward.

Alexander's laughter followed on their heels.

The night air was cool against Genny's face, and her natural instinct was to nestle into the warmth of her husband's body, pressed so close to hers that she could feel his muscled strength and inhale his sweet, intoxicating musk. But so angered was she that he had demanded she ride in this fashion, she sat rigid in the saddle, refusing to allow herself the sanctuary his heat and nearness seemed to offer.

The scent of his wife's hair floated to Tristen's nostrils, a delicate fragrance of lavender, like spring. The tendrils fluttered against his face in the breeze, inflicting tiny, stinging sensations that were not unpleasant but were unsettling. He could feel the rigidity of her body, but more unsettling still was her squirming around in the saddle, creating a distinctive warmth where her body met his. Even through her surcoat he imagined he could feel the warmth of her skin, and he did not have to imagine the rhythmical heaving of her breasts against his arm.

Was she deliberately attempting to arouse him with her movements? he wondered in irritation. Nay, it was simply the juggling ride producing such distracting friction between them. He damned himself now for not letting her ride her own mount. Anything would be better than these feelings she was stirring in him. The thought of her bare legs, their silky tautness testimony to the hours she must spend riding her huge Arabian steed, tormented him.

Genny's breath quickened as she felt Tristen's grip tighten. Why had he been so angry with her tonight? In riding to Sarah's assistance, she had only done what circumstance dictated. After all, the villagers were his people. Shouldn't he care what happened to them?

Nay, doubtless he was the kind of man who cared only about himself, Genny reasoned angrily.

A wife shouldn't think such things about her husband, she rebuked herself a moment later. She had been raised to know that a husband was due respect. But allotting him respect was going to be very trying if he was given to such frequent fits of rage.

The moment they were within the bailey of Ravenswood, Genny was anxious to rid herself of his presence.

Tristen dismounted hastily, turning to help Genny from the saddle. Although his manner was gruff, his touch was surprisingly gentle as his large hands encircled her small waist to set her lightly on the ground.

Genny inhaled sharply at the contact, and she sought his gaze, unsure what to make of this tender attention. His dark blue eyes seemed to be drinking her in, and her heart began to pound at his masculine appraisal. These unfamiliar responses to a man's touch, a man's look, were disturbing to Genny, and she knew not what to do.

"Lady Genevieve, lest you forget, our guests await," he said, his voice gently taunting, as if he was aware of her preoccupation. "Alexander," he said, turning to his friend, "have someone see to the horses, and let my family know that Lady Genevieve and I will join them shortly." Then he took Genny by the arm, led her through the arched doorway, and began propelling her toward the stairs.

"With your professed concern for our guests, you would squander more of your valuable time before joining them?" Genny challenged boldly, uncertain of his intent as they mounted the stairs.

"Your attendance is required as well, milady. And you are in no condition to welcome homage."

His assessment of her appearance suddenly made her feel exposed, vulnerable. "I am aware of my appearance," Genny countered in what she hoped was a steady voice. "However, I am fully capable of attending to it myself. I *am* a grown woman."

"Of that I am well aware." Tristen's suggestive tone disquieted Genny. "But your tendency to deviate from the expected requires that I take responsibility for ensuring your attendance."

"Methinks you would do well to consider the

welfare of your people above your own petty pride," Genny snapped, surprising even herself. They had reached the door to her chambers, and she found herself thrust none too gently within.

"You will cease your insolence, woman," Tristen commanded.

His deep voice resounded through her body, and something deep inside Genny cautioned her to hold her tongue.

"What are you waiting for?" he questioned impatiently. "Surely you have another gown more presentable than that which you are wearing."

Genny looked forlornly down at her once-resplendent gown, now wrinkled and soiled. Conceding to herself that she could not be seen in such disrepair, she chose another kirtle. and chainse. She stood motionless, holding the garments in her hands, awaiting Tristen's departure.

"Why do you delay?" he asked, seeming to take pleasure in her discomfort in his presence.

"Milord, you cannot mean to stay here," she said, a stain of scarlet fiercely coloring her cheeks.

"Have no fear, Lady Genevieve. My sole intention is to see that you are properly attired before we greet our guests. I have no desire to watch you disrobe." He paused. "I shall avert my gaze so that you may retain whatever modesty you may still possess." And with that he simply turned away from her to warm his hands by the fire.

Outraged at his insults, mortified at the notion of disrobing in his presence, yet oddly chastened by his cool indifference, Genny knew not how to contest his command. Her hands trembling with frustration and anxiety, she hurried to remove her ravaged apparel and cover herself up again.

The rustling of heavy velvet seemed uncannily loud to Tristen, audible even over the crackling of the fire, and he had to fight the images his mind flashed before him. Images of her petite body being slowly revealed, the creamy shoulders, the firm breasts he had but glimpsed earlier, the tiny waist he had clasped on their ride to Ravenswood, the delicately curved hips that had snuggled close to his groin.

Unnerved by his inability to control his thoughts, Tristen was even more unsettled by the fact that it was impossible to control his body's response. He caught sight of her, now dressed, as she sat to brush her hair. He watched as she futilely attempted to remove the pearls and satin ribbons that had become hopelessly entangled in her long tresses.

Without forethought to his actions, he moved behind her, took her hands from her hair, and proceeded to gently unwind the tangled ribbons.

The startling touch of his fingers against her scalp sent an unexpected jolt of pleasure through Genny, and though she knew that, in light of his earlier actions, she should protest, instead she felt her defenses weakening. As the ribbons fell free, she languidly reached for the brush settled in her lap, only to have her hand covered by his as he, too, reached for it. Raising startled eyes to his, their hands still touching, she was instantly lost in the depths of his compelling gaze, and his nearness caused a warm ache to spread throughout her body.

He held her gaze, his hand upon hers caressing as he brought his other hand to her face, touching her cheek as he lowered his head to hers. His kiss was hypnotically slow, almost thoughtful, and as his tongue traced the soft fullness of her lips, he whispered hoarsely, "Genny."

A delightful shiver of desire ran through her at the sound of his voice speaking her name.

The disturbing crescendo of his emotions rocked Tristen to the very essence of his being. Never before had he kissed a woman thusly. His impetus for doing so puzzled him. Why had he felt an overwhelming urge to embrace her so tenderly? And why did he now regret it so?

Abruptly withdrawing from her, he turned to glance around the room, seeking a safer outlet for his attention. He spied the long strand of pearls Genny had placed upon the table. Picking them up, he realized they were the very strand his father had presented to his mother when she had given birth to Tristen.

Lady Eleanor had always worn them on special occasions, and without really being aware of it, he had assumed she would have been wearing them tonight.

Struggling to rouse herself from the spell

Tristen's kiss had cast, Genny saw the pearls held aloft in his hand, noted his look of mild confusion. She stood to face him. "Your mother wanted me to wear her pearls tonight," she explained, unaware of their special significance.

"That is as it should be," Tristen intoned, unsure why he had responded so even as he acknowledged the fact that his mother had never expressed a desire for Kathryn to wear the necklace. "Allow me, milady," he offered gallantly, holding the loop aloft.

Stepping within the circle of his arms, so he might secure the clasp on the beautiful strand, Genny longed for the comfort those arms might have afforded her had the marriage they were about to celebrate been one of love.

Chapter 11

All eyes turned toward Lord and Lady Sinclair as they entered the great hall. Murmurs of approval surrounded Genny, word having spread about her successful assistance to Mistress Sarah.

Taking his place at the table of honor, Tristen sat at the head with Genny on his right, Alexander on his left.

Christopher stood, raising his goblet in the air. His voice carried throughout the hall. "A toast, to my brother and his new wife, Lady Genevieve."

All in the room raised their goblets and voices in affirmation. Genny sensed Tristen stiffening beside her. She raised her eyes to seek his, but he did not even glance at her as he drank.

Since leaving her chambers they had not spoken a word. He was visibly tense, and Genny was beginning to wonder if she had imagined the tender scene they had shared mere moments ago.

The food was brought to the table and served with a ceremonial flourish that befitted the festive occasion. It was an imposing banquet, with an elaborate array of delicacies. There was a large roasted boar's head and two enormous swans dressed and baked to perfection. There were platters of stuffed partridges and rabbits, stewed potatoes, and an endless number of pies, with sweet ale and cheese complementing the fare.

Christopher, seated at Genny's right, leaned over to speak in her ear in order to be heard above the gaiety. "I trust my brother had no trouble locating you?"

"He found me," she replied quietly.

Tristen focused his attention on Alexander and Lady Eleanor, while Genny told Elizabeth of the joyous addition to Sarah's household. The bride and groom stole glances at one another throughout the evening but did not once engage in conversation.

Thomas, one of the first among Tristen's men-at-arms to openly approve the new Countess of Ravenswood, stood upon one of the benches and offered another toast. "To Lady Genevieve!"

All the men raised their voices and tankards in a cheer.

"Lady Genevieve, please favor us with one of your dances," Thomas implored.

Another cheer rang out in support of the proposal. The musicians responded to the enthusiastic cries with a popular and lively melody, and the spirited guests posthaste demonstrated their endorsement by commencing to dance.

Genny glanced toward Tristen, but at that

moment Thomas took her by the arm and led her into the circle of dancers. Her mental agitation of necessity submerged in the merriment, she began to twirl and turn.

Tristen watched as the crowd enveloped Genny and she began to move gracefully in interpretation of the exhilarating tune. Her cascade of hair swayed with supple richness, and she raised her skirts above her slender ankles as she executed the intricate steps. Her face was aglow with delight, her dazzling eyes alight with laughter. Her joy was almost childlike, but the effect on Tristen was seductive.

"What think you now of your wife, Tristen?" asked Alexander, noting that his friend was unable to pull his eyes away from Genny.

"My opinion has not changed," he replied curtly.

"Come now, my friend, you cannot tell me she is the kind of wife you thought to reject so easily."

Tristen watched as Genny's hair flew about her face, heard her laughter above the music. It was a painfully sweet sound, alive and full of excitement.

"I grant you she is lovely enough to look at. That, however, does not change my dislike for this marriage," he retorted sharply, raising his goblet to drink.

"Really, Brother, I can think of many who would find wedlock with Genny no burden at all," interjected Christopher, overhearing the last of Tristen's remarks.

"I quite agree, Christopher," said Alexander, openly admiring Genny as she danced.

As the music grew faster-paced, the dancers, including Genny, grew bolder in their steps. They formed a cotillion, with the men comprising the outer circle, the women the inner, the men promenading in one direction while the women commenced to move in the other. The circles began to move faster and faster, keeping time with the music.

From time to time the music paused and the men clasped the ladies about the waist and lifted them into the air, and it soon become an unspoken challenge to see which man could hold his lady the highest and the longest.

Genny, caught up in the gaiety, refused to heed Tristen's scowls, and she did not notice who next grabbed her around the waist to lift her high in the air. But as the powerful arms ever so slowly lowered her, her eyes were captured by those of her husband. She knew a searing blush was staining her neck and face, and her senses began to reel as she felt his warm breath upon her neck, felt the unnerving friction as he slid her down the length of his body. Her heart jolted and her pulse pounded, and as if she were touching fire, she quickly removed her hands from where they rested upon his shoulders.

"Milord, I did not know you danced," she said, her voice fluttering in her nervousness.

"There are many things you do not know about me," he replied softly. Then he abruptly added, "However, my men seem to know a lot about you."

"I have spent more time with them than with you, milord," she said simply.

"So it seems," he said, suddenly releasing her waist as though she were hot to the touch.

Genny watched his eyes flash with anger, but before she could find speech, a male voice intruded on the moment.

"Lady Genny, I would be honored to have this dance."

Genny turned to see Alexander's handsome, friendly face.

"That is, if your husband does not object," he added, looking at Tristen.

"I have no objection. My wife enjoys the pleasure of dancing with many men." With that Tristen turned on his heel, leaving Genny with Alexander.

Genny lowered her head to hide her embarrassment and confusion at her husband's rudeness.

"I am sorry, Lady Genny. Tristen does not seem to be himself tonight. He is not usually so vicious in his comments to ladies."

"You need not offer apologies for my husband, Sir Alexander," she murmured.

"Would you like to go back to the table? Perhaps you are tired. You have had a most unusual night, Lady Genny," he said with genuine concern.

"Aye," Genny agreed with a smile, "it has been that. I should like, however, to have this dance with you, sir," she said, determined not to let her husband see the hurt his words had inflicted.

Alexander guided Genny across the floor with aplomb, and they conversed with ease while dancing.

Tristen watched the display with rapt interest, gripping his goblet with acute pressure, his eyes never leaving the couple on the dance floor. He did not fail to note the spontaneity with which they conversed, nor that the flush in his lovely wife's cheeks from the dancing made her all the more appealing.

He stiffened, forcibly reminding himself that this was a wife he did not want. True, she was proving different from what he had expected, but all the same, any woman who had so many men clamoring at her feet had to be wanton, regardless of her chaste appearance. He saw the looks the men gave her—the same kind of looks men had given his first wife, Kathryn.

What a fool he had been then. He had thought that, like himself, the men had merely admired Kathryn for her beauty. He had thought her innocent. In truth, she had been nothing but a common harlot shrouded in finery. She had known exactly what she was doing. She had calculatedly sought his affection, then lied outrageously, even disgracing him on her dying day.

His eyes narrowed as he glanced up at the couple now quitting the dance and approaching the table. He was again married, and this woman's veins coursed with the same inferior blood as did Kathryn's. Well, by God, he would not lower himself to join this one in the marriage bed and risk offering up his affections in vain sacrifice again. He would not be made a fool twice.

"I fear, Lady Genny, we are being regarded with a most harsh scowl," remarked Alexander, observing Tristen.

"That look, sir, seems to be the only one my husband knows to grace me with," Genny replied quietly.

They took their seats, and Tristen replenished Alexander's goblet while addressing Genny.

"I trust you have enjoyed yourself tonight?" His tone indicated he did not care if she had or had not.

"Aye, it has been a most pleasant evening."

"Good. Then I think it is time we bid our guests good night and retire. I am sure you are most worn out from this eventful night." He rose from his chair and extended his hand to her.

Startled, Genny placed her quivering fingers in his.

"Good friends and family," Tristen said loudly, instantly gaining the crowd's attention. "We thank you for this gift of celebration. We retire now and leave you to your gaiety."

Chapter 12

Tristen awoke with his head pounding, his mouth dry, and his body aching. After escorting his wife to her chambers last night, he had later returned to the hall, drinking himself into such a stupor that Christopher and Alexander found it necessary to assist him to bed. The place from which, at this moment, he was valiantly attempting to rise.

Why, he asked himself, did this new wife of his have him behaving in such an inane manner? He'd been married but a few short months, and the wench was wreaking havoc in his life. He hadn't drunk himself into such a stupor since he had been a callow young knight attempting to prove his mettle. Even after Kathryn's betrayal he had never felt a need to immerse himself in such a way.

Thoughts of his first wife only enhanced his foul disposition toward his new one. Perhaps some fresh air and exercise would provide release from that and the lingering effects of his overindulgence.

Approaching the practice field, Tristen nearly

stumbled as he caught sight of his wife standing between Christopher and Alexander as Christopher released an arrow from his longbow toward the target downfield. Genny's laughter floated to Tristen when his brother leaned down to speak to her.

Jealous rage, an emotion Tristen would never admit existed within himself, welled up inside him at her open camaraderie with the two men.

"Christopher," cried Genny, "you have improved greatly!"

"I could not let you continue to humiliate me in front of the men any longer," he replied jovially. "However, Genny, I fear our Alexander here will prove a worthy adversary for even you."

Genny turned and looked up at Alexander, a mischievous smile lighting her face. "Thou art accomplished, sir?" she asked.

"With all humility, milady," said Alexander with a bow, enjoying the banter, "I am very accomplished."

"I should like to judge the merits of your boasts for myself, sir," Genny replied with enthusiasm.

"As you wish, Lady Genny. Christopher, if you would please set the targets."

Tristen watched in livid silence as Alexander and Genny rivaled one another in good humor. Each accurate arrow Genny released seemed to pierce more deeply into his mind, enhancing his anger. He could not believe that a lady would purposely learn a man's skill and so flagrantly flaunt that ability. The endorsement his brother and best friend were so obviously granting such unseemly behavior only heightened his displeasure.

'' 'Tis a pity not all our men are as diligent in their practice or as accurate as Lady Genny.'' Sir Marcus, having approached unnoticed, interrupted Tristen's silent observation.

"She comes here often?" asked Tristen with shock and disgust.

"Aye, milord. But fear not. I keep watch that naught happens to the lady while she is here," he said, evidently thinking this the reason for his lord's disapproval.

Tristen gave no reply to the man's assurances. He simply walked, unobserved, toward the merry trio.

Watching as Alexander's last arrow hit the center of the target, Genny exclaimed with delight, "You are indeed very accomplished, sir!"

"No more than you, milady. Where did you learn to shoot with such accuracy?" he asked in obvious admiration.

'' 'Tis an interesting question. I, too, would like to know where she acquired such skills,'' said Tristen from behind, surprising them.

Genny stiffened at his implicit rebuke. "Milord, I did not think we would see you so early today," she said with mock sweetness, obviously referring to his overindulgence of the previous night.

Christopher cast his eyes downward as Tristen glared, knowing that only two within Ravenswood could have informed her of his excess.

"I am sorry to disappoint you, Lady Genevieve."

"One must expect something before one can be disappointed, milord. I expect nothing from you," she retorted. "As to your inquiry, I was taught my skills by the captain of the guard at Montburough."

"Your father condoned such instruction?"

"Seeing that I possessed a certain proficiency in weapons, he conceded to my training," she said, not bothering to mask her air of defiance.

" 'Tis a shame he did not invest as much time in having you instructed in the skills of a lady," said Tristen rudely.

"I am as efficient in household matters as any lady," replied Genny, meeting his accusing eyes boldly.

"Perhaps. However, you obviously have not been instructed as to the proper behavior of a wife."

Genny's breathing hitched painfully with her anger and hurt. When she spoke, resentment tinted her voice. "When I am treated as a wife, then perhaps I shall behave as a wife."

Alexander and Christopher stood in awkward silence as Tristen clenched his fists in anger.

"Milady, one must prove one is worthy of a position before being awarded the privileges of that position," he said caustically.

She swallowed the despair in her throat, forcing herself to address him. "Yet a wife need do nothing to earn the denunciation of her husband, it seems." And she whirled on her heel and stalked away.

Tristen turned back to his brother and Alexander, ignoring their disapproving expressions. "I have come here for exercise. Should you care to join me, you may do so—on the condition that you do not utter one word concerning my wife," he said with grim finality.

"Christopher, you may choose to stay," said Alexander. "However, I find I am exceedingly hungry after my strenuous competition this morning. I am going indoors to seek out the remains of last night's feast."

The mere mention of food unsettled Tristen's queasy stomach.

"I am sure there is plenty of cold boar and sweet ale for the taking," Alexander added, turning to go. He had taken only a few steps before he called back over his shoulder, "I shall see you two at supper." And his laughter echoed through the yard at his sight of Tristen's pallor.

Genny mumbled a pithy suggestion as to where her devil of a husband might find a suitable home as she went to the stable and asked Edmund to saddle Apollo. Once she was past the gates and out in the open countryside, she pushed the Arabian into a gallop.

The fresh air and vigorous ride did much to soothe her agitated state of mind, and after she had put a comfortable distance between herself and Ravenswood, she slowed Apollo's gait, assuming a pleasant pace as she entered the dense woods.

Even in the morning sunlight the trees, though barren of leaves, cast heavy shadows, giving the forest a mysterious and slightly foreboding allure. Winding her way among the trees, Genny began to have the uneasy feeling that she was being watched. Suddenly Apollo snorted loudly and skittered sideways, and Genny became aware of another horse and rider.

Attempting to control Apollo, she finally saw to her relief that she recognized the approaching rider. It was Thomas on the riding path.

"Lady Genny," he called in greeting.

He sat tall upon his horse, his slender build and perfect posture making him appear even taller. His dark hair accented tawny brown eyes, and his handsome features were flawed only by the scars left by a childhood disease that had nearly taken his life.

"Thomas," she greeted him.

"You are enjoying your ride, milady?"

"Aye. 'Tis a lovely day, perfect for riding."

"I do not think Lord Tristen would approve of your riding alone, however. I would be most honored to accompany you," he offered.

Genny lowered her eyes. *No, sir, you are wrong. Lord Tristen would not care what happens to me,* she thought sadly.

She had wanted to be alone, but it appeared that that was not to be. She nodded. "I thank you for your kind offer."

When they reached the cliffs that had been

her destination, she dismounted, welcoming the brisk autumn air on her face as she gazed at the churning waters of the Bristol Channel below.

" 'Tis cold, milady. Perhaps we should return to Ravenswood," Thomas suggested.

"Nay," Genny replied, shaking her head. " 'Tis one of my favorite spots. I want to stay for a while, but please do not feel that you must linger. I will be fine alone."

"I would not think to leave you here alone. Perhaps a walk, milady, would warm us," he said, offering his arm.

After securing their horses to a nearby tree, they walked a long while in silence, Thomas taking much time to observe the woman. Since her arrival at Ravenswood, she had been the only thing on his mind. Day after day he had watched Lady Genny, intrigued by her vivacious spirit, overwhelmed by her fair beauty. His body tensed as he thought of this delicate creature married to the crude Lord Tristen. The blackguard, though mighty, didn't deserve a woman as enchanting as Lady Genevieve.

"So you ride here often, milady?" he asked.

"As often as I can. I love the beauty and solitude it offers."

"And I have intruded."

The man's apologetic tone made Genny feel guilty for her earlier irritation.

"Nay. I enjoy the companionship. At home I spent much time in the company of my father's men."

"They were fortunate to have a mistress such

as you," he said graciously. "I would venture your home was much different than Ravenswood."

Genny sighed deeply before answering. "Aye. I am afraid that I was ill-prepared for the turn my life has taken."

"Should you have any need of support, milady, I am, as always, your servant," Thomas said, placing his other hand upon hers where it rested on his forearm.

So moved was Genny by the man's sincerity that she unthinkingly disregarded propriety, allowing his hand to linger.

The sound of pounding hooves caused them to stop walking. Genny turned around as her husband reined in Demon, who reared within inches of them.

"Ever I find you in the company of men, milady," Tristen said, looking down pointedly at Thomas's hand resting upon hers.

"Ever I find your temperament foul, milord," retorted Genny.

"You may return to the castle, Thomas," Tristen commanded, pinning the other man with a hard stare.

Thomas bristled at being thus dismissed by the earl, certain that if they had not been interrupted, Lady Genny would have turned to him for comfort in her loneliness. He looked down into her face, trying to read her thoughts, reluctant to abandon her to her angry husband. However, he knew he had no other choice. Not for the moment, anyway. He turned and went to seek his mount, tethered back near the cliffs.

After Thomas departed, Tristen dismounted Demon and stood gazing at his wife. The crisp autumn air had added a pleasing pinkness to her face. Or maybe the company of another man had evoked the glow? Now that he thought of it, he had seen that same radiance on Kathryn's face many a time when she was in the presence of men. She had adored their attentions, had encouraged them, taking delight in provoking him.

"I have warned you before, Lady Genevieve, that I will not be made the fool."

"And I have told you 'tis not I who makes you appear so, milord," Genny retorted.

"You would do well to control your tongue, milady. I am not a man of limitless patience," he growled.

For once Genny remained wisely silent as he escorted her back to Apollo and helped her mount.

Tristen was inwardly fuming. He wanted to shake this woman and wring her beautiful neck. She was fast becoming the bane of his existence. Was he, he wondered on the silent ride back to the castle, fated to wed women who were faithless and deceitful?

Chapter 13

Genny was filled with apprehension as she reread the message Aunt Beatrice had sent a fortnight ago, stating that she and Philip intended to visit. In truth, she had missed Philip, though she had yet to rid herself of perplexity and remorse over the disconcerting way they had parted.

Knowing also that she must consult her husband before granting consent to their visit, Genny had agonized for days before approaching him, wondering if Christopher had told him of her cousin's possessive behavior. Not that Tristen would worry over her affections; rather, he would likely think she had done something to entice Philip's attentions. But Tristen had reacted with nonchalance, and Christopher had not yet returned from his mission to some of the outlying villages, where he had gone to ensure that preparations for winter were well under way. Genny suspected that, after the incident at Montburough, he would not greet Philip gladly. Indeed, she was unsure if she could. Nonetheless, her aunt and cousin were now on their way.

They arrived late one afternoon, barely missing the first flakes of winter that began to fall as Genny stepped out into the bailey to greet them.

"Genny, my dear, it is so good to see you after all these months!" exclaimed Aunt Beatrice, hugging her niece.

"I have missed you also, Aunt."

Slowly Genny raised her gaze to Philip, who was standing next to his mother. Not without pain did she take in her cousin's familiar, handsome visage as he clasped her winter-chilled hands.

"I, too, am glad to see you, Genny," he said quietly. "I feared you would not grant my visit after my appalling behavior at our parting. I have come to beg forgiveness for my transgressions." His abject manner and genuine request tore at Genny's conscience and evoked her kind disposition.

"Philip, I, too, wish to put the incident behind us and resume our previous friendship," she said with sincerity.

"I am afraid that I behaved rashly when I learned of Genny's marriage to the earl," Philip offered by way of hasty explanation to his mother, who evidently had not heard of the unpleasant incident between the cousins. He turned back to Genny. "I was only thinking of your welfare, Genny."

"Indeed, we were all taken aback by the

swiftness with which my brother arranged your marriage," Beatrice interjected.

"How fares my father?" Genny entreated.

"As well as can be expected," replied her aunt. "Sad to say, he seems to worsen in your absence. The men your husband sent to manage Montburough are not as interested in keeping him informed of matters as you were. I fear that Montburough will become sorely neglected," she said, sighing dramatically.

Though the news would otherwise be grim, Genny knew her aunt was not above twisting the truth to suit herself and suspected she was doing so now. Genny, who was certainly not blind to Tristen's faults, could not take exception to the way he administered his responsibility to his people and lands.

"How long will you be staying, Aunt?" she inquired, partly to change the subject and partly because she feared Aunt Beatrice's abrasive presence might place additional stress on her already strained marriage.

"Oh, I promised my dear brother we would stay as long as it took to assure that you are well settled here. Your father does so worry about your happiness."

"I assure you, I am quite content," Genny asserted with what she hoped was convincing bravado. For if they required additional proof of her happiness, they would be staying on at Ravenswood for a very long time. She shuddered slightly at the thought of their discovering the disarray of her marriage and reporting the distressing news to her father.

Noticing her shiver, Philip suggested, "Genny, it is much too cold for you and Mother to be standing out here." Taking her by the elbow, he led her into the castle, his mother following close behind.

Genny quickly saw them settled into chambers purposefully distant from her own, not wishing them to become aware of her chaste union, then bade them a good rest until supper.

Having changed into a fresh kirtle for the evening meal, Genny was preparing to leave her chambers when a discreet knock sounded at her door. She found Tristen standing there, handsomely clad in a forest-green tunic, its rich hue a match to the finely loomed knit of his hose. The tunic was belted with a wide leather girdle that emphasized the breadth of his shoulders.

The unexpectedness of his visit nearly took her breath away, but more startling still was the surprising smile on his face. "Milord, is something amiss?" she asked quickly.

"Nay, I have but come to escort my wife to supper." He looked amused at her confusion. "Are you not ready?" he queried, for all the world as if this were a common nightly occurrence for the two of them, when in fact this was the first time he had deigned to escort her to the hall since their marriage feast.

Secretly, Genny was grateful for the attentive gesture, which would better enable her to make a show of marital unity in front of Philip and Aunt Beatrice.

Upon entering the hall, Tristen seated

Genny at the table, then merely nodded to
Philip before greeting his former mother-in-law.

"Mistress Aldred," he said formally, his face
giving away nothing of his feelings at the awkward meeting.

Tristen thought back on the few occasions he
had found himself in the presence of Kathryn's
family. Always such encounters had left him
disgusted. The weak, frivolous Philip and his
ambitious, calculating mother all but nauseated
him. Looking at them now, seated at his table,
Tristen could only hope they had mellowed fa-
vorably with the passage of time.

With a slight nod, Beatrice replied, "Lord
Tristen."

Although the atmosphere remained somewhat subdued, the meal was, on the surface,
congenial enough. Lady Eleanor was gracious,
endeavoring to confer a sense of ease to an ex-
traordinarily strained situation.

Beatrice Aldred, on the other hand, sat rigidly upright throughout the meal, her hawkish
face and penetrating, high-pitched voice adding
to the tension. Genny noticed that her aunt all
but ignored Tristen while appearing totally fascinated with Sir Alexander, who sat next to her
at the large table.

Alexander, who over the years had become
accustomed to the flirtations of women of all
ages, was friendly but reserved in response.

Genny was embarrassed by the way her aunt
was fawning shamelessly over the younger man
and caught Alexander's eyes in silent supplication, pleading his forgiveness of her relative's

behavior. Never before had Genny seen Beatrice behave so piteously.

Philip seemed oblivious of his mother's flirtation, spending the majority of the meal being excessively solicitous to Genny. Even though he was amiable toward Tristen, Genny sensed an underlying enmity between the two men, which heightened her discomfort.

Finally, to her relief, Tristen suggested that their guests, having traveled for several days, were most certainly in need of rest, thus putting an end to the strange ordeal.

Tristen mumbled curses to himself as he walked the length of the courtyard. Since the arrival of their guests more than two weeks ago, the snow had fallen almost without interruption—a sign, Tristen was sure, that God, too, did not tolerate their presence very well. Each day had become a labor of patience to endure their objectionable company.

Beatrice spent each night vainly vying for Alexander's regard. How his friend managed to eat—and keep his meal down—was a mystery to Tristen. Beatrice's coquetry was so unseemly, like that of a faded harlot well beyond the age of usefulness. Yet, despite her years, how like Kathryn this woman behaved. For the first time he clearly saw the unattractive desperation of such women, whose only ambition was to be coddled and adored and indulged in their every whim. He cringed to realize that Beatrice was the woman Kathryn, had she lived, would have become.

Caught unaware as a lump of snow landed smartly on his right cheek, Tristen cursed again, losing his footing on the slippery ground. A familiar laugh floated across the yard. Righting himself and looking around for the source of the laughter, he spotted Philip and Genny running through the snow-covered garden.

As he approached the frolicking figures, he caught fragments of the merry banter the two exchanged.

"Philip, you always had a bad aim. You take your eyes off the target too soon," chided Genny as his next snowball flew harmlessly to the right of her, missing its intended mark.

" 'Tis only your quickness and size that save you," he replied, dodging another of her well-aimed shots.

Genny ducked behind one of the benches and quickly crafted a small mound of snowballs. Giggling, she gathered them into a fold of her heavy woolen cloak, and, rising, she quietly stalked Philip, who was occupied with preparing his own defense. Retrieving one of the snowballs from her makeshift pouch, she took careful aim and hurled it. The accuracy of the shot was evidenced by Philip's outcry. Unwilling to give her cousin any chance for reprisal, Genny sent more snowballs through the air in rapid succession, each as accurate as the first.

Philip finally managed to launch a counterattack, hurling one large snowball that caught Genny squarely in the chest.

"You will pay dearly for that, Philip," warned Genny with a laugh as she prepared to

send another snowball sailing toward her
cousin.

Philip artfully dodged the flying ball by
crouching, leaving clear the path to Tristen,
who still observed the pair.

Genny blanched at the sight of her husband,
her misguided snowball falling in clumps from
his scowling face. Then, unable to control herself, she burst into peals of laughter at the vision he made. Unfortunately, her mirth only
seemed to make his temper worsen.

"Good shot, Genny!" exclaimed Philip,
joining her in her laughter.

Noting Tristen's clenched jaw and his obvious failure to appreciate the humor of the mishap, Genny finally repressed her laughter.
"Milord, my apologies. 'Twas not my intent to
hit you. 'Twas intended for Philip," she offered. Genny turned to Philip. "Had you not
moved, it would be *your* face covered in snow."
She giggled again at the thought.

What angered Tristen was not the snowball,
or even his wife's amusement at his expense,
but the obvious pleasure she took in Philip's
company. In the weeks since her cousin's arrival, Tristen had observed them sharing many
such carefree and intimate adventures. Of
course, he mused, Genny seemed to be able to
laugh and enjoy herself with everyone *but* her
husband. During her family's visit they had so
far maintained a convincing facade of compati-
bility, but she was never totally at ease in his
company.

Something taut inside him suddenly gave

way, and he purposefully strode forward.
Stooping down next to Philip, he thoughtfully
retrieved several snowballs from his stockpile.
Then he advanced meaningfully upon Genny,
projecting his first snowball.

Belatedly recognizing her husband's surprisingly playful intent, Genny breathlessly reached
into her cloak, only to find that she had depleted her cache. In an attempt to elude the on-
slaught of snowballs that suddenly arced
through the air at her, she turned and ran.

Rounding the corner of the stables, she hurried along the stone wall until she discovered a
niche created by an unused doorway. Hearing
Tristen's heavy footfalls as he rounded the corner, she swiftly hid herself, placing her hand to
her breast to still her heavy breathing and the
rapid thundering of her heart.

Once her breathing had quieted somewhat
she listened intently for her husband's approach. She heard nothing, and each second
she waited seemed like an eternity. Slowly she
eased her head out to peek.

Tristen pounced, and Genny shrieked as his
large body backed her against the wall. With his
hands flat against the stone, he trapped her
within the confines of his arms. His broad
shoulders heaved as he inhaled deeply, and he
locked his eyes with hers even as the white va-
por of their labored breathing merged in a cold
cloud suspended between them. His gaze traveled over her face, then searched her eyes once
more.

"Genny," he murmured.

His voice, deep and sensual, sent a rippling awareness through her, and Genny realized that the only other time he had ever called her Genny had been on the night of their marriage feast, when he had kissed her so tenderly. His nearness, as well as the memory of his lips upon hers, sent a shiver through her body.

Lowering his head to hers, he whispered her name again.

"Oh, there you be," hailed Philip, spotting Tristen, who was only partially concealed in the recess of the doorway.

"Damn," Tristen muttered under his breath as he quickly withdrew from her.

Philip scowled as he got close enough to observe Genny's face glowing with a soft blush.

"You must excuse us, Aldred. Lady Genevieve has become quite chilled," said Tristen. And he quickly led Genny away.

Philip glared at their retreating backs, thinking to himself that Genny had looked anything but chilled.

Tristen did not release his hold on Genny's arm until they entered his chamber. He then stepped over to the hearth to add even more wood to the already roaring fire.

"Come, sit here and warm yourself," he said to Genny. "I would not have you take ill. Your leeching relatives would delight in using that as an excuse to prolong their stay."

"Milord?"

"I grow weary of accommodating the Aldreds. It was tiresome in the past, and it is unbearable now," Tristen said. Again he considered Genny's friendship with Philip. He was tired of watching the man so blatantly pursue his wife while he provided him and his mother with food and shelter.

Genny did not blame Tristen for wanting to rid himself of Beatrice's presence. The woman treated him with cool indifference, barely maintaining a civil tongue in his presence. When he was not around she made scathing remarks that, ironically, had Genny continually defending her husband's honor and integrity. Not only did Aunt Beatrice continue to be critical of his dealings with his lands and people, but she never missed an opportunity to ridicule Tristen's every directive. Such behavior had also worn Genny's considerable patience thin.

Although she and Philip had sought to reestablish their friendship, it was not, and perhaps never would be, the carefree, easy companionship it had once been. Philip was changed somehow, different. His presence had become almost suffocating. He seemed always to lurk nearby, watching her, especially when Tristen was around. At first he had made a few carefully caustic comments regarding her husband, but Genny's unfailing defense of Tristen had quickly arrested any overt attempts at criticism.

Most important, however, Tristen had become more attentive to her during their stay, no longer raising his voice or degrading her as he had before their arrival. Genny had come to enjoy the reprieve, the fragile peace of the past weeks. And she knew that, with the departure of her aunt and cousin, her husband's feigned devotion would cease.

Genny felt torn by her own desires to see Aunt Beatrice and Philip gone and her selfish yearning to prolong her truce with her husband. But Tristen's next words rendered her ambivalence pointless.

"I shall expect them to be gone in two days," he commanded.

"Two days, milord?" Genny questioned. "Milord, two days is not enough time to prepare for their departure. Besides, the roads are not fit to travel in this weather."

"There is but a small amount of snow. It will not hamper their journey," he said airily, discounting reality.

"The travel in this cold will be hard on my aunt," Genny pointed out.

"It will be a greater hardship on her should she stay any longer," Tristen declared. "They must go before the season is fully upon us. I'll not have them here for the duration of the winter."

Though Genny could not wholeheartedly disagree with his assessment of the situation, his imperiousness sparked her to challenge him. "Are you so heartless, milord? I know that my aunt has not been the most agreeable of visitors, but other than my father, she and Philip are the only family I have. I have no desire to demand they depart so precipitously."

"I hold it is not your fellowship with your aunt you fear will be disrupted. I surmise the departure of your cousin is the genuine motive behind your entreaties.'' At her startled expression, he continued darkly, ''I have watched you both this past fortnight. He is forever your shadow. Wherever I find you, he is also. Did you think I had not noticed your inappropriate behavior, milady? He goes, I say, and you . . . you, Lady Genevieve, shall comport yourself as befits the role of the Countess of Ravenswood.''

''And what might be proper comportment for the Countess of Ravenswood, milord?'' queried Genny, her ire increasing by the moment. ''Shall I cower and await your approval before I run the slightest errand or perform the simplest task? Shall I seek your approbation for every conversation I have? Is it your desire that I hold you in abject idolatry, regard your every word a divination? Or perhaps you hunger for me to bow down and simper at your feet, as the young maidens in the keep do every time you deem to smile at them.'' Her tone was unmistakably bitter.

''You go too far,'' Tristen growled. ''Even my first wife knew when to hold her vile tongue.''

''Finally you deem to discuss Kathryn with me. All these months no one has even so much as mentioned her name. It is as if she never existed! When my aunt speaks of her, everyone around here scampers away, as if the mere mention of her name were a curse.''

Tristen swore and turned to stare into the fire.

Genny thought back to yesterday, when she had successfully evaded Philip long enough to take Apollo on a brisk ride to the cliffs. Upon her return she had entered the great hall to find Aunt Beatrice and Lady Eleanor conversing and embroidering while a handful of servants prepared the room for the evening meal.

"There you are, Genny," Beatrice had exclaimed, setting her needlework aside. "Philip has been looking everywhere for you."

"I was riding," Genny had replied, experiencing a twinge of guilt that she had deliberately evaded her cousin's company because she had felt the need to be alone with her thoughts.

"By yourself?" her aunt had questioned, scandalized. "Your husband certainly allows you more freedom than he did my Kathryn."

The room had grown ominously silent, as if all activity had ceased as at some dreadful invocation. The eerie hush had been interrupted only when Lady Eleanor had discreetly cleared her throat and issued some trivial commands. Genny had looked around as the servants scattered quietly out of the hall.

"If you will excuse me, Beatrice, I would like to rest before we sup," Lady Eleanor had said. And as she had risen, she caught Genny's eye.

"I, too, must excuse myself, Aunt. I'm certainly not dressed for supper," Genny had said on cue, her customary good manners masking her curiosity about the reaction to Kathryn's name.

Genny now lifted her eyes to look at Tristen, who still stood before the fire, his back to her. Here was the man who could answer all her questions. Yet evidently he refused to do so.

"She was your wife. Can you disregard her so easily?" she inquired.

Genny was unprepared for his vicious reply as he spun around to face her.

"She was even less of a wife than you."

Genny gasped at the malicious remark.

"I have no desire to discuss my first wife with you. Ever," Tristen proclaimed with finality.

Genny was speechless as Tristen glared at her. In the past his anger had irritated her, but this was different. This time she sensed a deep rage that might push his temper beyond his control. Unlike any of their previous confrontations, this one made her afraid. For the very first time, she became aware of his absolute power and authority over her.

Tristen angrily watched the emotions play across Genny's face. Though he had not meant to frighten her, he would have his bidding done. Not only were Beatrice and Philip a constant reminder of Kathryn and her deception, but even a blind man could not help see the affection Philip had for Genny.

Nay, he would not sit by this time and again be betrayed by a wife, especially with another dishonorable Aldred. No doubt Philip was as amoral as his sister, seeking pleasure wherever he might, regardless of the laws of man or God. It was now glaringly apparent to Tristen why Lord Warren had beseeched King Edward's advocacy in finding his daughter a husband. No father could be expected to sit by and watch a scoundrel like Philip Aldred prey upon his daughter. How unfortunate, though, that he himself had been the one chosen to deliver her from his clutches.

"They will be gone in two days," he commanded, adding emphasis to his words by holding two fingers aloft.

"Aye, milord," replied Genny obediently, knowing no other response would be acceptable in his present temper.

"You may go," he stated, turning his back to her as she rose from the chair and walked silently from the chamber.

Chapter 14

The chamber was silent except for the harsh breathing of the man as he rolled off the woman's soft body.

"Are you contented, sir?" asked Beatrice, running her fingers through the springy dark brown hair on Thomas's sweat-slick chest.

"Very," replied Thomas, smiling to think of the past two weeks spent in this woman's bed. Despite her age, with her dark hair and startling blue eyes, she bore an amazing resemblance to Kathryn. Better still, from the moment they'd met, her admiration for him had been obvious, her pursuit of him bold. Her excuses to seek him out had been many and varied, and she had quickly put an end to the game of cat-and-mouse when she requested his assistance in moving a trunk in her chamber. Once in the room, she had wasted no time before inviting him to share her bed, an invitation Thomas had been more than willing to accept.

"I had best leave," he said now, disentangling himself from Beatrice.

"Must you?" she implored softly as he rose

from the bed. "This will be our last night together. Philip and I leave in the morning."

"I hadn't realized you would be going so
soon," Thomas said, unsure how he felt at the
prospect. Due to the possibility of discovery,
their secret trysts had held for him a profusion
of misgivings. He was glad Beatrice's chamber
was far removed from those of the Sinclair family, somewhat lessening that threat.

He smiled again, recalling how the opposite
had once been true—how it had heightened his
excitement to take this woman's daughter in the
very bed she shared with her husband, the Earl
of Ravenswood.

Even when the earl had discovered Kathryn's
infidelity, she had protected Thomas, giving her
husband the name of another young knight as
her companion. Lord Tristen had violently
spent his anger on that knight before turning
the man out of Ravenswood.

Thomas's mouth twisted into a cynical smirk
as he recalled how the arrogant Lord Tristen,
believing the matter ended, had left Ravenswood to continue his service to the crown. His
smile broadened as he remembered the months
that had followed, the countless nights of pleasure he had shared with Kathryn in the earl's
absence.

Thomas knew he'd been fortunate that he
had never been caught with Kathryn, and he
certainly did not relish detection of his illicit
couplings with her mother. Not when there was
so much hanging in the balance. He had no intention of forfeiting the possibility of obtaining

the affections of the woman he truly yearned for in exchange for a few nights of diversion with Beatrice.

Lady Genny. Just the thought of her made him ache with wanting. How often he had imagined her lying with him, her supple form pressed willingly to him, her abundant energy exhausted from long hours of passion in his arms.

Thomas flinched as he felt Beatrice's cold hands encircling his waist from behind.

"I'll miss our nights together," she said, brushing her lips across his back. "Had it not been for Lord Tristen, I'd be staying here with you. I don't know how my niece can tolerate being married to that man."

"Nor do I," muttered Thomas darkly.

Hearing his remark, Beatrice sensed she had found a kindred spirit in this man. He, too, despised the earl, then. To what extent, she had yet to discern.

"I will never understand why my brother settled for such a man as Sinclair over Philip," she ventured.

"Your son wished to marry her?"

"Aye. Indeed, Montburough should have been his with or without its heir. My son, fool that he is, believes himself in love with the girl," Beatrice snarled.

Thomas tensed. The fact that Philip Aldred had been with Genny constantly since his arrival had not escaped Thomas's attention, but it had never occurred to him that perhaps she felt more than familial affection toward the man.

Turning to face Beatrice, he asked, "And does she share his feelings?"

"It hardly matters, now that she's married to the Earl of Ravenswood. She belongs to him, and, unfortunately, so does Montburough." Bitterness infiltrated her shrill voice.

"Is it Montburough or Genny your son desires the most?"

"They are the same," she said blandly. "If Philip had only listened to me, there would have been no problem. Genny I could have handled, but the earl . . ."

Beatrice looked into Thomas's tawny brown eyes, attempting to ferret out his thoughts. This was a strong, virile man, who, if he could be persuaded, would be an asset in her plans for reclaiming Montburough.

Rubbing her naked breasts against his bare chest, she smiled, sure that she was just the woman to do the persuading—even if it took all night. Slowly drawing her pink tongue over her lips to moisten them, she began trailing kisses down his chest. Sinking to her knees, she paused to nip at the glistening tip of his now protruding manhood.

Looking up at him, she cooed, "We still have time. Stay with me a while longer."

Thomas's only response was a low groan in his throat as he wound his fingers into her hair and pulled her closer to his burgeoning desire.

Beatrice was issuing last-minute instructions to the servants who were packing her belong-

ings for departure when Genny entered the
chamber.

"Leave us," Beatrice curtly commanded the
servants.

After their hasty retreat, Genny addressed
her aunt. "I would that you not be so harsh
with the servants."

"Really, my dear," Beatrice said with a dismissive wave of her hand. "I wished to discuss
something with you privately. I feel it is my responsibility to you as your aunt, and because I
love you as a daughter, to speak with you on a
matter of grave importance." She paused to
settle herself into a chair. "I would be remiss if
I did not warn you of your husband's cruel-
ties."

"Lord Tristen has never been cruel to me,"
Genny said defensively, weary at the thought
of having to deflect yet another of her aunt's
derisive tirades.

"You have been married but a short time, my
dear. He was not cruel to Kathryn at first either,
but it did not take long for his abuse to surface."

"Aunt Beatrice, I do not think I should be
discussing my husband's private affairs with
someone other than himself."

"But certainly you should know matters of
import concerning his previous marriage—you
must be prepared for what will surely happen.
Kathryn told me time and again of his temper
and his infidelity. He broke her heart, spawn-
ing treacherous lies about her to conceal his
own indiscretions."

"Surely you are mistaken," Genny suggested nervously.

"I doubt Sinclair was faithful to my Kathryn for above a month. He did not even have the decency to hide his faithlessness. On more than one occasion she discovered him with any one of a number of common wenches, rutting like a boar in the very bed he had shared with her on their wedding night," Beatrice related with relish.

"Aunt, please stop," Genny pleaded, too startled by what she was hearing to offer a stronger response.

"Nay. There is more you must know. I should not have waited this long to tell you," Beatrice said, continuing relentlessly. "Kathryn confronted him, begging him to be discreet in his conduct. That's when the beatings started. Not only did he subject her to abuse at his hands numerous times, but when he learned that one of his young knights had befriended her, he beat the man nearly to death before exiling him from Ravenswood."

Beatrice paused significantly before continuing. "Poor, dear Kathryn was unable to endure his cruelty. Her death was a direct result of his blatant mockery of their marriage. Everyone at Ravenswood was a party to his behavior. Have you not noticed how they refuse to discuss Kathryn? They harbor their own guilt at her demise. My dear, you must be careful not to be misled by their apparent felicity toward you. They were seemingly kind to my Kathryn, too. However, they stood by silently and watched her wither away from Lord Sinclair's abuse and neglect.''

Genny was apprehensive. Perhaps there was some truth in what her aunt was saying. Although Tristen had never raised a hand to her, she had been the recipient of his angry words more than once, and his unjustified, jealous accusations, his refusal to discuss Kathryn, would seem to support her aunt's charges.

As for his infidelity, she had seen the looks many of the castle wenches exchanged with him, and she knew he was not devoid of masculine urges. His indiscriminate proposition to her upon their first encounter proved he was not. Only after his discovery that she was his wife had his desire waned. Aunt Beatrice knew naught of their unconsummated union, and yet here she supplied what was a plausible reason for his reluctance to share the marriage bed with her. If he already had so many at his beck and call, then he most certainly had no need of her as a woman.

That she might have encouraged his advances on the few occasions he had chosen to display his lustful nature was now, in light of Aunt Beatrice's revelations, mortifying to Genny.

Beatrice watched as the seeds of doubt took hold. Beginning her long-awaited revenge gave her such satisfaction that she had to fight hard to disguise her delight. Sinclair would pay for his rejection of Kathryn, and through Genny, naive Genny, her brother, Richard, would be made to suffer for his rejection of Beatrice's son as the rightful heir to Montburough.

Dredging up tears to give her performance authenticity, she murmured in distress, "The beast would not even allow me to be present at Kathryn's burial. Me, her own mother."

"Oh, Aunt, I grieve for your pain. I did not know of his cruelty, truly. He never speaks to me of Kathryn."

"Of course he never speaks to you of her. He does not want to admit to his vicious treatment of my daughter," Beatrice spat in disdain.

"I promise you I will discuss this matter with my husband straightaway."

"Nay!" Beatrice called in obvious fright. "Do not say anything! He will only deny the truth, and I fear for your well-being," she rushed on, voice rising in shrill desperation. "Promise me you will not mention a word of this to him. I could not live with myself if harm were to come to you! You must promise me!" she begged.

Genny had never seen her aunt so frantic, and though she knew the woman's accusations demanded an airing, she knew naught else to comfort her, save to yield to her persistent pleas. "Calm yourself, Aunt. I promise to say nothing if it worries you so."

"Please be careful, my dear. Your father would be inconsolable should anything untoward happen to you," Beatrice said, clasping Genny's hands and looking utterly anguished.

"I shall be careful. Now you had best prepare for your departure," Genny said, squeezing the woman's hands in gentle reassurance.

"I love you, my dear. Like a daughter. Remember that," said Beatrice, hugging Genny, a smile briefly touching her lips.

"And I love you, Aunt."

Chapter 15

With the departure of Philip and Beatrice, the household soon resumed its normal activities, but Tristen found his marriage even more strained than it had been before. Still, he told himself it was for the best that he and Genny saw little of each other and spoke together even less. He was, however, somewhat confused by Genny's deepening aloofness toward not only himself but also the rest of the family. She remained faultlessly polite and kind to the other Sinclairs, but something was indefinably different in their relations.

Further, he would catch her staring intently at him during meals, more times than not a look of bewilderment furrowing her brow. Had the harsh words he had used when he demanded the Aldreds leave spawned this sustained anger at him? he wondered.

Though he was loath to admit it, he missed the fleeting harmony they had shared while the Aldreds had been at Ravenswood. He missed hearing her laughter, seeing her infectious smiles, even if they had been false.

He hadn't seen Genny at all that morning, and he reckoned she would be in the stables. Making his way to the grooming stalls, he was rewarded with the sight of her tightening the saddle on Apollo's back.

Genny had just grabbed the reins and placed her slippered foot in the stirrup to mount Apollo when she felt strong hands encircle her waist from behind and lift her into the saddle. Startled, she turned to look down, and her heart quickened at the sight of her husband standing there. He looked so handsome. Shafts of early-morning sunlight filtering into the stable fell across his face, and his deep blue eyes twinkled brightly with obvious enjoyment at having caught her off guard.

Trying to sound nonchalant even while her heart fluttered in her throat, Genny said, "Oh, 'tis you." Unfortunately, she missed her mark, and instead of cool she sounded dispirited.

"Aye. Sorry to disappoint you," Tristen said tautly, taking a step backward and bringing his arms back to his sides, his open, happy expression of just moments before now replaced with his usual scowl of disapproval for her. "You ride again, milady?" he questioned sharply.

Noting the abrupt change in his demeanor, Genny answered defensively, "I find great pleasure in a daily ride."

"I would hold that the mistress of a keep the size of Ravenswood would have little time for trivial activities."

Genny's grasp on Apollo's reins tightened, and the horse's head bobbed in protest.

"I assure you, milord, I do not neglect the duties I am permitted to consummate."

Tristen bristled. Was she making blatant reference to their bedless marriage? "What do you imply, milady? That I disallow you certain duties you would wish to be burdened with?"

She gazed at him. "I imply nothing, milord. A wife's lot is merely to comply with her husband's wishes."

He stared at her, unable to determine her thoughts. "Finally we are in agreement, then," he grumbled flatly.

"Finally. And on that harmonious note, I take my leave. Apollo grows restless," Genny asserted. Not waiting for a response, she set the huge animal in motion with the slightest movement of her wrist.

"I, too, grow restless," murmured Tristen, staring after her retreating form as she exited the stable.

Anxious to escape her husband's disturbing presence, Genny nudged Apollo into a brisk trot through the bailey. Struggling to free herself of the turmoil brought on by this latest confrontation with Tristen, she spurred Apollo to an even more vigorous pace the moment they left the courtyard. So familiar had the path become to both horse and rider that almost before she was aware of it, Apollo had taken them to their destination.

Genny sighed, looking out over the cliffs from the place that had become her refuge. If only this tranquil setting could impart to her the serenity for which she longed, she thought as she dismounted. But no, just as she had feared, the fragile peace she'd shared with her husband had collapsed when her aunt and cousin departed.

Now, however, Genny knew she could no longer lay the blame for that solely at her husband's feet. For no matter how hard she tried, she could not rid herself of the doubts Aunt Beatrice had aroused. And those doubts were contributing greatly to her tension in Tristen's presence.

So absorbed in thought was Genny that she jumped at the sound of a voice behind her.

" 'Tis a chilly day to be riding, milady," said Thomas, who, still astride his horse, had quietly made his way to the edge of the cliffs.

"I am quite warm," Genny replied, pulling her cloak about her as she watched the man dismount.

"Were you my wife, I would not allow you to linger in the cold so long."

"Then I am fortunate my husband is not so demanding," said Genny, "for I find great contentment in my daily rides."

"Ah, but my wife would find contentment with me," Thomas countered softly as he moved closer.

Genny stepped back, suddenly ill at ease with the conversation. "Pray, excuse me, Thomas, I must return to Ravenswood."

Genny stepped around him and was almost past when his hand latched on to her arm.

"Stay a while longer, milady," he pleaded, his soft voice in marked contrast to his firm grasp on her. "I but long to be in your presence."

Genny's uneasiness became alarm. "Pray, release me, Thomas. Need I remind you I am the Countess of Ravenswood?"

Her words and emphatic delivery caused Thomas to stop in his tracks. Both were all too familiar to him. The declaration—and the pain it was meant to inflict—were still fresh in his mind from when he had received them from Kathryn. When she had become afraid their illicit relationship would threaten her prestigious status, she'd used her cruel tongue to belittle him. And now, here again, echoed those same wounding words: *I am the Countess of Ravenswood.*

"Countesses, too, have needs, milady," he growled now in sneering response. "Needs I am capable of fulfilling." And he pulled her roughly against his chest.

"How dare you!" gasped Genny. The stinging slap she delivered to his cheek left an angry red mark, and she quickly stepped away, appalled.

Slowly he slid his gaze back to hers, and reason took hold once more. He didn't want to anger her further and risk evoking the wrath of the earl. Instead, he would summon up charm, seek to placate her.

"I am sorry, milady. Your beauty makes me forget myself. Pray, forgive me," he implored, dropping to bended knee and lowering his head.

For a moment Genny stood silent, willing away her trembling and weighing her options. She knew she could not tell Tristen of this; he would but accuse her of encouraging the man's affections. Still, she would have to firmly discourage Thomas, even if she could not invoke the threat of retribution. Calming herself, she reflected that the man had been naught but kind to her in the past, and she was almost appalled at her own violent reaction to his momentary lapse.

"You are forgiven, Thomas," she said kindly, finally recovering her composure. "But while your attentions might be flattering to another woman, you must heed that I am steadfast in my marriage."

"I understand, milady," he said gravely. "And I thank you for your indulgence."

"Now I must go," she said, retrieving Apollo's reins.

"Take care, milady. The wind grows cold," said Thomas, rising to help her mount.

Genny glanced down at him, again oddly uneasy, then urged the horse into a gallop.

Thomas stared intently at her retreating form.

Chapter 16

Genny pulled her woolen cloak tightly around her shoulders to guard against the crisp night air. Claiming a genuine weariness, she had supped alone in her chamber and retired early, but sleep seemed impossible these nights. She walked slowly toward the stables, knowing but not caring that walking out alone at night would be yet another breach of comportment her husband could fault her for. She sought the quiet companionship Apollo could offer.

So many confusing thoughts roiled within her as she stood stroking the horse's neck. This husband of hers seemed such a bundle of contradictions. He had seemed so lusty and spirited at their first meeting—until he had learned who she was. Then he had become as a man made of ice.

In all fairness she had to admit that wounding him probably had not secured an auspicious beginning for their union, but there had been misunderstanding aplenty for both of them on that confusing occasion. Further, it could not

165

explain why he had become furious with her when she danced at their marriage feast, but been tender when he joined her, holding on to her longer than had been strictly necessary. His behavior at the stables the morning he had found her with Alexander was abhorrent, yet when he had taken her in his arms, all else had faded away under the magical spell of his kiss.

Her heart raced at the memory of that kiss, and of the tender moment they had shared in the snow. Both, however, had been fleeting, quickly blotted out by his anger.

Genny fought to quell the anxiety that knotted her stomach as she recalled Aunt Beatrice's words: *I fear for your well-being.*

What had happened to Kathryn? Despite her cousin's fragile appearance, Genny had known her to be a headstrong, determined woman more capable of breeding heartache than succumbing to it; she had witnessed the decimation of many a young swain's heart at Kathryn's hands. If any man Kathryn had consented to marry had sought gratification of his lust in the arms of common wenches, Genny did not doubt that her cousin would have retaliated forcefully. Her withering away was scarcely believable, even if one were to deem Aunt Beatrice's account of Tristen's violence credible.

Yet Tristen's adamant refusal to discuss his first marriage seemed a possible confirmation that he was indeed guilty of *some* wrongdoing. But what, Genny was unsure.

"Oh, Apollo, I do not begin to understand this husband of mine. I have seen signs of his harshness, but he has also displayed a gentleness that makes my heart melt."

The horse merely snorted calmly.

"Are you finding this new home as hard to adjust to as I am? No, not the home . . . It is the lord of the home. He is so different from any man I have ever met. He is pigheaded, pompous, arrogant . . . and, unfortunately, so handsome. Why does he have to be so handsome?"

Apollo began to whinny and shake his head from side to side.

"Ah, yes, you are beautiful, too, my jealous beast." She laughed, patting his front leg, then stroking his regal mane.

Hearing a muffled rustle behind her, Genny began to turn around, only to be stopped by an intense, searing pain tearing through her skull. She stumbled forward into the horse, causing him to buck and twist against her as she tried desperately to hold on to him.

But her hands slipped through his golden mane, and blackness overtook her.

"Fire! Fire!"

Frantic shouting awakened Tristen from drowsing in his chair.

He had retired to his room early, hoping to capture some of the much-needed sleep that had eluded him so often since Genny had come to Ravenswood. But tonight had proved no different from any other night. Indeed, every time he closed his eyes he saw the image of a golden-haired, green-eyed beauty. Even strong drink did nothing to dull the seductive daydreams that flitted through his weary mind. Finally he had succumbed to a restless dozing, slumped uncomfortably in his chair before the fire.

He stared blankly for a moment, then shook his head in an attempt to clear it. Then he heard frantic whinnies of the horses in the yard. Recalling the cries that had roused him, he quickly pulled on his boots and bounded to his feet.

Rushing into the courtyard, he was transfixed by the sight of the flaming roof of the stables. Men were frantically leading frightened, frenzied horses out of the burning structure, and within moments Alexander reached his side. As they raced forward to assist in the rescue attempts, Tristen shouted to one of the younger squires, ''Has Demon been led to safety?''

''Aye, milord. But the mistress's horse is still trapped,'' he answered.

Both Tristen and Alexander ran toward the stables in search of Apollo.

They worked their way through the burning building, the heat intensifying as they proceeded. The men outside continued to fling buckets of water onto the roof, bravely trying to save the horses still within. The smoke made it almost impossible to see, but Apollo's frantic whinnies guided them to the Arabian's stall.

Tristen's heart skipped a beat at the sight before him.

Genny lay motionless in the now smoldering hay. In his frenzy Apollo was bucking violently, his eyes rolling wildly in fear, his hind legs striking the ground dangerously near Genny's head. Alexander rushed to the Arabian, swiftly grabbing the horse's mane in an attempt to control the terrified animal.

The heat inside the stable was nearly intolerable, and the billowing smoke was suffocating and blinding. Tristen blinked rapidly to clear his stinging, watering eyes while dropping to kneel at Genny's side. "Get that beast out of here!" he yelled back over his shoulder to Alexander as he quickly gathered her limp, seemingly lifeless form into his arms.

The heat was near searing as Tristen carefully picked a pathway through the burning hay and flaming debris falling from the quickly disintegrating rafters. Alexander followed closely with Apollo. Finally the large archway leading into the open yard loomed before Tristen's streaming eyes, offering the promise of salvation. But then they heard, and felt, a great explosion as the stone archway fractured, sending burning beams catapulting, collapsing the passageway.

Apollo reared wildly at the flying rubble, and Alexander, struggling to maintain control, removed his tunic and threw it over the horse's head, hoping that, thus blinded, the beast would became more docile.

"This way!" Tristen shouted, turning in the direction opposite the tumbled wall and heading back through the sweltering, perilous inferno.

After what seemed like hours of negotiating Lucifer's abyss, the two men finally burst into the open air, inhaling great draughts that seemed to sear their already laboring lungs. In

spite of the pain, Tristen dragged himself and
Genny away from the burning structure, turning to glance over his shoulder to assure himself that Alexander and Apollo, too, had
escaped the hellish destruction. Thus relieved,
he carried Genny as far as he could into the
cool, dark night.

"Oh, God, please let her be alive," he rasped
as he finally eased himself to the ground, holding her tightly within his arms. She looked so
fragile, so white and lifeless. As he examined
her carefully for injuries, he felt something
warm and wet upon the arm that cradled her
head, and his heart began to pound fearfully in
his chest when he saw the red stain upon his
tunic.

"Oh, Jesu!" he moaned. Then, rousing himself, he shouted, "Alexander, have Tilly summoned to Genny's chambers immediately!"
And, gathering her in his arms again, he raised
his eyes upward to silently beseech the heavens, *God have mercy. Please let her live.* Then he
looked back down at Genny's ashen pallor and
hastened her away from the inferno and into
the castle.

Tristen was gently lowering Genny to the bed
just as Matilda rushed into the room, Mary following closely upon her heels.

"Lord Almighty, what happened to the girl?"
she exclaimed.

"She has injured her head. Send someone to
the village to fetch Thisbe," he directed Mary
as he lightly touched Genny's pale brow.

"While we await Thisbe's arrival, we had best

get her out of her garments," the older woman dictated.

"Perhaps . . . perhaps I should call Elizabeth," Tristen said weakly, loath to leave Genny's side yet suddenly awkward with the thought of undressing this woman he had not yet made his wife.

"You are her husband, are you not?" Tilly snapped.

Tristen cursed fluently under his breath, but he reluctantly moved to obey Tilly's instructions.

"Remove her kirtle while I fetch a bedgown," the woman commanded as she took off Genny's slippers.

Gently Tristen raised Genny to a sitting position, with her upper body resting against his chest, while he fumbled with the belt that encircled her small waist. Upon removing the belt, he slowly raised the kirtle up her hips, over her midriff and breasts, and then her arms. Damn her, he thought, ashamed at the surge of desire he felt, yet holding her close as he lowered his head to rub his cheek lightly against her soft golden tresses. Chastising himself for his errant thoughts, he gently pulled the kirtle off over her head, mindful of her injury, and lowered her delicately back to the bed. Then, taking a deep, fortifying breath, he untied the ribbons of her chainse and began easing the undergarment down.

Willing himself not to notice the delicately rounded breasts now being bared to him, he lowered the chainse down her midsection and over the curve of her hips. Her skin felt like silk beneath his hands, and his fingers began to tremble slightly. With the last of her clothing now removed, he tried to pull his gaze away from her complete and utter exposure, but the effort merely rendered him rapt and motionless.

At that moment Matilda appeared at his side, shaking the wrinkles from a soft white bedgown before handing it to him. ''Put this on her while I fetch the herbal water,'' she said briskly.

Deliverance, Tristen told himself as he held the gown in his hand. Still he remained motionless, absorbed by the physical perfection of the woman lying naked on the bed.

She is only a woman! he chided himself next. A beautiful woman, yes, but then, Kathryn had been beautiful as well. Genny's beauty did not alter the fact that she was a wife he did not want, he told himself firmly.

Having thus tentatively replaced his unwanted passion with the comforting familiarity of anger, he quickly if awkwardly drew the gown about her naked body and hastily tucked the coverlet around her.

Unsteady from the combined forces of the terror of the fire, his anxiety for Genny's wellbeing, and the torrent of emotions unleashed by her undressing, Tristen pulled a chair beside the bed and sat, trying to regain his scattered wits. Some soldier he! he scoffed at himself, hoping thus to shame himself into stolidity.

To no avail. He leaped to his feet as Tilly entered the room, with Elizabeth and Lady Eleanor trailing behind her.

"Oh, Tristen, how is she?" questioned Elizabeth, obviously shaken.

"She has yet to awaken," he answered, looking down at Genny's pale face.

"Does anyone know how this could have happened, my son?" Lady Eleanor asked, her eyes filled with concern as she observed Genny.

"Nay. I do not even know why she was in the stables at this late hour. Alexander and I discovered her as we were freeing Apollo."

"Will she be all right?" asked Elizabeth nervously.

"She has sustained an injury to her head. I have sent for Thisbe," replied Tristen while Tilly began bathing Genny's wound with the herbal water.

Slumping back down into the chair, Tristen felt a hand upon his shoulder.

"Genny is a strong woman," said Lady Eleanor. "I am confident she will be fine." His mother squeezed his shoulder reassuringly as he placed his hand over hers.

"She is my wife. I am supposed to protect her."

"Even you could not know something like this would happen," she answered gently.

"She has too much freedom, Mother. She should never have been out there in the dark by herself. I must put a stop to this bizarre behavior of hers," he said, welcoming the harshness that might mask—and hold at bay—the tender feelings that had so recently assailed him.

"I grant you Genny is somewhat unusual, my son. But I caution you to be careful when you clip her wings. You must leave her still able to fly."

Chapter 17

The next three days blurred into a prolonged bout of agony for Tristen, who had not left Genny's bedside since the night of the fire. His face was drawn, his chin covered with stubble. Dark smudges encircled his weary eyes.

He cared naught for his appearance or comfort. The long hours spent in vigil had merely intensified his feelings of guilt at having failed to adequately protect his wife. If he had been a real husband, he reflected angrily, she would have been sharing his bed and would not have been alone in the stables in the middle of the night.

What she had been doing there was a question that haunted him incessantly. He had spoken briefly with Christopher and Alexander the morning after the fire, and each of them had vowed to uncover the cause of this disaster. But so far no results had been forthcoming.

Thisbe tended to Genny, pronouncing her head wound the only injury she had suffered. Although the old woman did not say so, Tristen could tell, as one day stretched endlessly into another, that the healer grew more apprehensive about Genny's apparent inability to break free from her deathly sleep.

Soft, pale moonlight illuminated the night as Tristen stood in Genny's chamber gazing out the window at the charred rubble that remained of the stables. Slowly he flexed his legs to relax the cramping muscles, which screamed in protest from days and nights of sitting at the bedside.

He turned with a start when he heard a low moan. Looking at the small, motionless form on the bed, he wondered if he had only imagined the sound. He walked slowly to the side of the bed to look at the face of the woman who had dominated his every thought since the fire and, if he were honest, since the very first day he had met her.

Gently he reached down and took hold of her hand. How he wished he could will her to return to life, to him. She seemed so far away, and, strangely enough, he found he couldn't envision his existence without her. The recollection of her infectious laughter rang softly in his ears. Her subtle smile, starting slowly and warily but eventually spreading across her whole face, appeared in his mind. He was forced to admit that he even missed her stubbornness, a trait that had so often resulted in arguments between them, he thought with an ironic smile. He caressed Genny's hand, tenderly stroking the back with his thumb.

Genny groaned softly, and her head stirred on the pillow.

Tristen took a sharp breath, willing her to awaken, to speak. When she did not, however, he reluctantly released her hand and thundered across the hall to bang on the door of the chamber that Thisbe had been occupying since coming to Ravenswood to tend Lady Genny.

"Thisbe, come quickly!" he shouted.

The door flew open on its hinges as the healer rushed to obey his command. "Has she awakened?" she asked as she hurried to Genny's chamber.

"She moaned and stirred," Tristen said, standing anxiously at the foot of the bed while Thisbe examined Genny.

"Saints be praised," she murmured. Her examination complete, Thisbe gradually straightened her crooked form and turned to face Lord Tristen. "She'll be fine now, milord. She has come back to be among the living. All she needs now is rest," she pronounced.

After placing a fresh cool cloth across Genny's forehead, Thisbe turned once more to Tristen. "Milord, you could do with some rest yourself," she suggested, looking up into his weary eyes.

He made no reply. Instead, he turned as a soft glow of candlelight appeared in the doorway, illuminating Lady Eleanor's face. "Mother," he greeted her.

"We heard your shouts," Lady Eleanor said, walking to the bed as Tilly rushed through the doorway, gasping to catch her breath after her hasty flight up the long staircase.

"Thisbe says Genny will be all right now, Mother," said Tristen, relief flooding his voice.

"She merely sleeps now, but she will awaken again," Thisbe reassured them.

Lady Eleanor studied the gaunt face of her son. She had been openly displeased with his treatment of Genny since Beatrice and Philip Aldred had departed. Yet he had sequestered himself in this room for three days, allowing no one save Thisbe and himself to care for her. Mayhap he felt guilty about his callous handling of her? Or was he finally beginning to fall under her spell? Genny had affected many at Ravenswood in such a short time. Why should her son be immune to her charms? Indeed, if he would but admit it, he was not.

"Tristen, you look weary, my son. Go lie down. I shall care for her till you have rested and washed," she admonished gently, touching her son's cheek fondly.

"I quite agree, milady," Matilda said. "Now be gone with you, milord, till you be more presentable," she commanded as she herded Tristen to the door.

"I surrender. I know when I am defeated." Tristen chuckled lightly with relief and joy, threw his hands in the air, and left the room.

"Thisbe, we are so grateful for your care of Lady Genny," said Lady Eleanor sincerely.

" 'Twas not so much my care as Lord Tristen's presence that milady responded to. Please summon me if you have further need of me," said Thisbe, curtsying stiffly before leaving the room.

"What think you, Tilly?" asked Lady Eleanor as she seated herself at the bedside.

"Milady?"

"Come now, Tilly. You know my son as well as I do," she said with a soft smile.

"I think he does not want to admit it."

"But it is there, is it not?" she asked hopefully.

"Aye, 'tis there, milady. Now 'tis just a matter of her being strong enough to find it," Tilly answered as she looked down upon Genny.

"She is a spirited young woman. If anyone can kindle his love, it will be Genny," Lady Eleanor pronounced with an indefinable sense of rightness.

Bright morning sunlight streamed through the chamber. Tristen had intended to rest only a short time before returning to Genny's side, but once he had laid his head upon his mattress, he fell into a deep, much-needed sleep. It was the noise of the men working to clear the remains of the stables that finally roused him.

After washing and changing into fresh clothes, he resumed his vigil at Genny's bedside. Looking down at her, he wondered what it was about this woman that so absorbed his every thought. From the moment he had set eyes on her, she seemed to permeate his very being. Her golden locks and emerald eyes drew him in. Deeply. Too deeply.

Indeed, many men were drawn to her, he reflected bitterly. Yet still, there seemed to be a certain innocence about her that he could no longer dismiss.

Genny slowly opened her eyes, narrowing them against the sharp stab of sunlight. The pounding in her head was dull but constant, and only slowly did she turn toward the light. And there she met the intensity in her husband's dark blue eyes.

"How do you feel?" he asked in his deep, resonant voice.

Placing her hand on her brow in an attempt to still the pounding, she replied in a quiet voice, "I should think I would feel better had I no head."

He laughed softly. "I fear it will be so for a while longer."

"How long have I been thus?" she asked in confusion as she belatedly took in her surroundings.

"You have been away from us for over three days."

"Three days! I do not understand," Genny said, her eyes questioning. "Milord, what happened? I—I do not remember anything."

"There was a fire in the stables, and—"

"A fire!" Genny broke in, distressed. "Are the animals safe? What of Apollo and Demon? They were not injured, were they?"

"No, they were not injured. But you were, and I would be most grateful for some answers," he replied, his voice harsher than he had intended.

Genny stared at him. His mood had changed

so quickly. His voice was now demanding, where only moments ago it had been gentle.

"I told you, I remember nothing."

"Why were you at the stables at night, alone?" he demanded.

"Likely I could not sleep," she snapped, angry and hurt at his abrupt inquisition.

"I would expect a better answer than that, milady. Perhaps you had planned to meet someone there?" he offered cruelly, responding to her tone and to whatever inner demons controlled him in discourse with his wife.

Genny inhaled sharply, then winced at the acute shooting pain that raged through her head. Her anger and pain at his unfair accusations made devilment with her tongue.

"There are so many I meet in secret, milord, I would barely be able to recall who it had been that night."

"Do not try my patience, milady," he rumbled.

"I was not aware that you were possessed of any patience, milord," she countered.

"You wouldn't be," he muttered. "But we digress. My patience is not the issue. We were discussing what you were doing in the stables."

"We weren't *discussing* anything. As usual, you were accusing me of disloyalty."

"And, as usual, you were denying it. Play me not for a fool!" Tristen thundered.

At that moment the door opened, with Tilly entering the room bearing Tristen's midday meal.

"Ah, Lady Genny, it is good to see you awake."

Matilda's affectionate tone was a welcome relief from her husband's harshness. "Thank you, Tilly," Genny replied sincerely.

"I will take my leave, milady, " Tristen murmured. "You are in need of rest. But we will continue this discussion soon," he added forebodingly before he left the chamber.

"You gave us quite a fright. We have all been so worried," Tilly told Genny.

A soft knock sounded at the door, and Tilly turned to answer it. It was Alexander. Tilly took her leave to carry "milord" his meal, promising to return with broth and tea for Genny.

"Ah, Lady Genny. It does my heart good to see you thus," Alexander said gently.

"Thank you, Sir Alexander," she replied, motioning for him to sit with her.

"I will not stay long. I know you are in need of rest. Especially with your husband dancing attendance for so long."

"Indeed, he promises to return forthwith," she replied bitterly.

"Ah, I perceive you two have resumed your skirmish."

"Aye. It appears my marriage is a constant battle of wills, does it not?" she asked, her voice laced with sorrow.

"Aye, and I would that it were not so," he answered with concern.

"You are such a loyal friend to him, Alexander," she said, reaching for his hand. "Even through the trials he puts upon that friendship.''

''Friendship does not mean that you agree with all your friend does or says. Friendship is much like love, Genny. The bad things will not chase you away from the good,'' he replied, squeezing her hand lightly. Then he bade her a hasty recovery and left her to ponder the full meaning of his words.

Chapter 18

The days of Genny's convalescence seemed endless to her. Elizabeth made effervescent conversation on her daily visits, keeping Genny informed of all that was afoot at Ravenswood, and, sensing the patient's boredom, began bringing her children, Blakely and Abigail, to visit. Although Genny was cheered by their energetic company, she was eager to be well and active again herself.

Edmund attempted to distract her with reports on the welfare of the stock and the progress of the reconstruction of the stables, but his narrative only served to heighten her restlessness, since she could not be a party to any of the goings-on. He had even brought Sarah, Lionel, and little Gerald for a visit in the hope that it would relieve some of her boredom at the forced inactivity.

The well-intentioned efforts of her friends and family made Genny ever more impatient with her own uselessness, and, against Thisbe's wishes, she insisted on being up and about much sooner than anyone had anticipated.

Nonetheless, Genny had had far too much time to reflect upon her last confrontation with her husband. Despite his threat to return anon to pursue their bitter dialogue, Tristen had left on a trip the day after she regained awareness, and without so much as a parting word to her. Elizabeth had related the news of his departure.

The days stretched into weeks as, fully recovered, Genny attempted to proceed with her life in spite of her husband's uncaring rebuff.

This morning she was watching the men finish rebuilding the stables, taking advantage of a brief unseasonal respite from the cold winter weather. As the workers completed their final tasks, Genny began laying out fresh hay so the animals could once more be sheltered comfortably.

"It is good to see you so well, Lady Genny," said Thomas as he entered the stable where Genny was working.

"Thank you, Thomas," replied Genny, looking up at the scarred but handsome man.

"Milady, we were all so worried for you after your . . . ah . . . accident."

"I appreciate your concern for my health, Thomas. However, I assure you I am well now," she replied, continuing to spread the hay onto the floor and hoping to curtail any further exchange.

"Has Lord Tristen discovered the cause of the fire?" asked Thomas.

"I have not discussed the matter with him," she answered as she hurried in her task, wishing to put an end to the conversation.

"I am confident it will be only a matter of time before Lord Tristen uncovers the reasoning behind this unfortunate mishap," he said, his face showing no emotion as he shrugged his shoulders dismissively.

Alexander entered the stable, his mere presence giving comfort to Genny. "Lady Genny, you look fatigued," he complained as he approached them, his eyes narrowing on Thomas. "Allow me to escort you back to the hall," he entreated, offering her his arm.

"If you will excuse me, I have duties to attend to," said Thomas abruptly. "Milady, Sir Alexander." He bowed formally before taking his leave.

"You look distressed. Has Thomas been disturbing you, Lady Genny?"

"Nay, he only desired to voice his happiness at my recovery," she answered.

"Indeed, we are all quite relieved that you are well. Now, will you not come indoors so that you may stay that way?" he urged.

But Genny shook her head and recommenced spreading the hay.

Alexander frowned in mock indignation. "Very well. Since you will not rest and insist upon performing this task, then I shall have to assist you," he said. And he grasped a large armful of hay and tossed it high into the air.

"You are no help, sir!" Genny laughed while bits of hay tumbled into her hair. And she grabbed an armful of hay herself and threw it directly upon Alexander.

"You shall pay dearly for that," he threatened through his laughter.

Soon the stable air was filled with particles of hay and wild bursts of riotous laughter. Finally exhausted from their merriment, the pair sank to the ground, Genny holding her sides, for they ached from all her laughter.

Tristen, who had just returned to Ravenswood, observed them from the archway of the new stable. Genny's sweet laughter filled the air and Alexander, too, appeared at his most playful. As Tristen watched, he discerned that his friend's look, his posture, seemed most intimate, and he felt his gorge begin to rise. It was obvious his wife had not lacked companionship in his absence.

"What the devil is going on here?" he thundered.

Genny jumped at his outburst and promptly began to rise to her feet. Alexander readily gave her assistance, despite the threatening presence of her glowering, jealous husband.

"Nothing untoward, I assure you, milord," Genny answered sharply. "I was simply spreading fresh hay for the horses. If you will excuse me, milord, I will finish the task," she added, glaring up at him.

In a voice of deadly calm Tristen said, "My wife does not spread hay for horses. Is that understood?"

Rage shot through Genny. Such moments he chose to acknowledge her as wife! "Aye, milord," she replied through clenched teeth.

Tristen moved closer, taking her chin in his large hand.

"Lady Genevieve," he said, "my name is Tristen. That is how I desire you to address me from now on."

Genny felt an unwelcome excitement race through her at his touch. She tried desperately to ignore the warmth of his hand, the smell of leather and spice that was unique to him, but most of all his lips, which were only inches from hers. But suddenly she was unable to move, to think, or even to react.

"As you wish, mi—Tristen," she replied, her voice barely above a whisper.

"Good. Now go clean yourself," he snapped.

The spark his touch had ignited vanished instantly at his harsh command. " 'Go clean yourself.' 'Go change your clothes.' That is all he ever says to me," she mumbled under her breath as she turned on her heel and stomped from the stable.

Tristen watched her leave, mildly amused at her grumblings, before he glanced back to confront Alexander. "Alexander, you take much interest in my wife."

"We are but friends, Tristen, and well you know it," he answered calmly.

"Indeed. Why is it my wife seems to have so many men as . . . friends?"

"Mayhap because of her beauty and her sweet laughter, or simply her infectious zeal for life. Can you stand there and tell me you have yet to see any of these things in her?" asked Alexander.

"Aye, I have seen them, and I am not sure what I should do," he replied solemnly. "Alexander, well you know that I did not want another wife. And she above all was not my choice."

"Lady Genny may not have been your choice, my friend, but she is your wife. Mayhap if you took time to learn of her, you would find that you have sorely misjudged her," he said.

"Are you so convinced of her innocence?" Tristen asked bitingly.

"Are you so convinced of her lack of it?" Alexander demanded. "Genny is not Kathryn, Tristen. She deserves to be judged for herself, not by the transgressions of others." He ended thus abruptly, taking his leave to give Tristen time to ponder his remarks.

Tristen sat in his dark chamber, staring blindly into the glowing embers of the fire, cursing himself as he drank deeply from his goblet, trying to force thoughts of Genny from his mind. Even during his recent trip, which he knew he had made not out of necessity but merely as a means to elude her seductive presence, he had not been able to erase her image. There seemed to be no escaping her.

He had never been through such a torturous experience as tending to her after she had been hurt. He had watched her lie deathly still for days, observing every small detail of her beautiful face, hour after agonizing hour.

He began to ache with desire, remembering her perfect body as he had undressed her. Her

small, firm breasts, her tiny waist, which he was
sure he could span with his hands. He tried
desperately to forget the soft golden triangle of
curls resting at the apex of her ivory thighs. He
groaned aloud to the silent room at the image.

Hearing Genny's dulcet tones through the
door as she and Mary passed his chambers
caused him to redouble his efforts to blot out
her nearness. Climbing into his large bed, he
buried himself beneath the covers, furrowing
deep within them, determined to ignore her
velvet presence in his ironclad heart.

Genny slipped into bed, feeling weary yet
taut as a bowstring. Suddenly she saw her life
laid out before her as wife to a man who did
not want her. Tristen was cold and oft inhuman
toward her. Yet the few times he had touched
her, he had evoked such warm feelings within
her. Feelings she did not entirely comprehend,
for they were foreign to any stirrings she had
ever experienced before. To be condemned to
suffer these newfound longings seemed worse
than had she never discovered them.

Genny awoke from a light, fitful sleep to a
soft rapping at her door. Donning her robe, she
opened it to discover Edmund standing in the
hall nervously wringing his hands.

"Milady, I am sorry to disturb you."

"What is amiss, Edmund?" she asked anxiously, knowing he would not have crossed the
bounds of propriety by coming to her chamber
unless the situation was of utmost importance.

"It is the gray mare, milady. She is dropping

Demon's foal early and is in distress. I know that you have waited anxiously for this foal."

"You were right to come for me," she said, aware that he sought reassurance for his breach of protocol. "I will dress and join you straight-away at the stables."

Genny and Edmund worked feverishly for hours, trying to help the mare. She seemed un-able to pass the foal and grew increasingly weaker with her attempts. Against their better judgment, they had finally decided to lay the mare down to assist her.

"We will have to hurry, milady. Her breath-ing is already shallow and labored. She cannot stay this way for long."

"Aye," replied Genny with much concern. "You will have to hold her still while I pull the foal from inside her."

Edmund took hold of the horse's hindquar-ters, attempting to get a tight grasp on the top leg. Genny swiftly plunged her hands into the mare, prompting shrill screams of pain. She managed to dislodge the front legs of the foal, but the slippery secretions kept her from gain-ing a firm enough hold to pull it from the moth-er's body. Desperate, she retrieved a rope hanging on the wall of the stall, then rapidly tied it to the front shanks of the foal. Then she stood once more and pulled with all her strength. The mare let forth an agonized shriek, but at last a midnight-black foal slipped onto the hay. A perfect miniature replica of Demon.

"Oh, Edmund, it is too small!" she sobbed, looking down at the tiny, perfectly formed, motionless foal. The mare fought for each breath, looking at Genny as if in silent supplication for her to do something for her foal.

Genny blew softly into the foal's nostrils again and again, but it soon became apparent that the foal was too small to live. Genny sat back, her clothes and arms wet with birthing fluids. Her hair hung in sweat-sodden strands, some of it clinging to her wet clothes, her eyes filled with tears that began to slip unhindered down her cheeks.

Tristen cautiously entered the stables. He had walked alone in the cold night air as small flecks of white descended from the heavens, falling serenely upon the land. The few hours of fitful sleep he had managed to secure had rendered him even more restless than before. He had hoped a solitary stroll would help clear his mind of the golden-haired vision that plagued him. But a faint light flickering from deep within the new stables had caught his attention. When he drew near, he heard faint sobs from inside. Upon entering, he was taken aback at the sight before him.

Genny sat weeping into her hands, her hair hanging around her like a golden curtain, concealing her face from his view. He looked at Edmund, who mutely returned his gaze, his eyes mirroring Genny's pain. Edmund lowered his gaze as Tristen knelt down beside her.

"Genny?"

Slowly lowering her hands from her face, she gazed into those familiar dark blue eyes. "I could not save him. He was too small," she said through her tears.

"Come, Genny," he entreated as he gently raised her to her feet, his strong arms encircling her waist.

Tristen's heart slammed heavily in his chest as he gazed into her sorrowful eyes. "I will see to Lady Genevieve, Edmund. Please do what needs to be done here," he instructed.

Within minutes Genny was seated before the fire in his chamber, wrapped tightly in a warm wool blanket.

"Drink this, Genny. It will help," he said, handing her a goblet of wine. Obediently she took the goblet from him and sipped slowly.

Mary entered the chamber, followed by two men carrying buckets of hot water, which they emptied into the bathing tub. Mary then sprinkled some of Genny's favorite lavender fragrance into it.

"Will there be anything else, milord?" she asked, glancing nervously at her shockingly disheveled mistress.

"Nay, you may leave. I will care for Lady Genevieve."

With a quick curtsy, Mary was gone.

"Genny, you are filthy. You need a bath," he stated quietly.

Genny finally looked at him with some semblance of recognition. "I am too tired to bathe," she murmured through her fatigue.

"Then I shall assist you."

Startled, she looked away, aware enough to blush at the implication of his words.

"After all, I am your husband," he added.

Her chin raised slightly, but a quaver inflected her voice as she muttered softly, "A husband who does not want a wife, remember?"

Tristen exhaled slowly and lowered himself beside her chair. Taking her chin in his hand, he slowly lifted her face to meet his gaze. His touch soft, his voice gentle, he replied, "I may not have wanted a wife, but I most certainly have one. And right now she is in need of a bath and is too tired to bathe herself."

Slowly he raised her to her feet. The blanket fell from her shoulders, landing softly on the floor. Then he lifted the kirtle over her head and tossed the ruined garment aside.

"Your actions unnerve me, mi—Tristen," she said with a catch in her voice, as his hands slid up her arms to her shoulders, now vulnerably clad only in her winter chainse.

"I mean to undress you, Genny, not unnerve you. It is not my intention to frighten you."

His voice was a soft caress, but it sent shivers across her skin. Genny trembled as he lowered the undergarment from her shoulders, down past her breasts, her waist, her hips, finally to billow unheeded to the floor. Suddenly her nakedness before him was complete, and Genny shuddered, crossing her arms uselessly in front of her to shield herself from his probing eyes. Her entire body felt ablush, and she trembled violently at the unfamiliar sensations coursing through her. Never had she been so aware of her body, and never in her life had she felt so utterly vulnerable, so totally exposed, as she did in the presence of her towering husband with his piercing, midnight-blue gaze.

Cursing under his breath, Tristen scooped her into his powerful arms and carried her to the tub. Though she was as light as a feather, he staggered under the weight of his desire.

To his eyes she was perfect, with her delicate breasts, her slender waist, her supple thighs, the mound of golden curls nestled between her thighs. He fought to control himself, avoiding her eyes as he lowered her into the tub, lest she notice how profoundly she moved him.

Taking up the sponge, he daubed her tear-streaked, stricken face, then moved to wash her long golden tresses. Gently pushing away her trembling hands—raised to help or hinder? he wondered—he slowly worked the warm, scented sponge down her neck and over her breasts, groaning inwardly as her rosy nipples distended to the touch. Breathing with what he hoped was not an audible rasp, he guided the sponge down her midriff and across the glistening skin of her abdomen. Then he cupped his hands, making a ladle for the fresh warm rinse water the servants had left. The clear water ran in rivulets over her flawless body, seeming to accentuate her delicate curves in a manner designed to taunt his heightened senses.

Genny felt as though she were on fire. Her body had quivered beneath the sponge's softly rough caress, but now Tristen's hands were replacing that gentle friction. She gasped to feel his fingers slide across her belly, then down to the sensitive skin of her inner thighs. Just as she wondered what he was about, he began to provocatively explore her most intimate, feminine region.

Genny reeled with abject confusion and surprising curiosity. The feel of his calloused hands upon her soft, moist skin was oddly exciting, and she found herself longing for him to continue to touch her thus daringly, even though her mind kept telling her she should resist him. Her body would not respond to her inner voice, and her breasts began to heave, her breathing to quicken as she strained in perplexity beneath this masculine invasion.

"Come," Tristen said, his voice sounding raw to her ears.

Taking her trembling hands in his, he placed them upon his shoulders. Then, encircling her waist with his strong arms he lifted her, dripping, from the tub. Genny's legs wobbled beneath her as he set her down and she once more stood naked—and still more vulnerable—before him. But before she had time to contemplate her weakness, he quickly wrapped her in a soft blanket, using more to gently dry her hair. Then, turning her around to face him once more, he stared into her eyes, his own brilliant with some inner fire.

Slowly he lowered his head, and once again the nearness of him lit a flame within her. Her arms, of their own accord, slid up around his neck, and she closed her eyes, her chin uptilted, her lips awaiting his.

She felt the heady sensation of his mouth beneath her earlobe, bringing the delicate flesh alive with his ministrations. His tongue seared a path down her neck, onto her shoulders. She moaned as he lifted his head, and her lips found their way instinctively to his.

It was a kiss into which her entire being seemed to dissolve. His tongue parted her lips in a bold, soul-searing caress, and he proceeded to plunder the recesses of her mouth.

Even through her blanket she could feel the heat of his body course the length of hers, could feel her soft curves molding to the contours of his lean, muscular form. Then, with a low moan and seeming reluctance, he ended the kiss, raising his mouth from hers to gaze into her eyes.

"Why do you do this? Why do you offer me what you are not willing to give?" she questioned weakly, her voice quavering, her breathing ragged.

"I assure you, Genny, if I offer something, I will give it. And right now, I am offering," he replied as he captured her lips once more, holding her tightly to him.

Genny swayed into him as the kiss deepened, and the blanket around her slipped to the floor. He caressed the still-moist skin of her back and shoulders, and his mouth traced a sensuous path down her neck, pausing here and there to nip at the soft skin. Genny felt her knees weaken uncontrollably as Tristen's hand cupped her breast, and she thought her legs would give out completely when he lowered his head to suckle the tantalizing bud now swollen to its fullest.

No longer fatigued, her senses fully awakened, she began to comprehend the extent to which she had allowed her passions to undo her. She stiffened as she became fully aware of the hardness of Tristen's desire pressing against her nakedness, sensing that he wanted her only as a man would want to use a woman, not as a husband who loved and adored his wife. If she gave in to the flaming desire he fanned within her, he would merely be fulfilling a moment of physical desire, while she would be allowing him to tear apart her soul.

Tristen continued to boldly caress her, cupping now her buttocks, now her breasts, stoking her wantonness. It was not until she pushed hard against his chest that he raised his head and looked, startled, into her eyes.

Seeing that her passion had suddenly fled, Tristen grew angry. That she would close herself to him when she was so willingly attainable to other men was an outrage. With a growl of disgust, he abruptly set her away from him.

"Do not worry, wife," he spat. "I have no intention of forcing myself upon you."

His voice, no longer softly murmuring approval and encouragement, was once again laced with bitterness and anger, and Genny felt her heart constrict within her. She fought hard to control the tears that threatened to spill forth, knowing he had wanted her only to quench a temporary lust and thus could, his wits returned to him, rebuff her so easily.

Feeling naked and vulnerable, utterly ashamed, Genny quickly stooped to gather up the discarded blanket to cover herself. Then she fled the room, angered and confused, tears blinding her as she hastened to her chamber, where she flung herself across her bed, sobbing. Naked and exposed and wanton as she had been, this rejection was the hardest to endure. His prior disapproval of her unladylike behavior paled in comparison to this spurning of her as a woman. That she had temporarily whetted his masculine desire was no consolation in view of the fact that he refused to make her his wife.

Genny had breakfast sent up to her chambers the next morning, unwilling to risk confronting her husband after the events of the previous night.

Afterward she made her way to the stables. The air was cold, but the snow had stopped, leaving it a perfect day to visit Sarah.

"Edmund, could you please ready Apollo? I should like to ride to the village today."

Edmund nervously shuffled his feet. "I beg your pardon, milady, but Lord Tristen has left orders that you are not to ride alone."

"What do you mean?"

"After your accident, Lord Tristen left orders that you are to go nowhere unescorted," he replied, unable to look her in the eye.

"Well, we shall straighten this matter out immediately," Genny replied, turning on her heel and storming from the stables.

She made it only halfway across the court-yard before she saw Tristen walking with Alexander and Christopher. Her anger was such that she did not even acknowledge the presence of the other men.

"Milord, I would like to know the meaning behind your order."

"What order might that be, milady?" he asked calmly.

Genny's temper flared. He was deliberately baiting her. "The order that I am not to be permitted to ride by myself," she responded, her cheeks crimson with humiliation as she noticed the uncomfortable expressions Alexander and Christopher wore. "What is the reasoning for this directive?" she continued nonetheless. "I am not a child, milord. I ride as well as any of your men. I am not in need of a keeper."

"I am quite sure you are capable, Lady Genevieve. However, have you forgotten it has been but a short time since your accident?"

"Nay, I have not forgotten, but I hardly think a ride to the village will cause a relapse."

"I did not say you could not ride to the village. Only that you may not ride unescorted," Tristen said, each word condescendingly slow, as if to imply she was incapable of comprehension otherwise.

"I will not be treated as a child. I am a grown woman," Genny said as she threw back her head and placed her hands on her hips.

"I am well aware that you are a woman," he said pointedly. "My orders are merely meant to assure myself of your well-being. You are, after all, my responsibility.''

"Your professed concern is touching. However, I am capable of seeing to my own welfare," she declared. Giving him no chance for rebuttal, she left the three men standing open-mouthed in the courtyard.

Walking briskly to the stables, she muttered myriad invectives regarding the fate of her husband's soul. Edmund stood anxiously watching as she saddled Apollo herself. The task completed, she mounted the horse and rode from the stables, passing Tristen and his companions at breakneck speed.

"Alexander, have Edmund ready my horse," commanded Tristen as he watched Genny ride out of sight.

"She has a mind of her own, does she not?" asked Christopher cheerfully.

"I am not sure the woman has a mind at all," replied Tristen angrily as he headed for the stables.

Chapter 19

The children swarmed to Genny as she entered the village, their affectionate laughter and chatter bringing a smile to her face, her outlook having greatly improved during her ride in the cool winter air.

"Lionel, how fares your mother?" asked Genny, handing him Apollo's reins.

"She be fine, Lady Genny, and will be pleased to see you."

After he had secured the Arabian, Genny took Lionel's hand, and he led her into the cottage, where Sarah was seated in a chair, nursing the baby.

"Lady Genny, how good it is to see you."

"Sarah, you look wonderful. The babe, he has grown so big!" she exclaimed, looking wistfully at the tiny bundle nursing at his mother's breast.

"Aye. Would you like to hold him?" Sarah asked, releasing Gerald's small pink mouth, which continued to suckle greedily.

"May I?" Genny asked with yearning.

Sarah gently handed the infant to her.

"Sarah, he is beautiful. You must be so proud."

"I am. And we are ever grateful to you. He would not be here if it were not for you. Nor would I," she added meaningfully.

"How fares Edmund's courtship?" asked Genny with a teasing smile, recalling the unconventional birthing of the child she held.

"Fine." Sarah blushed, she, too, remembering. "We are to be married in the spring," she added demurely.

"Oh, Sarah, that is wonderful! Please let me hold the wedding at Ravenswood!"

"Oh, I could not, Lady Genny. You have already done so much for us."

"Nonsense. I am fond of both you and Edmund, and there will be no further discussion. The wedding will be at Ravenswood. I am confident Lord Tristen will agree," she said, though inwardly she wondered just what his reaction to another marriage would be.

"I do not know what to say."

"Say nothing. It has been decided," Genny replied, smiling.

The door to the cottage swung open as Lionel raced in. "Lady Genny, Lord Tristen is here!"

"Damn," Genny muttered under her breath as she reluctantly handed the sleeping infant back to his mother. "I think my visit will be cut short, Sarah. Come, Lionel, let us go see what the lord and master has to say." Grabbing Lionel's hand, she walked outside.

A sudden chill ran up Genny's spine as she approached a glowering Tristen, his eyes so cold and dark. Beside him stood the smiling but silent Alexander.

"Milord, what a happy surprise," she said caustically.

"Indeed."

Just as the heavy silence that hung between the two threatened to darken the bright winter day, a loud cheer rang out. Genny gazed about, searching for the source of the jubilation.

Lionel tugged at her sleeve. "Come, Lady Genny, let us go watch the ice games!" he cried joyfully.

"What a wonderful suggestion, Lionel. Lady Genny should see the ice games at least once before the winter is over," said Alexander mischievously, taking charge of the awkward situation. "Go and get your mother's permission, and we will meet you at the site." Leading Genny by the arm, he escorted her in the direction of the hubbub, while Tristen scowled at their retreating figures.

Approaching the clearing, Genny saw the village children and some of Tristen's men, each clutching a broom, huddled in two groups upon the small frozen lake. The recent snowfall had been swept away, leaving the surface smooth and slippery. Genny observed a young girl precariously crossing the ice to place a small round object between the two groups.

"What are they doing?" she asked.

"The idea, milady, is to move the wooden block past the opposing team with one's broom, all the while attempting to stay on one's feet," Alexander explained.

"Oh, that sounds like fun!" she exclaimed. "I should like to try it."

"Do you think that would be wise?" Alexander admonished.

"Sir Alexander, do you think I am in need of yet another watchdog?" she said as she proceeded carefully onto the frozen lake.

Approaching the team closest to her, she noticed Tristen hailing the other team. "Could you use another player?" he called out to the group. His question was met with resounding agreement.

Genny hesitated, but she had already been espied by Sir Marcus, one of the participants.

"Will you join us, milady?" he asked, handing her one of the brooms.

"I would be delighted to, Sir Marcus," Genny replied, knowing it was too late to back out now.

"Our goal is marked by the wooden barrel behind the other team, and theirs is marked by the barrel on the shoreline behind us," Marcus informed her. "Do you prefer to defend the goal, or would you like to advance against our opponents?"

"I prefer to advance, if you please, sir," Genny said with a gleam in her eye.

"I quite agree, milady."

At a whistled signal, both teams moved toward the center of the lake, brooms wildly flying to reach the rounded block first. Genny weaved her way across the ice, slipping and sliding around other players doing likewise.

His wife's laughter floated to Tristen's ears,

and he watched her progress intently—until he crashed to the ice. Looking up, he saw that Alexander had joined the fray and had recklessly cost him his footing.

At that moment Genny, caught up in the merriment of the game, skidded to a stop before him, a huge smile on her face. Seeing his position, she gamely offered to help him right himself. And to his surprise, he allowed her to.

He held her eyes for a moment, noting she was rosy-cheeked with the cold air and exhilaration of the game. The healthy flush heightened her beauty all the more, he decided.

"Thank you, milady," he said, touching his lips lightly to the back of her cold hand.

As the wooden block struck Tristen in the boot, he reluctantly released Genny's hand and returned to the game. He quickly captured the block with his broom and, rushing around numerous opponents, made his way with agility to his intended goal. Shouts of approval rose up from his teammates.

When next the block slid toward her feet, Genny moved into action, taking it with authoritative grace past many members of the opposing team. Raising her head toward the goal, she noted her only remaining obstacle was Tristen.

His lips curled into a smile of anticipation. She guided the block to the left, and when Tristen moved his body in response, she quickly reaimed and sent the block skidding to the right, where it found its goal with a resounding thud.

"Well done, milady," Tristen said quietly. But

a crowd surrounded them before Genny had time
to respond to his uncharacteristic praise.

"Congratulations, Lady Genny," Sir Marcus
declared. "We did well to have you on our side.
Better luck next time, Lord Tristen!"

Genny looked around with a perplexed expression.

"The game is over, milady. You have won
the game," Tristen explained, sensing her confusion.

"Really?" she asked excitedly.

"Really." He chuckled, entranced with her
childlike enthusiasm.

Sarah, who had joined the spectators with Lionel and a thickly swaddled Gerald, awaited the
couple as they and Alexander stepped off the
frozen lake. "I propose that we warm ourselves
with a celebration toast," she said, glancing
shyly at Edmund, who now stood beside her.
"Would you kindly accept our hospitality?"

"Lady Genevieve and I would be pleased to
accept your invitation," replied Tristen, taking
Genny's arm.

"Tristen, the men and I shall head back if
you have no further need of our services," said
Alexander, winking and not waiting for a reply.
"Perhaps another time, Mistress Sarah," he
added, flashing his garish smile.

Back at the cottage, Sarah heated the pun-
gent wine while Edmund stoked the fire.

Tristen watched Genny closely as she sat
holding little Gerald. Observing her tenderness
as she soothed the babe, he felt a sudden, unexpected yearning deep within his chest.

It should be his babe she was tending.

If only he had met her before . . . Before
Kathryn. Before he had come to know women
for what they were—faithless, self-serving,
wanton creatures. Perhaps then he could have
deluded himself into believing in a marriage of
love.

Gazing upon Genny, he had difficulty con-
juring the unscrupulous image he had been trying to maintain of her. Could it be that his
opinion had been unjust? Was Alexander right?
Perhaps she was just what she appeared to be,
a beautiful, compassionate, untethered spirit.
Was it possible?

His reverie was broken as Edmund joined
him at the table with the wine.

"A toast to our health and our friends," the
young man exclaimed, raising his goblet.

After they drank, Genny proposed, "I would
like to toast your upcoming marriage."

"Thank you, milady. We owe it in large part
to you," Edmund said with good humor.

"Marriage, you say? Then a toast *is* in order.
When will the ceremony take place?" Tristen
inquired with what Genny thought was uncharacteristic cheer.

"Sarah tells me the spring would be most
proper. I hold, however, that the sooner the
better," replied Edmund as his arm encircled
Sarah possessively around the waist.

"I have heard it said that women hold dear
their notions pertaining to weddings. I dare say,
Edmund, you shall enjoy spring nuptials."
Tristen chuckled. After a moment's thought he

added, ''The chapel at the castle would be an ideal setting. Lady Genevieve and I would be most pleased to hold the wedding at Ravenswood.''

Genny was astonished to hear the invitation she had, just hours before, extended to Sarah reissued in his voice.

''That is a wonderful proposal,'' she agreed smoothly. ''We would be delighted if you would consider having the wedding at Ravenswood.'' And she gave Tristen an appreciative look.

''We would be most honored, milord and milady,'' replied Sarah, quietly drawing closer to Edmund.

''Then it is decided. A toast to the bride and groom!'' proclaimed Tristen, raising his goblet high. As the evening wore on, the men's talk turned to war and the affairs of state. Genny stole glances at her husband from time to time, marveling at the significant role he evidently played in the whole. More than once he turned his eyes upon her, too, with that potent, enigmatic blue gaze she seemed powerless to resist.

Darkness began to fall, and Tristen and Genny conveyed once again their good wishes, preparing to take their leave. Outside, Tristen silently boosted Genny onto Apollo before mounting Demon, and slowly they headed the horses out of the village and back toward home.

Chapter 20

In the stillness of the night, interrupted only by the clopping of the horses' hooves, Genny attempted to reflect on the events of the day. But her contemplation served to further confuse her. What sort of man was her husband? She remembered his tenderness and subsequent withering cruelty of the night before, his obstinacy this morning. Then she smiled, recalling how carefree and youthful he had looked while he played upon the ice, his thick hair tousled, giving him an almost boyish appearance. And she remembered his cheer and warmth and generosity back in Sarah's cottage.

"I thank you, mi—Tristen, for offering the use of Ravenswood for the wedding," she said, finally breaking the moonlit silence.

"I am not as devoid of generosity as you would believe me to be."

"Aye, it would seem I have many things yet to glean of you," she replied solemnly.

He gazed sharply at her but said simply, "If we are to reach home before dark, we had best make haste. It will soon grow even colder."

A little annoyed at his evasion of the conversation, Genny felt a spurt of mischievousness arise in her breast.

"I quite agree. I, however, will be warming myself before the fire when you arrive," she stated.

"A challenge, milady?" questioned Tristen, obviously startled yet intrigued by her playfulness. "What will be my reward?"

"It matters not, since I will most assuredly prevail," she pronounced.

"Such confidence," he said, smiling that boyish smile she was so coming to cherish. "Then I would assume you will have no objection when I propose that the loser must do the victor's bidding for an evening. What say you now, milady?"

Genny swallowed hard while staring into the depths of her husband's now twinkling blue eyes. To do his bidding for one night . . . for him to do hers . . . Though blushing at her thoughts, she quickly rallied to the occasion.

"I accept," she announced, nudging Apollo to a full gallop before Tristen became aware of her intent.

Laughing in amazement, Tristen followed her lead, kicking Demon into action.

Their shouts rang out through the glen as they raced to the castle. Genny looked back over her shoulder to see Tristen advancing fast upon her. Lowering her body over Apollo's neck, she spurred the Arabian headlong up the steep incline. She was almost to the top when her saddle shifted beneath her, sending her tumbling to the ground.

Tristen, intent upon the race, scarcely had time to react as he witnessed Genny's terrifying fall. He pulled up hard on Demon's reins to prevent the horse from trampling her where she lay, and the animal reared and thrashed the air, coming down only inches from Genny's side.

Leaping from his mount, Tristen rushed to Genny, sheer black fright knotting his stomach. She moaned softly as he gathered her into his arms.

"Genny, are you all right?" he asked anxiously, cradling her head against his chest, where his heart beat erratically.

"I . . . am a bit dazed," she replied weakly as she struggled to regain her breath. "Is Apollo . . . is he . . . injured?"

"Nay, he fared better than you," replied Tristen, gathering her closer.

Genny could feel the warmth of her husband's body and the uneven strength of his heartbeat as he held her close. She drank in the familiar scent of leather and spice that was all his own. As she slowly recovered from her shock, she felt a shiver unrelated to the cold night run through her body.

"I . . . I should like to stand." Her voice sounded weak even to her own ears.

Assuring himself that she was not injured, Tristen encircled her waist with his strong arms and helped her to her feet. When he saw that she was steady enough, he reluctantly released her and went to the horses. As he returned,

Genny noticed that Apollo's saddle was hanging loosely off his back. Stepping forward, she ran her hand underneath the Arabian, feeling for the saddle girth.

Lifting her eyes to Tristen, she said, "The girth broke. That is why the saddle shifted under me."

Tristen crouched down to look, frowning as his hands came upon the frayed leather ends. Even without his seeing the girth, his fingers told him it had been cut.

"I cannot conceive how this happened," said Genny. "The saddle was fine this morning."

"Nor can I," replied Tristen, saying nothing about his discovery for fear of alarming her. It was, however, a matter he intended to give considerable attention once he had Genny safely back at Ravenswood. He rose to his feet.

"You shall have to ride with me," he said, dismissing any further talk of the incident. "We will lead Apollo back."

Genny watched as Tristen secured Apollo's reins loosely to Demon's saddle. Moving to mount, she felt strong hands clasp her waist, and Tristen gently set her upon his horse. The leather creaked as he hoisted himself into the saddle behind her. As he grabbed the reins with one hand, his other arm closed around her, pulling her snugly against his chest as he nudged Demon forward.

Still weak and shaken from her fall, Genny leaned back into the security of his arms, her head resting against his massive chest. As she settled into his secure, comforting embrace, she mused how unlike the first time it was that they had shared a saddle.

Tristen felt her relax in his arms. Since their encounter of the night before, he had longed to feel her close again, and he had been able to think of little else. Try as he might, he could not forget her soft, silken skin bare and dewy beneath his tingling fingertips. The memory of their kiss, of their closeness, lingered in his mind. He had been powerless to concentrate on his duties all day, his mind insisting upon replaying every nuance of her petite, provocative nakedness in the intimacy of his ardent embrace.

A delicious shudder coursed through Genny's body when she felt her husband's warm breath against her cheek. Then her heart fluttered wildly in her breast as his lips brushed her neck, the feather-light touch more of a caress than a kiss. Was it an accident of their jostling ride? she wondered. Nay, she realized breathlessly, for next his mouth seared a path downward, exploring the soft skin, making her quiver like a bowstring. His lips left her briefly as he murmured her name, and she heard herself whimper as the hand at her waist slipped beneath her woolen cloak. Her breasts tingled, and his touch grew bolder, his hand roving intimately, cupping, possessing, tracing the circle of her nipples. Her body instinctively arched toward him in response to the urgency and heat he stirred within her.

But as the horses crested the final hill and Ravenswood appeared before them, the night guard noisily heralded their arrival, shattering the moment of passionate surrender. The soft crunching of snow beneath the horses' hooves finally permeated Genny's desire-addled mind, and she straightened decorously as they came to a halt before the great hall.

Tristen dismounted and helped her to the ground. '' 'Tis unfortunate we were unable to complete the challenge,'' he said huskily.

"I would have won if the girth had not broken,'' she teased breathlessly.

"We will never know, will we?'' he retorted with a soft smile, his hands lingering on her waist.

Genny, overly aware of his closeness, stepped back. "Mayhap I shall give you a chance for a rematch.''

"I should like that,'' he replied. "I was looking forward to your doing my bidding for a whole night,'' he murmured.

His dark blue eyes seemed to stare into the depths of Genny's soul, and her heart pounded so loudly in her breast she was sure Tristen could hear it from where he stood. Unnerved by her wanton urge to return to his embrace, bereft that their tumultuous day was ending, she found herself able to do naught but retreat from the certain disgrace of yielding her pride to him completely.

"Good night, milord,'' was all she said as she turned to flee him and her churning emotions.

Tristen stood silently watching her ascend the castle stairs until she was out of sight.

* * *

Tristen warmed his hands at the blazing fire, impatiently awaiting the arrival of Christopher, whom he had summoned. Although it had taken him but a few moments in the cold stable to confirm that Apollo's girth had indeed been severed, the long wintry day and the disturbing knowledge that someone had deliberately intended to harm Genny left his body chilled to the bone.

The sound of Christopher's footsteps finally broke the silence.

"You wished to speak with me?"

"Sit down, Christopher. I have need to talk to someone. We have a problem."

"Problem? What kind of problem?" asked Christopher, seating himself.

"Genny's fall from her horse when we rode back from the village tonight." Tristen's voice dropped deeper. "It was not an accident."

"What are you saying, Tristen?" Christopher questioned intently.

"Someone tampered with her gear."

"Are you sure?"

"I examined it myself after we returned. The girth had been cut almost in two, leaving but a small section to tear as she rode."

"Who would do such a thing?"

"I was hoping you could assist me in ascertaining an answer to that most perplexing question," replied Tristen.

"I cannot envision anyone at Ravenswood who would do harm to Genny. Everyone loves her, as well you know."

"Obviously not everyone," Tristen commented pointedly.

"I have not heard anyone so much as speak an ill word of her. No one except . . ."

"Me," finished Tristen solemnly.

Genny gently pulled the brush through her long, tangled curls. Though it was usually a task reserved for her maid, Genny welcomed the mindless soothing rhythm of the rudimentary activity. But tonight not even untangling her tresses could untangle her perplexing thoughts or emotions. Setting the brush down and wrapping herself in her robe, she decided that maybe a late-night raid on the pantries would help ease the hunger in her soul.

Quietly she padded toward the stairs, but the sound of voices attracted her attention. Slowly she moved in their direction. Though everything in her upbringing screamed in protest at her listening in on a private conversation, still she could not stop herself. Her steps faltered slightly at the familiar baritone voice.

"Now is not the time to discuss how I handle my wife," declared Tristen angrily.

"When is the time, Tristen? It seems to me you never wish to discuss Genny, at least not with any sort of civility," retorted Christopher.

"Save your breath, Brother. You are but one in a long line to defend the lady to me."

"Does that not tell you something? She is your wife! We should not have to defend her to you."

"A wife I did not ask for!" Tristen roared.

He sighed deeply before continuing. "I don't mean to hurt her, Christopher, but I can't bring myself to trust her."

Genny's knees went weak at his words. After today she had allowed herself to hope that perhaps, just perhaps, he was adjusting to their marriage. Obviously she had misread his tenderness once more.

"She is not Kathryn. Genny has done naught to earn your distrust."

"I suggest we continue with the problem I proposed to you and leave me to deal with my wife," Tristen advised, clearly vexed that another man chose to defend Genny to him.

Hearing her husband's declaration, Genny lost her appetite and abandoned her initial intention to pursue a late-night repast. Slowly she walked back to her chamber, her heart heavy with the impact of Tristen's words. Sleep eluded her for many hours as his words echoed over and over in her head: *A wife I did not ask for. I can't bring myself to trust her.*

Had she stayed to listen to the remainder of the conversation, she might have found sleep even more difficult to achieve.

"It is my belief that the stables fire was no accident either. The injury to Genny's head was not sustained from falling timbers. The stables were afire but still intact when Alexander and I found her. At this point, I am also unconvinced it was caused by Apollo's thrashing. I need you and Alexander to assist me in looking into this matter. Whoever has been doing these deeds will not go unpunished." Tristen's voice was firm, his resolve absolute.

"We will find out who it is, I promise. I would be loath for any further harm to come to Genny," Christopher said, concern lacing his voice.

"So would I, Brother. So would I."

Chapter 21

Winter hung on for several more weeks, shrouding Ravenswood in a white blanket of snow. Although all its occupants despaired that the cold would ever leave, gradually it did. And with the first fragile budding of the trees, Edmund, in his impatience to wed Sarah, declared that spring had arrived. Sarah, however, insisted they wait for the flowers to fully blossom before she, too, considered the season to be truly upon them. The date having thus been set, the following weeks were filled with a bustle of preparation for Genny.

Although Sarah's enthusiasm was infectious, Genny remained somewhat subdued. Despite Tristen's peculiar insistence that she remain close to the castle, she refused to curtail her daily rides, which provided her only solace. Much to her chagrin, however, it seemed that everywhere she went she was constantly attended by either Alexander or Christopher. Tristen, on the other hand, remained aloof, though bodily he, too, seemed never to be far away.

Spring unfolded with splendor all over Ravenswood, and what was once barren in winter was now blossoming lush and green in the warmer weather. The wedding day having actually arrived, Genny's somber manner of late finally gave way to cheery enthusiasm.

Making her way to the courtyard, she was greeted by the happy chatter of her niece and nephew and the village children, who awaited her arrival to take them to gather fresh wildflowers to place in the hall and the chapel. As the boisterous procession meandered through the gates to the open fields, Genny was stopped by Alexander.

"Milady, I would enjoy the honor of escorting you and your flower gatherers."

Genny took in his warm, friendly smile.

"What say you, children? Do we allow the gallant Sir Alexander to accompany us on such an important mission?" she asked, her eyes twinkling.

Shouts of favor rang out as Alexander offered his arm to Genny, and the two of them led the merry group on their way.

"I would surmise milord could find a duty more befitting his right-hand man than guarding his wife at flower picking, Sir Alexander," said Genny.

"You wound me greatly, milady. I can think of no other place I would rather be than with you. And perhaps in addition you underestimate your worth to your husband."

"I think not, sir," replied Genny, dancing away from his side to join the children on the hillock.

Alexander sat watching in silence as Genny roamed among the children, helping them with their baskets of flowers, their chatter and laughter floating delicately on the spring air. A while later a rustling of leaves behind him alerted Alexander to someone's presence. He espied Tristen approaching.

"I had not meant for you to have to gather flowers," said Tristen, looking down at the basket Genny had given Alexander when she went to fill another.

"I merely carry. Your wife gathers," replied Alexander, smiling toward Genny and the rambunctious children.

Tristen was unable to pull his gaze away as he watched his wife running through the meadow. So petite was she, one could almost believe her to be one of the children.

Alexander observed the softening in Tristen's eyes. "She is good with children," he ventured. "She will make a wonderful mother, don't you agree?"

Making no reply, Tristen lowered himself down beside Alexander.

"I have received orders from King Edward. We are to leave for Wales in a fortnight."

"Have you told your wife yet?"

"Nay. I hardly think she would find it of interest. Indeed, she may miss you, my friend, but I imagine she will not even notice my absence."

"Perhaps if you gave her a reason to miss you . . ."

"Meaning?"

"Meaning, if she were my wife, I would not leave if she were not firmly branded mine." Turning his gaze to Genny, Alexander said blithely, "And from what I have seen, you have yet to lay claim."

"And I do not intend to. You know well my feelings," replied Tristen curtly.

"Aye, I know what you have said. I also know what your eyes reveal." Prodding a little further, he queried, "Do you deceive yourself into thinking a woman does not have the same needs as a man, my friend?"

"Bah! Genny's only need for me seems to be as a target of hatred. She has said scarcely a word to me in the past several weeks."

"Do you not agree that one who hates so passionately will also love passionately?" Alexander insinuated softly. He rose and placed his basket in Tristen's hands. "Milord, I leave you to your wife." And he left with a twinkle in his eye and a tune upon his lips.

Frowning, Tristen turned an appraising gaze back toward Genny. Her long golden hair flowed loose and free in the soft spring breeze. Most women wore a circlet covering their tresses, but rarely did Genny. She was not one for the conventional or the expected. Nor had he done aught to make her biddable, he mused darkly.

As she bent over to pick up one of the baskets, Tristen was afforded a fleeting view of her

creamy white breasts straining against the linen
of her chainse. A familiar tightening arose in
his loins, one he had become accustomed to
since being married to Genny.

Raising her eyes, Genny caught his gaze, and
a blush rose to her face as she straightened and
slowly approached him.

"I would not think flower gathering would
be of interest to you, milord," she said as she
placed her full basket next to Tristen.

His eyes moved slowly over her body, and
he replied in a husky tone, "I had not thought
I would enjoy it this much either."

"Uncle Tristen, Uncle Tristen, play with us!"
exclaimed the small, dark-haired boy who unceremoniously dumped himself into Tristen's
lap.

"Please, Uncle Tristen, please. You hide and
we'll try to find you," pleaded his little sister
with the woeful aqua eyes of her mother.

"Blakely, Abigail, I am sure your uncle has
other duties," reprimanded Genny, pulling
them off Tristen's lap.

"Nonsense," Tristen proclaimed. "I would
be happy to play," he added, watching Genny's astonished expression with amusement.

Cheers rang out across the field as Blakely
declared himself *it*. Children scattered to find
hiding places as Tristen grabbed Genny by the
hand and led her behind a row of bushes.
Caught up in the excitement, she scarcely had
time to react to his surprising agreement to join
in the children's game. She giggled as they
crouched behind the leaves.

"Shh." Tristen placed a finger to her lips. "If you make a sound, he will find us. He is very good, you know," he whispered.

Genny held her breath as she heard Blakely's approaching footsteps. He stopped suddenly, searching very close to them. Genny glanced up at Tristen. Looking down at her, he again pressed a finger to her lips to assure her silence. Her mouth tingled from the contact. Soon Blakely moved on, and Genny breathed a sigh of relief.

"How long do we wait here?" she asked in a whisper.

Genny could feel Tristen's warm breath upon her skin as he murmured close to her ear, "Till we are found." Turning his head, he moved his mouth to within inches of hers. "Do you wish to be, found, milady?"

Her breathing was rapid, her heartbeat so loud she was sure it alone would give them away. When at last she spoke, it was a breathless whisper. "Nay."

At that his mouth descended upon hers. All else seemed to vanish at his touch, her only thoughts of him and his kiss. It was demanding, urgent, but at the same time infinitely tender. Genny found herself longing for the touch of his hands on her, felt her breasts straining against her gown. And at that moment his hand slipped down to fondle one small globe. Her nipple surged at the intimacy, and she arched toward him as his other hand sought to explore the soft lines of her back, her waist, her buttocks. The stroking of his fingers sent jolts of unexpected pleasure through her body, and she whimpered in urgent desire.

At the sound, he laid her back against his thighs, and his lips recaptured hers, proving even more demanding this time. The touch of his mouth on hers, the feel of his hands on her body, set her totally aflame. She gasped as he fleetingly released her lips, and then his hands and mouth were everywhere, touching and caressing, adoring her. She reveled in the unbearable pleasure of it.

Raising his head, he looked into her passion-filled eyes. Then he slowly moved his hand under her skirts. Sliding his fingers beneath her chainse, he began to leisurely explore her legs, slowly tracing a path up her calf and thigh to the curve of her hip. Just as Genny thought she would burst with her aching desire, the laughter of the children intruded close upon their seclusion.

Despite the potential for embarrassment at being caught in such a position, Genny felt searingly bereft at the loss of his touch as Tristen quickly pulled her gown back down to cover her legs. Near drunk with desire, she forced herself to move off his lap, barely righting herself before hearing Blakely's exclamation of delight at having found them.

Thankful that the children would think nothing of her flushed appearance, Genny rose on trembling legs and proceeded with the group to the hall to ready the flowers for the wedding. As the children chattered and laughed in their excitement, Genny studiously avoided looking at Tristen, afraid she might see his familiar accusing look, abashed at the wanton way she had once again behaved in his arms.

Chapter 22

During all the wedding preparations Genny had been so busy designing a gown for Sarah and implementing the banquet plans, she had not taken time to have a gown made for herself. Nonetheless, she had a perfectly appropriate gown that she had worn only once. Oddly enough, she reflected sadly, it was to have been for her own wedding feast.

Walking through the chapel making sure all was in readiness, she uneasily contemplated the events of the morning. Why had her husband tried to seduce her in the field? Were his kisses and caresses the act of a cold, foreboding, uninterested mate? What were his motives? A blush stained her skin as she remembered how she had once again given herself to him with utter surrender. She knew that, had they not been interrupted by Blakely, her husband would have taken things further . . . and she would have let him.

Genny sighed in dismay. She was no closer to an understanding of this man than she had been on the day she married him by proxy.

That day itself seemed to be from some other maiden's memory. Such expectations, such great hopes she had had for the marriage. Even without benefit of ever having met her husband, she had believed that he would one day come to care for her and she for him.

Seating herself on one of the intricately carved stone benches interspersed throughout the garden, she reached over and plucked a fragrant blossom from a nearby plant, inhaling its delicate perfume.

"Genny, my dear, you look lovely sitting here among the blooms," Lady Eleanor greeted her as she entered the garden. "This has ever been my favorite spot in all of Ravenswood," said the older woman, gazing fondly around her.

"My mother, too, had a garden such as this at Montburough. I was so young when she died, it is one of my very few memories of her. I remember that she would take me to her garden and hold me upon her lap and sing to me. She had such a beautiful voice, I never tired of sitting there listening to her."

"She would be pleased that you have such pleasant memories of her. I feel a mother's ache for her that she did not live long enough to see what a beautiful lady you have grown to be."

Genny laughed lightly, though tears threatened. "I fear, Lady Eleanor, that she would not entirely approve of the manner in which my father chose to raise me."

"Oh, Genny, how could she not? Your spirit

and independence are part of what we have all come to love about you.''

''Not all,'' replied Genny softly, lowering her eyes from the older woman's intuitive gaze.

''Ah . . . and therein lies the reason we have missed your smile of late?'' asked Lady Eleanor, gently cupping Genny's chin to look into her eyes.

''Aye,'' Genny answered as her tears finally spilled forth.

''As wise a man as my son has become, he is still, I fear, a fool in some matters.''

''Nay, Lady Eleanor, you cannot fault Tristen for rejecting what he cannot possibly accept. I know I am unlike other women,'' she said in sorrow.

''Oh, aye, Genny, that you are!'' exclaimed Lady Eleanor happily. ''And I am so pleased that you are.''

Confusion furrowed her brow as Genny looked at the woman, unsure of the meaning behind her words.

''Genny,'' Lady Eleanor began, ''Tristen was very young when he married the first time. He did it, I fear, largely due to my constant pressures for grandchildren. More to the point, an heir for Ravenswood. I have come to sorely regret my interference, for I now realize I played a significant part in bringing sorrow and turmoil to my son's life. Your cousin was beautiful, Genny, and my son was no more able than other men to resist her. Where I beheld cruelty, he beheld kindness. Where I beheld lies, he beheld reason, and where I beheld slyness, he beheld tenderness. He desired her, as many did."

A pain flashed in Genny's heart as she pictured Tristen touching Kathryn in the intimate ways he had touched her just this morning.

"It eventually became apparent to my son that Kathryn was not what he had perceived her to be, but by then it was too late. They were already married. In youthful ignorance, Tristen sought to distance himself from her, thinking this the simple answer to their dilemma. But Kathryn merely sought other companionship." The older woman's eyes lowered as she continued. "I knew of it, but there was naught I could do." Her voice was filled with anguish. "I silently watched as she ruined her life, knowing it would also ruin my son's."

"Did Tristen know?" asked Genny quietly.

"Nay, not then. Kathryn was, if nothing else, somewhat discreet, and Tristen was away on crusade to the Holy Land. But, my dear, there are consequences to such dalliances. When we received word that Tristen would be returning, I was most anxious. It had been over eighteen months since I had seen my son. I hoped Kathryn, too, would be glad, that perhaps she would attempt to mend their marriage. However, my hopes were not to be realized. The closer the time came to his arrival, the more nervous and agitated Kathryn grew, further distancing herself from me and all others at Ravenswood."

A long silence impregnated the air.

"I found her, lying in her blood-soaked bed. Where she had managed to get the vile potion for such a deed, I do not know, but something had gone wrong, and she was bleeding.'' Lady Eleanor paused, shuddering, as she relived the moment. ''So much blood . . . the bleeding never stopped. She lived long enough to see Tristen one last time, but she refused to tell him whose child she had attempted to rid herself of. Her last words were a curse to him for ever marrying her. She died two years to the day after they were married.''

Genny paled at the shock of Lady Eleanor's disclosure. Kathryn had been her cousin, and thus Genny owed her love. But the woman had made a mockery of her marriage, dying while ridding herself of another man's babe. What utter shame Tristen had been forced to endure, and what vicious lies Aunt Beatrice had spat in defense of her deceitful daughter.

Genny felt shame that her cousin had so callously turned against her vows to God and to Tristen. But now, at last, she thought she understood her husband's aversion not only to their marriage but to the marriage bed. How could he trust her, a blood relation, after all, to his first faithless wife?

Lady Eleanor watched in silence as Genny sought to absorb all she had been told, to reckon the unknown demons with which she had attempted, vainly, to do battle.

At last Genny spoke. ''My sorrow runs deep. Not only for Tristen but, in a peculiar manner, also for my cousin. Mayhap Kathryn was unable to love, and that, too, seems too tragic for words.''

"My dear, your compassion is one of the things that makes you extraordinary. My son perhaps knows this somewhere deep in his heart. Unfortunately, he is fighting what his heart is struggling to tell him."

"Perhaps," Genny whispered, her voice trembling, "he, too, is unable to follow his heart."

"I sincerely hope, for you and for my son, that that is not true."

Chapter 23

Descending the long stairway to the great hall, Genny was captivated by the sight of Tristen waiting at the bottom. She had never seen him look more handsome. He was wearing a white tunic emblazoned with a black raven, dark hose, and black leather boots. The ever-errant lock of hair that brushed his forehead seemed to enhance the piercing blue of his eyes.

Tristen could no more take his eyes from Genny than she could from him. He recognized instantly the green velvet kirtle he had seen so briefly on the night of their marriage feast—the one he had insisted she doff while he had remained in her chamber. Although the chainse she wore today was different, the memory of how she had looked in her undergarment that night sprang afresh into his mind's eye. The strength of her will as she had breathed her own life into the motionless babe was permanently seared into his senses. That same strong will was what made her so rebellious when he insisted that she yield to his commands, he mused now.

He stepped forward, offering her his arm, oddly gratified to see that she once again wore his mother's long strand of pearls.

"You look enchanting," he murmured as he tucked her hand into the crook of his arm. And he led her into the hall so that they might take their places beside Sarah and Edmund.

As the ceremony began, Genny's thoughts drifted far away. Tears began to well in her eyes as she recalled her own wedding day. No flowers, no feast, no husband. She turned her gaze to Tristen, who was gazing back at her. Their eyes held for a moment before Genny lowered hers.

Tristen knew what she had been thinking. He had seen it in her eyes. Every woman remembered her wedding day. But what did Genny have to remember? The sadness in her eyes told him she had no memories to cherish, and he suddenly felt himself longing to cradle her in his arms, to ease her pain, to wipe away her sadness.

As Edmund repeated the vows, Genny once again raised her eyes to Tristen's. She beheld in them an expression she had never seen there before. His gaze was gentle and caressing, almost seeming to convey the message that Edmund's words espoused. Though his lips never moved, Genny almost thought she could hear the troth to love and honor his bride till death did them part in Tristen's resonant voice. As Sarah vowed aloud, Genny, too, silently af-

firmed to love and honor her husband in return. And as they looked into each other's eyes,
each other's souls, she realized that not until
this moment had they been truly wed.

Loud shouts broke into their unspoken com-
munion, making them aware that the ceremony was concluded. The chapel echoed with
merriment as well-wishers rushed forward to
congratulate the newlyweds.

Sounds of laughter and music rang throughout the great hall, where everyone had moved
to commence feasting and celebrating. Tristen
watched his wife mingle with his people, recognizing that women and men alike seemed enchanted by her, responding to her infectious
smile and energetic presence.

A frown settled on Tristen's face as he saw
her talk with some of the squires. For once, his
agitation was not provoked by those with whom
she conversed but by his concern over who
would want to harm her. What Christopher had
said was true; no one seemed to harbor any ill
will toward her. So why the accidents? No, not
accidents. They were deliberate attempts on her
life.

Turning her head, Genny was startled to see
the frown on Tristen's face as he stared at her.
But before she could puzzle out his mood, a
voice behind her distracted her attention.

"It is considered bad manners, milady, to be
as radiant as the bride."

Genny smiled as she turned to look up into

Alexander's ever-cheerful face. "You are too kind, sir," she replied, laughing.

"At last, that dazzling smile we have waited so long to see. If now you would honor me with this dance, my evening would be complete," he said.

"I wouldn't want to be responsible for your evening being less than perfect," she replied, conforming to their usual banter. "I shall, therefore, allow you this dance."

Alexander smiled at her words and offered his arm, and they quickly abandoned themselves to the lively music that filled the hall, oblivious of the scowl Tristen cast toward them.

The music floated into the garden, where the two men stood concealed in dense shrubbery.

"I do not wish to incur Lord Tristen's wrath," the first said, slurring his words slightly with both nervousness and drink.

"Come now, Daniel, you have seen how she behaves. Lord Tristen would more likely reward you. Her behavior has humiliated him beyond recompense." The second man paused, giving time for his words to take root. "Even you she has made the fool," he added goadingly.

Daniel remembered all too well the day Lady Genevieve had humiliated him in the archery contest. She'd made him a laughingstock in front of the other men. "Enough!" he thundered in drunken reply. "She will pay, I assure you," he hissed with undisguised menace.

"Good." The other man's satisfied smile

crept up to his cold, dark eyes. "And as I promised," he said as he dropped a leather pouch
into Daniel's hands, "it will be worth your
trouble."

Daniel closed his fist around the pouch. Feeling himself the victor in this duel of wills, he
held back his heady laughter. He would gladly
do what had been suggested for no pay, but so
much the better if this one was willing to
squander his silver to see the bitch get her due.
Returning to the hall, he hoped no one had
noted his absence.

Tristen watched Genny dance, first with Alexander, then with numerous others. She had,
in fact, not refused a dance to anyone who
asked. Tristen drank deeply from his cup, as he
had been doing all night, and the wine was now
beginning to dull what little sense he seemed
to possess when it came to his wife. His per-
ceptions narrowed till all that existed for him
was anger and seething resentment.

Genny was conversing with her newest partner, wishing the dance would end because her
feet ached and the room seemed hot and stuffy,
but even from across the vast ballroom she felt
Tristen's eyes boring into her like daggers.
When the dance ended, she quickly retreated,
making her way to the garden for a breath of
fresh air.

Winding her way down the path, she paused
to gaze up at the starlit heavens. A night for
lovers, she mused. Lovers, she thought sadly.

All her childhood fantasies of love and marriage had been shattered in the past several months.

Lost in poignant thought, Genny gasped as a hand shot forth from the darkness, taking hold of her upper arm. "Daniel! You startled me," she said, casting him a wary glance as the smell of ale overpowered her.

"I did not mean to frighten you, milady," the man said, but without letting go of her arm. "I have been hoping to meet with you alone for some time now." His tone was deep and somehow raw, and his eyes meaningfully raked over her form.

Genny refused to be intimidated. No doubt his boldness stemmed from too much celebratory drink, and he would be much chagrined at himself come morning. Her voice was calm and in control as she addressed him. "Daniel, I insist that you release me so that I may return to the festivities."

"I think not," he replied huskily, and he pulled her roughly against him.

Genny began to struggle as she felt the sickening touch of Daniel's wet lips on her throat, his hands groping at her breasts.

"You don't have to fight so hard, my pretty. You'll enjoy this almost as much as I will, I promise," he growled.

Panic momentarily overtook her till she saw the tall, familiar silhouette of Alexander nearby. He was withdrawing his sword as he approached them.

"Release the lady!" he commanded.

So consumed was Daniel in his plot of revenge that he failed to respond to Alexander's order, growling as he pursued his malevolent attack.

Alexander grabbed the man by the scruff of the neck, forcibly pulling him away from Genny. Caught off guard in his inebriated state, Daniel stumbled to the ground. Alexander planted his foot in the middle of Daniel's chest and pressed his sword tightly to the man's throat.

"You had best sober up before giving an account of your behavior to Lord Tristen."

"She deserved it. She's always enticing the men," Daniel sneered, his voice laced with fury.

Alexander pressed down slightly with his sword, piercing Daniel's flesh. "You will temper your words, or I will cut them from your throat."

Swallowing hard, the man sobered enough to realize he was in no position to object.

"Sir Alexander, may I be of service?" questioned Thomas, who now hurried across the garden.

Alexander did not lighten his grip on the sword as he looked up at Thomas. "I want this man taken to the knights' hall and guarded. Lord Tristen will deal with him on the morrow."

"As you wish," replied Thomas, unsheathing his sword.

"See to it he is guarded well," Alexander commanded, then jerked Daniel to an upright position.

Alexander finally sheathed his sword as Thomas led Daniel off into the darkness. Turning to Genny, he observed the faint glimmer of tears in her eyes, belying her attempt to appear calm. Silently he opened his arms, and Genny, still shaken, walked into his comforting embrace.

"Did he harm you?" he asked as he gently stroked her back in solace.

Her mouth formed words, but no sound would come. Tears slipped down her cheeks, onto his tunic, and he said no more, sensing her need just to be held.

This was the scene Tristen found when he entered the garden. Alexander saw him first and instantly became aware of the seeming impropriety of his embrace.

Genny felt his stiffening. Her head came up and her arms dropped from his waist. As she stood irresolute before him, only then did she glance in the direction of his gaze.

"I trust I am not intruding?" Tristen said bitterly.

"Genny was in need of comfort," replied Alexander hastily.

"My wife is most fortunate to have you as her champion. As ever," he added pointedly.

"Now, see here, Tristen, I did nothing more than protect your wife from someone who would take liberties with her," Alexander responded angrily.

"I am here now. I will see to her *comfort*."

Alexander noted the glitter in Tristen's eyes,

promising swift retribution for what he believed was dire betrayal.

Genny felt the perilous tension in the air.
"Alexander, I thank you. I shall be fine now,"
she interjected, wishing to circumvent any ill
feelings between the two friends.

Alexander glanced first at Tristen, then at her,
clearly reluctant to leave her.

"As you wish, milady," he murmured, then
drew himself up and walked past Tristen into
the hall.

After a moment of uneasy silence, Genny,
too, proceeded to make haste to the hall. But
Tristen's hands clamped down on her shoulders, halting her progress.

"Not so fast. I demand an explanation." He
spun her around to face him. "Your conduct is
inexcusable."

"As is yours, milord!" she shot back, struggling to free herself from his cruel grasp.

But he was beyond reason.

He was not merely angry, he was possessed
with a blind fury. He had found her in the arms
of another man, and the spectacle had unleashed some sinister emotion within him, some
primeval drive he had never felt before.

He crushed his lips to hers in a brutal and
vicious kiss, laying claim to what was his by
right.

Then tearing himself away from her lips, he
clasped her arm more tightly still and began
dragging her toward the hall. Leading her
through the back of the large room, he progressed unheeded by the merry participants en-

thralled in celebration. Genny struggled in his clutches, but he forced her up the stairs. As they reached the top, she spun and landed a swift kick to his shin, momentarily stunning him into releasing her. Raising her skirts, she fled down the hall. She had gone but a few steps, however, when Tristen lunged at her.

"You bitch!" he breathed, recapturing her. She tried to wrench herself free, to no avail. He dragged her into his arms and he carried her through his open chamber door. Setting her on her feet, he fastened the latch to the door. Genny instinctively started to back away from him, but his compelling eyes held her rooted to the spot. She gazed into those dark blue pools, trying to read the emotions submerged there.

Conscience and passion fought for mastery in Tristen's mind. Though he inwardly raged and planned to make free with this seductive, faithless wench, doubt took hold of him as she stood trembling before him. He had known many women. If her innocence was a sham, it was a convincing one. Lucifer! It was damnably hard for him to sort out *what* he believed when she was so close to him.

His gaze traveled over her face and once more searched her eyes for the truth. The vulnerability he beheld there finally sealed his decision. He moved forward and gently cupped her chin in his hands. His thumb brushed her cheek tenderly. Then, lowering his head, he pressed his lips to hers, caressing her mouth more than claiming it.

Genny was shocked at his tenderness and stunned by her own response. He stood so close she could feel the heat from his body, yet she moved nearer him still, impelled by her own uncontrollable passion. Despite her better judgment, she was once more completely immersed in him, his strength, his scent, his hypnotic presence. She wound her arms around his neck, clinging to him, trembling. Parting her lips, she boldly traced her tongue over the fullness of his mouth.

The touch of her tongue sent shivers through him, and Tristen groaned as he gathered her against him. Releasing her mouth, he trailed kisses down her neck to her shoulders.

"Genny," he moaned. "I want you. Tonight I shall make you mine."

"Yes, Tristen," she breathed pulling him back to her lips.

"Then you will no longer seek the touch of other men," he murmured against her mouth.

Genny stiffened. Anger flared within her breast. Even now he must accuse her! Placing her hands against his chest, she pushed hard. "Bastard!" she spat, and she slapped him hard across the face.

Sudden rage lit his eyes, and all reason fled him as he seethed. That she would resist him when she had so freely given herself to others was an outrage. By God, when he finished with her, she would know she was his and no one else's!

Without warning he grabbed hold of her kirtle, and in one swift movement he rent the fabric of her gown asunder, inadvertently breaking the necklace she wore, sending pearls scattering across the floor.

"Damn you!" Genny cried out, trying to fling his hand away.

With a vicious jerk, he swung her around, tossing her onto the soft mattress. Before Genny had a chance to move, he pressed his body down on top of her. Her strength was no match for his, and his weight was smothering, permitting her little movement.

"Let me go, Tristen!"

"I will not have a slut for a wife. I am your husband, and I say you will no longer seek comfort in another man's bed," he growled as he pushed her undergarment up to her waist.

Genny clawed viciously at his face, her efforts rewarded by a bloodied slash. With an angry roar he grabbed her wrists in one large hand, pinning her arms above her head, while he unfastened his hose, freeing his straining manhood.

His thighs settled heavily against the lower part of her body, the demanding hardness of his arousal pushing against her golden triangle.

Instinctively Genny tensed, sensing the violence about to descend upon her. Tristen's mouth settled into a cruel line, and in one swift motion he sheathed himself fully in her, ripping through the delicate membrane.

Genny cried out as rending pain sliced through her, and her body twisted in shock.

Tristen was stunned, but, having denied

himself the comforts of her body, as well as those offered by any other woman since he had met her, he was unable to halt the quick explosion of his seed deep within her. Then, groaning with shame at the brutal way he had just taken her virginity, he slowly withdrew from her before collapsing to the mattress beside her. Misery engulfed him at the realization that his actions—not only tonight but also in the past—were totally without just provocation.

"Genny?" His voice was etched with remorse and confusion as, fumbling, he pulled her undergarment down her legs and quickly refastened his hose.

Tears slipped silently down her cheeks, and she turned away from his questioning gaze.

"Why did you not tell me you were a virgin?" he questioned quietly.

There was something in his voice that gave her pause. A thread of guilt, an openness and a vulnerability she had never heard from him before. But she was not yet able to respond.

Raking his hands through his now tousled hair, Tristen sighed deeply. "Ever since you entered my life I have found myself in direct opposition to all the principles I have sworn to uphold. With this act you have caused me to forfeit my honor. What more can you do to me?"

His audacity defied reason, and outraged, Genny found her voice.

"You! *Your* honor!" she cried. "What of me, of *my* honor? I did nothing to you! It is you who have violated me!" she raged through angry tears.

Even in his guilt and confusion Tristen recognized the disillusionment, nay, the agony, in her voice. His chest tightened till he could barely breathe. He looked at the tears streaking her cheeks, the quivering of her lips, and the uncontrollable trembling of her slender body. Finally the full horror of what he had done to her began to penetrate his befogged mind. He reached for her, extending his arms in silent supplication.

Genny covered her face with shaking hands and gave vent to her agony.

"I am sorry, Genny. Forgive me," he pleaded, filled with regret, immersed in remorse.

Slowly, so as not to frighten her further, he blanketed her in his gentle embrace as she sobbed uncontrollably against him.

Genny was only vaguely aware of his soft murmurings of apology as he stroked her hair. Eventually his gentle ministrations lulled her into numbness.

Feeling her tension slowly dissipate, Tristen expelled the long breath he had been holding. How could he have done this to her? Whatever had possessed him to take such action, to say the vicious things he had said? No one had ever made him lose his self-control like this woman had, and yet that gave him no right to the wrongful deed he had performed. Would she ever be able to forgive him?

Hours elapsed while he held Genny in his

arms. When at last her sobs quieted, the slow, steady cadence of her breathing told him she had finally succumbed to sleep, leaving behind the atrocities that had been forced upon her that night.

That he had been the perpetrator of the assault left Tristen racked with guilt, unable to sleep.

Chapter 24

Tristen scarcely touched the food laid out before him the next morning. His lack of sleep and excess of remorse were manifest in the dark smudges beneath his eyes.

Alexander entered the hall, taking time to assess Tristen's temperament. Observing his friend, he detected no lingering anger from the night before, only anguish.

"There is a matter in need of your attention," he said quietly as he seated himself at the table.

Tristen's only response was to look at him blankly.

"Last night in the garden—"

"I would prefer not to speak of last night," said Tristen.

"We must. Last night at the celebration I noticed that Genny had left the hall. In compliance with your instructions to avoid leaving her unattended, I went in search of her. When I happened along in the garden, Daniel was accosting her. Fortunately, I arrived in time to rescue her, and I sent the blackguard to the knights' hall to be guarded till this morning, when you could deal with him.''

''Why did you not inform me of this last night?'' demanded Tristen, bounding from his chair.

''You were averse to explanations, if you will recall,'' Alexander replied crisply. ''But that is not important now, only—''

''You are correct. I want the man brought before me now!'' Tristen thundered in outrage.

''I would that that were possible,'' said Alexander softly.

''Why is it not?''

''He has escaped.''

''Escaped? I want the man responsible for this! Who was on guard?'' Tristen questioned in agitation.

''Thomas. However, he, too, has disappeared. It seems that neither even made it to the knights' hall. There are two mounts missing from the stables, and the men's personal belongings are also gone. I think perhaps we have solved the question of who has been committing these attempts on Genny's life. The motive, however, remains a mystery.''

''I want them found! Take as many men as you need, but do not fail to bring these knaves back to me,'' Tristen commanded.

Alexander rose from the chair. ''I shall not fail you,'' he pledged. As he strode to the door, he was halted by Tristen's voice.

''Alexander.''

Turning his head, Alexander looked back over his shoulder to his friend and lord.

"God keep you safe, my friend."

Alexander nodded without speaking, reflecting the unspoken bond of companionship and esteem each man held for the other. Then he turned and left the hall.

The gentle touch on her shoulder startled Genny awake, and Mary's sweet young face materialized before her in the muted sunlight. Struggling to focus her eyes, she became aware that she was in her own chamber, in her own bed.

Slowly dragging herself to her feet, she scrutinized her appearance. She had on the emerald-green velvet kirtle she had worn for the wedding the day before. She would not be able to make use of the gown a third time, she reflected morosely. It was ripped beyond repair, a brutal reminder of the ill treatment she had undergone last night at the hands of her husband.

As Mary prepared her bath, adding some of the precious lavender blend brought from Montburough, Genny was careful to avoid her maid's questioning gaze, having no wish to explain her dishevelment. Not even hours of sleep had restored her equilibrium or alleviated her acute sense of anguish and shame.

She remained in her room all day, avoiding contact with everyone, trapped by her memories of the night before.

How could a husband treat his wife as Tristen had treated her? She felt helpless, shamed, enraged . . . and tormented equally cruelly by her

softer emotions. For Tristen had viciously taken
what she would have given freely if he had but
asked. Then he had sought to soothe her in her
agony.

The contradictions in his character were diz-
zying; their consequences to her soul, devastating. After hours of agonized yet fruitless
reflection Genny finally resolved to confront
this tragic twist of fate with all the dignity she
could summon. Though her heart still felt bat-
tered beyond repair, she dressed herself carefully for the evening meal, hoping to mask the
turmoil that assailed her. Then she took a few
more moments alone to summon her inner
strength, knowing that facing the Earl of Ravenswood tonight would be the most difficult task
ever forced upon her.

Genny entered the hall, a vision of serenity
and composure. Tristen looked up, openly
studying his wife's controlled carriage. In silence she approached the table, gracefully seating herself next to him, giving no hint of inner
turmoil.

The meal proceeded awkwardly, conversation around the table stifled and sparse, as if in
deference to the excruciating tension between
Genny and her husband. Elizabeth alone attempted to alleviate the troubling drama with
pleasantries and chatter.

As all rose from the table at supper's end,
Lady Eleanor placed her hand on Tristen's arm.
"If you will take my arm, Son," she said qui-
etly, "there are some things I must discuss with

you.'' Addressing the others, she said, ''If you will excuse us?''

She led Tristen from the table and out into the garden. Walking slowly, seemingly deep in thought, Lady Eleanor stopped as they approached an elegantly carved stone bench.

''Tristen,'' she ventured as she lowered herself to the bench, ''perhaps your mother is the last person with whom you wish to discuss your marriage, but I should like us to try.''

Tristen gave no reply.

''When your father first brought me to Ravenswood, I was extremely apprehensive. I was so young and . . . so in love. We were fortunate in that we had come to care very much for each other before we married—our union was unusual, a marriage of love. Even if it had not been, I would have come to love your father, for he was honorable and steadfast in his duties and his life, a man of strong moral fiber. He was possessed of great strength, his bravery in battle never disputed. Also''—and here her eyes twinkled—''he was devilishly handsome.'' She sobered. ''Perhaps most important, however, he possessed a gentle spirit that we, as his family, were privileged to witness.'' Her eyes grew misty as they came to rest squarely upon her son.

He looked to have aged ten years in the past few months. Though her mother's heart went out to him, she also sympathized with Genny. For if the servants' whisperings were true, as they undoubtedly were, based on years of loyal service, Tristen had been unconscionably ruthless. A small frown clouded Eleanor's brow as she recalled her conversation with Matilda, which had been about that woman's interview with a most distressed Mary, who had nervously described the screams and angry shouts she had overheard. Indeed, if anything went on in the castle, the servants always seemed to be the first to know.

"Mother, I fail to see where this is leading," said Tristen dryly.

"You are so like your father in some ways," she said with a wistful smile, motioning him to join her on the bench. "Stubborn and sometimes unyielding in matters of the heart," she clarified, not without fond tenderness. "Tristen," she went on, "I know that this marriage was not of your choosing. However, it was not of Genny's choosing either." She paused, gazing into her son's dark eyes. "Yet because she is now your wife, she has been expected to adapt to a great deal."

"Genny does not seem overly fragile. Indeed, far from simply 'adapting,' she has completely conquered Ravenswood, from what I have beheld," he said defensively.

"I agree Genny is of strong mettle. But perhaps she uses that strength to cover certain frailties. For instance, a longing to be cared about. Everyone needs someone to love them."

"I advise you to abandon any lofty aspirations where my marriage is concerned," Tristen replied curtly, averting his gaze.

A long silence hung in the air before he continued. "Mother, my sins against Genny are too great," he replied in a dull and troubled voice, confirming his mother's worst suspicions.

"My son, no sin is too great if one seeks sincere penance." Lady Eleanor stood and placed a gentle kiss upon her son's cheek before taking her leave.

Genny had retired for the evening, her nerves no more settled than when she had awakened. The soft knock at her door startled her. As the door opened at her reluctant bidding, she looked up to see her husband standing there.

"I hope I have not awakened you," he said.

"Nay," replied Genny tentatively, wary of his disturbing presence.

"There is a matter of importance I must discuss with you."

When she made no response, he continued. "Last night . . ." He cleared his throat. "Alexander informed me this morning of the events of last night. It would appear that I was unjust in my assumptions."

"Nay, you were not 'unjust.' You were wrong and you were cruel," Genny said with quiet vehemence. "I wish to retire for the night. Pray, excuse me, milord."

His features hardened at her unforgiving reply, and he promptly abandoned any attempt at gentleness. "I beg your pardon, milady, for disturbing you. Nevertheless, you should be aware that Thomas and Daniel slipped away from Ravenswood last night. It appears that

they have been responsible for your so-called
'accidents.' ''

Shock at his implication that those accidents
had been deliberate attempts to harm her
drained all color from Genny's face. ''I cannot
fathom any reason why either man would do
me harm.''

''Nor can I, but when Alexander returns with
them, I intend to glean the reasoning behind
their actions. However, until they are returned
and secured, you will not be allowed to go anywhere unescorted,'' he said, a firm warning in
his voice.

Genny sat motionless on the bed. His gaze
dropped from her stricken face to her
slumped shoulders . . . and then to the out-
line of her breasts against her linen night-
gown.

Glancing up at him for answers to her pained
confusion, Genny noticed her husband's obvious appraisal of her. The smoldering flame she
saw in his eyes startled, frightened . . . and
aroused her. With a torturous pang she realized
that she longed for him to hold her in his powerful arms, to protect her. But she also feared
what that embrace would provoke. And so, in
miserable conflict with herself, she turned away
from him.

Tristen's expression was grim as he watched
her turn away. For a brief moment he had
sensed her vulnerability, and he longed to take
her in his arms and assure her that he would
let no further harm come to her. But her obvious rejection of him once again sharpened his

tongue, making his words harsh and insistent when he spoke.

"Do not disobey me on this."

Genny did not turn around till the slamming of the door echoed in her ears.

Chapter 25

G enny moved through the following three days like someone walking through water. Since the disappearance of Thomas and Daniel, she had not had a moment alone. Tristen, true to his word, allowed her to go nowhere unaccompanied. She was angered at her husband, resentful of his freedom. For every day he was gone long before the sun rose, returning only late at night, while she was constantly followed about by armed guards. They escorted her to the village, to the fields, everywhere. Their presence became a nuisance, as well as an uncomfortable reminder of the potential danger she would sooner forget.

As she stood brushing Apollo's mane in long, steady strokes, Genny was so absorbed in her grim thoughts that she did not hear whoever approached from behind her.

"I thought I'd find you here."

Genny jumped, nearly dropping the brush in her hands. Her edginess sharpened her tongue with irritation. "What do you mean by sneaking up and startling me like that?"

258

Tristen laughed softly. "My dear Genny, why would I sneak around my own stables? Indeed, I approached quite normally, and I have been standing here for some time watching you, but you were so deep in thought, you were oblivious of me. And a pretty picture you made, too," he added, walking to her side and brushing back a long golden curl draped over her shoulder.

Genny felt short of breath and unable to concentrate with Tristen standing so close to her, yet she spoke with a firmness of which she would not have believed herself capable. "You need not have bothered spying on me, milord. I am alone, as you can see." Her voice was heavy with sarcasm as she added, "Unless, of course, you would like to vent your spleen on Apollo."

Reaching out, he caught her hand in his. Genny started, then silently chastised herself for her fear. After all, what more could he do to her than he had already done? She swallowed hard, lifting her chin, and boldly met his eyes.

And what beautiful eyes they were! Today they seemed even bluer than usual, darker, and filled with ominous purpose.

"Are you afraid of me?" he asked, noting her response to his touch.

"Have I not reason to be?" she questioned, her voice shakier than she would have liked.

"Perhaps. However, I want you to know I do not make a habit of raping virgins."

"If I meet a virgin, I will pass along that information,'' Genny replied, letting her bitterness spill into her voice as she stepped back from him.

He flinched at her words. "You do not need to be afraid of me, Genny. Contrary to . . . what happened between us," he said with a small, wry smile, "not all my women have been forced to my bed. Some of them have even enjoyed the experience."

Her eyes widened. "I would be curious to know what kind of woman appreciates the treatment I received the other night," she spat contemptuously.

"None of them would have enjoyed the other night," he admitted softly, genuine remorse in his voice. "And for that I am most sorry."

But Genny was not to be swayed. "I do not need your apologies. I ask only that you leave me alone. We had an agreement, milord, one that you stipulated. I ask only that you now keep it."

"Nay. I have changed my mind about our 'agreement,' " he murmured.

Genny could feel the blood draining from her cheeks. Mere moments ago she had told herself that nothing her husband could do could be worse than what he had already done. Had she been wrong? Was he now demanding that she truly become his wife? Now, when her desire to do so had been so badly shaken? Genny looked at her husband in amazement. Did he truly believe that anything good or worthwhile could come from such a brutal beginning?

"I have taken the liberty, this morning, of

having your things moved to my chambers,''
he said, confirming her worst fears.

''Nay, I will not sleep with you!'' she responded sharply in panic.

''Genny,'' he remonstrated gently, ''you are
quick to say what you will not do. But I suggest
you devote some time to thinking about what
you *will* do. For from this day forward, you will
be my wife.'' His voice, though gentle, was un-
compromising. ''You will be my wife in all
ways. That I promise you.''

He sealed his vow with a kiss, cupping her
chin in his warm hand and touching his lips to
hers like a whispered pledge. And then he was
gone as swiftly and silently as he had come,
leaving Genny dazed and trembling.

The thought that occurred to Genny as she
wiped Elizabeth's sweat-slick brow with a cool
rag was that she had mercifully been spared the
ordeal of facing her husband that night at supper. The whole castle had been in an uproar
since early afternoon, when the time had come
for the newest Sinclair to make an entrance into
the world.

Christopher, who had listened fretfully
through the closed chamber door until Tristen
dragged him downstairs and helped him de-
plete a large supply of ale, was now at hand to
see his wife and newborn son.

Genny stepped back from the bed as the
proud if slightly inebriated new father leaned
over the squalling, red-faced bundle Elizabeth
held up for his inspection.

"He is beautiful, my love, as are you," said Christopher, tenderly kissing Elizabeth on the cheek.

Genny's eyes glistened as she beheld his obvious love and adoration for his wife. Silently she made her way toward the door, her eyes widening when she beheld her husband, who stood in the doorway observing the intimate scene.

Turning his gaze upon her, Tristen studied her intently for a moment. His face was unreadable in the flickering candlelight, but, ever so slowly, he extended a hand to her. Hypnotized by his gaze, Genny unthinkingly placed her hand in his.

"Come, Genny, you have had a long day," he said quietly.

He turned, and they walked silently from the chamber, leaving Christopher and Elizabeth and Matilda to fawn over the small bundle wrapped safely in his father's arms.

The door swung open easily at the touch of Tristen's fingertips. Slowly Genny walked into her husband's bedchamber.

After slipping the bolt, Tristen turned to his wife. He could see the fear in her emerald eyes, the tension in her petite form. Damn, he scolded himself even as his heart lurched at her beautiful presence here with him in his chamber.

"Get undressed, Genny," he said, his voice harsher than he had intended.

"I *will* undress for retiring—as soon as you leave," she replied.

He smiled. "This is my chamber. I have no intention of leaving."

"And I have no intention of undressing," she answered.

"You will undress, my dear, or I shall be forced to rip yet another of your fine gowns." He cursed himself for summoning the very demons he had hoped to quell. But, damn, her defiance provoked him every time! And it was too late to back down or wish for the delicacy that fled him whenever he neared his wife.

Genny's courage and determination faltered as Tristen moved closer. Slowly, with shaking fingers, she began unlacing the sides of the kirtle. She heard his sharp intake of breath as she pulled the gown over her head. Refusing to look at him, she unlaced her linen chainse and, as slowly as she possibly could, pushed it down her body, only reluctantly baring her breasts to him. With tears in her eyes she finally lowered the undergarment past her hips and let it drop to the floor. And there she stood, naked and ashamed, her eyes lowered, her cheeks flushed.

"Raise your arms," Tristen commanded with a slight catch in his voice.

Genny closed her eyes and drew a deep breath as she slowly raised her arms above her head, desperately wondering what further indignities were in store. She was startled to feel the soft brush of linen against her skin, and she opened her eyes to see her sleeping gown being pulled over her body.

Tristen gently lifted her chin with his fingers.

His touch was light, his eyes uncharacteristically gentle.

Against her will, those eyes pulled her in, and when he drew her into his embrace, though she trembled, she did not resist.

"I am sorry, love," he whispered into her hair. "When next we make love, you will feel no pain. I promise." His lips caressed her brow, her cheeks, and his strong hands tenderly caressed her back.

Genny cursed her own body, which now betrayed her. Her pulse was rapid, and she felt a tingling, a hot, deep longing, building inside. All her reasons for anger were becoming harder and harder to remember as his touch brought back the feelings that only he could inspire. How could she feel this way after what he had done to her? Why was the flesh so weak, responding to him despite everything? She despised him for what he had done to her . . . yet she could not deny that she desired him with shocking fervor.

Just as she despaired to think that she could never say no to this man, he abruptly put her away from him.

"Your hair," he said. "You will not want to retire with it thus."

Now completely unnerved and atremble, she walked unsteadily to the dressing table and began unbraiding her hair. Reaching for her brush, she paused as she beheld Lady Eleanor's pearl necklace lying upon the table. Every pearl had been expertly restrung. Recalling the cruel circumstances under which the strand had been

broken, Genny shivered, as if hearing anew the
cascade of pearls scattering over the cold stone
floor. Would that she, too, could be as easily
restored as this damaged strand. But such was
not to be. With trembling hands, she continued
her brushing until her hair hung loose and free
around her shoulders.

Tristen's back was to her when she finally,
slowly, turned around.

"Go to bed, Genny," he said flatly.

Obediently she climbed onto the large, soft
mattress and nervously wrapped the covers
around her, wondering whether she had thus
prepared herself for—or was to be spared—her
husband's attentions.

Tristen circled the room, dousing the candles
one by one, till only pale moonlight illuminated
the chamber.

Genny heard rustling as he undressed in the
dark, and she tensed when the soft mattress
gave way under his weight. He had slipped into
the bed beside her.

"You can relax, milady. I am merely going to
sleep." He rolled onto his side, and soon his
breathing was deep and even with slumber.

Genny's was anything but. She brooded over
the complexities of this man, her husband—and
over the tumultuous, conflicting emotions he
stirred in her breast. For even now she did not
know what she truly felt—relieved . . . or abandoned.

Sighing in a deep, perplexing frustration of
the soul, she gingerly shifted onto her side
away from Tristen, nestling her head into the

pillow in an attempt to get comfortable. Although the bed she had occupied alone for a time before Tristen's arrival at Ravenswood was mammoth, it now seemed tiny with her husband beside her. Even her senses conspired to rob her of sleep. She could feel the heat from Tristen's body, smell the leather and spice that lingered on the sheets.

Tristen groaned softly and rolled over, draping an arm around her waist. Genny carefully tried to escape his sleeping grasp, but his arm instinctively tightened, pulling her against him. She held herself rigidly still, afraid to breathe, afraid any further movement might awaken him. Worse, despite all her efforts to hold herself aloof from him, her flesh once more began to betray her.

The feel of his warm, naked body against her made her insides quiver. His breath upon her neck sent shivers through her, making her nipples harden against his forearm, which encircled her. Only his steady breathing managed to calm her slightly, and, unutterably weary, she finally began to relax into sleep.

Tristen smiled smugly as he felt Genny's body gradually conform to his while she drifted off into sleep. Knowing it would be hours before his own body and mind would quiet down, he was, nevertheless, content for the moment simply to hold her.

Over the next few days Genny saw little of her husband during waking hours, yet she was constrained to sleep in his bed at night. Never, though, did he do more than kiss her brow before dousing the candles and falling asleep. Many a morning she awoke to find her limbs closely entwined with his, her head resting on his shoulder or chest. Oddly ashamed, she would quickly remove herself before he awoke, or say a silent prayer on the mornings when he was already gone, thankful that she had not seen his face when he had witnessed this spectacle.

Watching Genny was torture for Tristen. She ate little or nothing these days, and deep hollows had formed in her cheeks. There were dark circles under her eyes, confirming his suspicion that she was not sleeping well. The worst was that he knew he was the cause of this somber change in her. He had damaged her spirit terribly that night—of this he was sure—and he knew not how to restore her, no matter how restrained he might be.

And his restraint required enormous strength. Night after night his body fought its natural desires as her soft curves innocently molded themselves to his harder, muscled contours. He was agonizingly aware of her warm flesh at his fingertips, and he wondered how much longer he could continue to thus torture himself.

Chapter 26

Tristen looked up at the sound of footsteps on the stone entry to the great hall. Taking in the sight of Alexander escorting his captive, he pushed away the remains of his meal. Rising to his full height, Tristen strode angrily to Daniel, whose hands were secured behind him with leather straps.

"Who are you sworn to, Daniel?" asked Tristen coldly.

"To you, milord," Daniel replied quickly, beads of sweat forming on his upper lip.

Reaching behind him, Tristen grabbed a leather bag off the table and spilled its contents at Daniel's feet. Gold coins clinked noisily and rolled across the floor. Daniel's face turned a pale shade of gray at the sight of what they had found in his possession.

"Think you this enough payment for my wife's life?" spat Tristen as he unsheathed his sword, his hand shaking from emotion.

"Nay, milord. I did not harm her," Daniel replied nervously.

"Where is Thomas?" Tristen demanded as he pressed the blade to the man's throat.

When Daniel swallowed hard but failed to answer, Tristen continued. "Alexander was lenient with you. I will not be." He bore down on his sword, causing blood to trickle over the blade's glistening edge.

Daniel swallowed convulsively before gasping out, "I swear on my life, milord, I only meant to scare her, not harm her!"

"I would not swear on your life. It is worth nothing to me," Tristen hissed. "Where is Thomas, and why did he want my wife harmed?" he thundered.

Again Daniel swallowed hard against the blade. "I know not where Thomas has fled, nor his reasons for anything. As for me, I only sought to give Lady Genevieve what she seemed to crave."

Tristen stiffened at the man's audacity. His eyes narrowed, his lips thinned in anger, his nostrils flared with fury. "You are a fool," he whispered, his voice deceptively calm.

"I but speak the truth. Any man would have done the same," Daniel protested.

"You are twice a fool, man!" Tristen roared. "No one touches what is mine . . . and lives!"

With that he raised the sword and sliced cleanly across the man's throat, all but severing his head from his shoulders, the body falling heavily to the floor. Sheathing his bloodied sword, he turned on his heel and stormed from the hall.

* * *

Having seen Edmund in the bailey, Genny had thought the stable would be empty. Thus she was surprised to come upon Alexander.

"Sir Alexander, I had not been told of your return," she said.

"I arrived early this morning."

"Did you find the missing men?" she asked eagerly.

"Only Daniel. Thomas was not with him."

"Has Tristen spoken with him?"

"Aye," he said grimly.

Just then Tristen entered the stable, leading Demon by his reins. He had ridden long and hard in an attempt to clear his mind of the savagery he had perpetrated in his overwhelming obsession to avenge and protect Genny from further harm.

"Milord, I was just welcoming Alexander home," said Genny nervously. "He informs me he was successful in finding Daniel. Will the man—"

"Daniel is no longer a threat. He is dead," said Tristen bluntly, his voice as cold as ice.

Genny paled. "And Thomas?" she asked shakily.

"Tell me, milady, do you fear Thomas, or are you afraid for him?" he questioned malevolently.

Genny lifted her chin, meeting his accusing eyes without flinching, but she had no intention of acknowledging his implied allegation. Squaring her shoulders, she turned and walked away from him.

Tristen merely glanced at Alexander's disapproving scowl before he, too, took his leave.

Alexander watched the gentle sway of Genny's hips as she left the stables. He shook his head vigorously to dislodge the less-than-platonic thoughts ricocheting through his mind and reverberating throughout his body.

"Tristen, you are a fool," he mused aloud. "You possess that which makes a man weak yet fills him anew with vitality."

He offered up a silent prayer that his friend and lord would soon discover what treasure he possessed.

Chapter 27

That night, and several tankards of ale later, Tristen, swaying slightly, made his way up the staircase to his chamber. Entering the room, he focused through the dim candlelight on the woman lying in his bed, the covers twisted loosely about. She was so petite that she appeared dwarfed by the massive feather bed. Her hair fanned out in golden waves, while her small, slender hands rested beneath her cheek, cradling her head.

After removing his clothes, Tristen sank wearily to the mattress and stretched out his long frame. In her sleep Genny sought him out, seemingly drawn to his body like a moth to flame. Tristen molded her tightly against the length of him. She moaned softly against his shoulder, moving into his arms as though they provided safe harbor from frightening dreams. As he shifted slightly to accommodate her, a hot surge of desire swept through his loins.

Genny awoke at his husky voice in her ear. "Relax, love," he whispered gently, molding her body more closely to his. He heard her breath catch as he ran a finger down her cheek, raising her chin.

It was at that moment that he felt the cold steel against his neck.

" 'Tis you who must relax, milord. 'Tis most unwise to assault one who slumbers if the slumbering one bears arms," said Genny, finding perverse pleasure in the expression of shock on her husband's face.

Tristen swallowed lightly as the blade of the dagger rested at his throat. Mentally he chastised himself for not remembering to hide it when he had had Genny moved to his chamber. And he could not fail to notice that, though she had identified her nocturnal assailant, she had not yet lowered her weapon.

"Genny, you will not rid me from our bed," Tristen declared, his mouth beginning to twitch with amusement.

" 'Tis I who possess the dagger, milord."

"But 'tis I who wield a mightier dagger, milady. One whose power you will not be able to resist," he huskily whispered as his warm hand gently closed over her wrist.

He gazed deeply into her eyes, and together they slowly lowered the blade as he captured her lips in a gentle, persuasive kiss. Without thought Genny opened her hand, releasing the dagger to him, and Tristen tossed the small weapon heedlessly to the floor.

Everything within Genny cried out that she should resist this man, but when he raised his head, she could do no more than gaze into those intense blue eyes filled with desire for her.

Slowly he again lowered his mouth to hers, and she felt his skillful fingers nimbly unfastening the ties of her bedgown.

Despite wanting her desperately, Tristen struggled to control the overwhelming sensations coursing through him, for to give in to them would surely frighten her. He had promised himself he would tread gently with her, a promise he now fought valiantly to keep. He raised his head slightly to look down into her beautiful face. Her cheeks were flushed, her lips parted from their kiss. Tristen groaned inwardly that this tiny slip of a woman had him trembling as no woman ever had before. He kissed her again deeply as he slipped the gown off her shoulders.

Genny drew back, trying to cover her breasts. Gently pulling her hands away, Tristen rasped, "Do not hide, Genny, my love." His hands cupped the firm, full mounds, causing the pale pink nipples to pucker beneath his caress.

Genny gasped in surprise at the throbbing pleasure that pulsated through her. His touch was almost unbearable in its tenderness. Instinctively she arched her back, thrusting herself into his gently massaging hands.

Lowering his head, Tristen fixed his mouth over one taut pink bud. He felt her quivering against him, heard the low moans that emanated from deep within her throat. Pleased, he moved to lavish attention on the other bud.

His musky male scent surrounded her, and a warm, intense ache began to throb in Genny's center. Of their own accord, her arms slowly wound themselves around his neck as he raised himself to once again feast on her lips.

"Your heart is pounding so swiftly," he said as he kissed the fluttering pulse at the base of her throat. His fingers moved slowly over her rib cage and silky abdomen, finally reaching the golden curls that hid her woman's treasure from him. Feeling the soft flesh of her womanhood moistening to his touch, he reveled with satisfaction even as his own desire brought him nigh to bursting.

He heard her gasp as his gently probing fingers found their way to her center. As he attempted to ease his way into her, he felt her tighten to repel him.

"I will not hurt you, Genny. I promise. I only want to give you pleasure," he murmured. And, fiercely reining in his own rampaging hunger, he continued his expert caresses until he felt her begin to give way. She timidly ran her fingers through the coarse raven hair that covered his chest, and he pressed himself against her so she could feel his desire for her hot against her thigh as he claimed her mouth again.

Moving very slowly, he finally raised himself atop her, teasing her breasts with his hair-roughened chest. Genny gasped but did not protest as he guided his straining manhood to her threshold and slowly, gently, pressed himself into her. Panting, her breasts heaving, she grasped him tightly to her, pulling him deeper within.

"Ah, Genny!" he moaned.

Genny writhed beneath him, crushing her breasts against his chest, her hips thrusting toward him as if possessing a will of their own, which seemed to further ignite him. A fire raged within her as he drove fully and deeply into her. Nothing mattered but the indescribable pleasure that washed over her as she rose higher and higher on the waves of desire.

Moans of ecstasy sliced through the air, growing more intense with each thrust.

"Tristen!" Genny's voice shook as her body seemed to explode from within. An instant later Tristen reared above her and cried aloud as he spilled his seed deep within her.

Rolling sideways to remove the burden of his weight from her delicate form, Tristen pulled her along in his strong arms, and they lay in united silence as their breathing slowly returned to normal.

Placing a kiss atop Genny's head where it rested against his chest, he heard her soft, even breaths, assuring him that she had fallen asleep. He breathed a sigh of release and amazement. Never before had a woman inflamed him so, nor responded with such wondrous, wanton pleasure. Just remembering her soft, small body moving beneath him made him ache again with wanting.

A frown puckered his brow. True, he had proved he could make her burn with desire for him, but had he truly made her his, body and soul? Or was there something he was missing? And should it matter?

It was a long while before he succumbed to

sleep, his mind uneasily echoing that it did
matter, yet he knew naught else to do.

The next morning, Genny awoke first. Pushing herself up on her elbow, she looked down
upon the face of her husband.

Yes, her husband. After last night, she no
longer felt remote from nor held any fear of
him. He looked so gentle in slumber, so young
and handsome, with his dark tresses mussed
about his head.

Tentatively she reached out and touched the
curly hairs on his chest. Slowly she moved her
hand across the well-defined muscles. Her mind
reeled with emotion as her eyes feasted on his
perfectly formed body.

She was thoroughly amazed by last night's
experience. Amazed that she had given this
man total control of her body, her self. He had
done things to her she had never imagined,
evoking desires and sensations she had never
before realized.

She sobered as the reality of their relationship loomed before her. She was married to this
man who could bring her such ecstasy, and she
had yielded herself to him completely. Yet he
did not love her and thus had not ceded any of
himself. The imbalance was stark, the consequences grim, and suddenly all Genny's fears
came rushing back.

Only one comforting thought came to her.
Perhaps, just perhaps, she mused, if he could
continue to desire her this way, he could eventually grow to care for her. Since she now knew

that his abusive words and actions had arisen not from genuine malice but from his own inner torment, perhaps somehow, some way, she could solace his soul and win his love. She would have to. She had already given him hers.

"Do you like what you see?" he murmured, teasing her. "Or is something wrong with my body?"

She was so intent on her musings that she had not sensed him awaken. She jerked her hand away, blushing furiously. "Oh, nay!"

"Nay, you do not like what you see, or nay, there is naught wrong with my body?" he asked, continuing his teasing.

"Nay, there is naught wrong with your body. It is beautiful," she added quietly, lowering her gaze to hide her embarrassment.

"Men's bodies are not beautiful," he replied in mock disdain.

"I have not seen many men's bodies, only those of the villagers I tended with Thisbe. And I can tell you, their bodies did not look like yours. Yours is . . . beautiful."

Tristen laughed lightly and pulled her down across his chest. "I, too, am pleased, with *your* body," he said, hugging her tightly. "Very pleased," he added huskily, running his hands over her delicate curves.

Genny could feel his heart beating swiftly against her own breast, and as he trailed hot kisses down the curve of her neck, she sighed with the pure pleasure of it. "Why are we always quarreling?" she murmured.

"I do not know. But I think we have found a

place for peace. Perhaps we should stay in bed all the time.''

'' 'Tis morning, milord,'' she protested mildly, though in truth she longed to stay where she was.

"Art thou shy, Lady Genevieve?"

"They await our arrival downstairs."

"Let them wait," he replied as his busy hands continued to roam freely over her body.

Genny was almost beside herself with frustrated excitement. ''But they will think . . .''

"And they will be absolutely right," he rasped as he rolled her over, pinning her body beneath his, letting her feel how much he wanted her.

Now his warm mouth began worshiping each place his fingers had touched. Slowly he moved down her body as his lips slid across her silken belly, downward to the swell of her hips. His hands, never losing contact with her skin, explored the soft lines of her waist and hips and breasts.

The tension within her building to a crescendo, Genny frantically clutched at the strong tendons in the back of his neck. Unutterably aroused, she attempted to draw him closer to her, desperately needing more of him. Her breasts heaved as she ran her hands feverishly over the solid muscles of his shoulders and back.

Shifting his position, he gently took her hands, encouraging them to further explore him. Tentatively she rubbed his masculine nipples, let her fingers rake his massive chest, his taut abdomen. Then, quivering, her fingers crept lower, seeking and finding his erect shaft. Her touch grew bolder at his tormented groan.

His hands became more demanding, roving over her smooth breasts, cupping and squeezing. His tongue caressed her sensitive, swollen nipples; he suckled her with tantalizing possessiveness.

Their impatience grew to explosive proportions, their mutual desire demanding immediate fulfillment, and Genny cried out with unbearable pleasure as she welcomed him into her body. She reveled in the heat of him deep inside her, flesh within flesh, man within woman, and together they found the tempo that bound their bodies.

"Tristen!" His name echoed through the chamber as Genny's passion reached its height, her heart pounding madly within her chest, every inch of her atremble. And she once more surrendered utterly to the tumult that had brought them to their tentative, temporary peace.

"What will you do with this day?" Tristen asked sometime later as he began to dress.

"Edmund and I are to start breeding the mares today," she said, unaccountably blushing at the factual revelation. As she hurried to clothe herself, she added nervously, "After each mare has been covered, then she must be marked."

"How do you intend to mark them?" he asked.

"I braid the manes. Those bred with Demon

are braided differently than those covered by Apollo.''

Tristen took a long moment to study her as she finished dressing. She was radiant this morning. Her cheeks glowed with color, and her simplest movements seemed imbued with innocent seductiveness.

''While you tend to the mares, Alexander and I are going to ride to the villages to survey the progress of the planting,'' he informed her as they descended to the hall.

For some unexplainable reason, Genny found comfort in his sharing his plans with her, and as he took his leave of her, placing a kiss on her eager lips, she felt an emptiness, an incompleteness, at the prospect of his absence.

Genny's eyes widened as Edmund led a prancing, snorting Demon to the whinnying mare. The mare bucked and huffed with primitive instinct as Demon mounted her, her nostrils flaring, her eyes rolling wildly. Savage mating sounds filled the air, and the mare pushed back farther to accommodate Demon's powerful thrusts.

Genny felt the hot breath on her neck before she heard the whispered words.

''Would that I could have spent my day as Demon has,'' Tristen murmured in her ear.

Genny blushed violently but retorted airily, ''Indeed, milord? Do you think you have Demon's stamina?''

''Are you prepared to find out?'' Tristen asked, nibbling on her earlobe.

"That sounds like a challenge, milord. Are you up to it?" Genny questioned, leaning back against him. Even through the fabric of her kirtle and his tunic, she could feel the hard ridge of his manhood straining against his hose.

"Need you more proof, milady?"

"Nay, milord," she whispered, her breath catching as his arm wrapped around her just below her breasts. His presence, his touch, were so powerfully masculine, so compelling. "I did not expect you back so early," she said haltingly.

"Would you believe me were I to tell you I had rushed through my day in order to spend more time pleasuring my lady, as does Demon?" he said, continuing the banter they were sharing.

Genny blushed still more deeply. " 'Tis true *Demon's* lady does not seem to object," she replied, rising to the suggestive sparring.

"Nor did *my* lady object. Not last night, nor this morning," he whispered, watching the vein in her neck pulsing, the rapid rise and fall of her breasts. He ached to strip away the clothing that kept him from claiming those breasts with lips, teeth, and tongue, and he sensed that Genny shared his urgency. He heard her breath catch as Demon reared above the mare, his savage cry of release piercing the air, and he felt her shudder in his arms.

It was several moments before either of them moved, and then it was to help Edmund secure a satiated Demon and the mares in their stalls.

They had yet to endure the lengthy main meal of the day in the hall before they could be alone.

Genny found it impossible to concentrate on the conversation at table. She kept gazing longingly at her husband, then shyly lowering her eyes when she thought anyone noticed. More than once questions were repeated for her benefit, and her replies were short and sometimes incoherent.

Lady Eleanor watched in silent amusement. Her son suddenly seemed most fascinated with his wife. Many a time she had seen that look in his father's eyes. It had stirred her heart and body beyond thought when Stephen had looked at her thusly. She smiled, thanking God for sending this small, spirited woman to her son.

Loudly attributing Genny's inattention to fatigue, Tristen escorted her upstairs as soon as was decently possible.

They had not even stepped fully into the bedchamber before he grabbed for her. A soft moan escaped Genny's lips as Tristen wrapped his arms around her from behind, her breasts resting lightly on his forearms. Her head rolled back against his chest as he trailed kisses down her slender throat. Heat swirled in her belly as he reached to cup her breasts.

As he moved his hips against her backside, flashes of Demon and the mare played through Genny's mind, and her breathing became still more rapid. Tristen quickly unlaced her gown and helped her to undress, then groaned with his desire for her. After rapidly tearing off his own clothing, he lifted her into his arms and carried her to their bed.

"Genny," he breathed as he pulled her into his embrace. "I have been wanting to . . . do . . . this . . . ever since . . . I left you this morning," he murmured between fervent kisses. She melted against him, wrapping her arms about him.

"Love me, Tristen," she whimpered.

His hands ran hungrily over her hips, her abdomen, her breasts. Deliberately he aroused her nipples to small, firm buds, then suckled them at leisure. Genny arched her back toward the tender torture of his mouth and tongue.

"Tristen . . . do not . . . stop," she begged, thrusting and writhing, offering her body to him in utter abandonment.

His lips did not leave her skin as he pressed hot kisses up her neck, making his way to the small, delicate shell of her ear. "Genny," he moaned. "Let me love you as Demon loved his lady."

Although she did not comprehend his actions, when he rolled her onto her stomach, she made no attempt to protest. He wrapped an arm around her small waist, lifting her effortlessly to her knees while placing moist, tantalizing kisses on the nape of her neck. Weak with longing, dazed by desire, yet Genny cried out with surprise as Tristen fused their bodies from behind in a most primitive joining. Then the raw sensuousness of the act carried her to greater heights, and she quivered with passion and a sense of oneness with her mate.

Tristen brought her to peak after peak of pleasure, and as he continued to rouse her passion higher, his own grew ever more urgent. Finally, reveling in her outcries, he allowed himself to join her. With one final, powerful thrust, his pent-up passion exploded into liquid fire before he collapsed beside her on the soft feather mattress.

Exhausted by the ferocity of their mating, Genny soon fell asleep, a curious smile curving her lips, her head resting securely on Tristen's shoulder.

Tristen, too, was exhausted, but rather than finding sated slumber, he shook his head in an agony of bemusement. This wife of his was having a most strange effect upon him. Perhaps it was a good thing he would be leaving shortly. Enjoying one's wife in bed was one thing, but losing one's wits—maybe even one's heart?— that was another matter. He shook his head again, trying to dislodge the faint tinge of fear that accompanied the thought.

Genny reveled in the ecstasy of her nights with Tristen. While she attended to her many daytime duties, her mind was often filled with thoughts of their lovemaking. Of how Tristen drove her half mad with new arrangements and strange caresses, until she lost all control and burned wildly with wanting him.

Many a time in the throes of their intimacies she longed to confess her love for him, but she held back. He had not made any declaration of love to her. More likely, he cared only for what they shared in the privacy of their chamber. And while she would not trade their physical passion for the world, she was beginning to fear that, if desire remained all, they might never navigate the depths of their marriage.

Chapter 28

The woman's touch startled Thomas awake.

"Your hands are cold," he protested, blearily focusing on the face of Beatrice Aldred.

"You did not complain last night," she purred. "But neither did you tell me why you have come to Aldred Keep."

"When I arrived last night, you gave me little time to explain," said Thomas, "so avid was your lust."

Knowing Sinclair would not give up his search for him, Thomas had sought out the one person who might help him, albeit unwittingly, gain revenge against Lady Genny. In the two weeks since Daniel had been captured, he had kept to the woods, avoiding contact with anyone while he made his way to Aldred Keep. Although eager to set into motion the new plan he had formulated, he was aware that he must first secure Beatrice's support.

"I am giving you the opportunity now," replied Beatrice tartly as she rose from the bed and put on her robe.

"I have decided to help you in your efforts to gain control of Montburough."

"Why did you wait so long to come to me?" she asked suspiciously.

"I am here now. That shall have to suffice."

Beatrice eyed him warily as she handed him a goblet of ale.

"Are you not sworn to Lord Tristen?"

"He is no longer my liege lord."

"By his say or yours?"

"It matters not," he replied tightly.

"How do you propose to help me gain Montburough?" asked Beatrice, somewhat vexed by the arrogance of the man.

"There is but one obstacle between you and Montburough—the Earl of Ravenswood. Should the earl meet an untimely death, Lady Genevieve would then be free to marry your son." Thomas paused, thinking of Philip Aldred. Did the fool really think Genny could care for someone like him? He wet his throat with a draught of ale. "Will Philip be a problem?" he asked.

"Leave Philip to me. My concern is how you think to best the Earl of Ravenswood."

"I have been in service to the earl for many years. I know his weaknesses," Thomas said pointedly after he finished his ale. "And I know of men who will follow any order if the payment is generous enough."

"And what do you hope to gain from this?"

Thomas rose from the bed and crossed the room to stand in front of Beatrice. "Need you ask?" he said seductively before drawing her into his arms.

Beatrice responded convincingly to his kiss while her suspicious and cunning nature dismissed his answer as false. She knew he had not betrayed Lord Tristen for her sake, and so she resolved to watch this man carefully. Very carefully.

Chapter 29

Genny was awakened by a stinging slap to her bare bottom.

"Arise, milady. We have a busy day ahead of us," said Tristen as he rose from the bed. "Dress for riding," he instructed her mysteriously.

"Riding? Where to, milord?"

"That, my dear, shall reveal itself in its own good time," he said as his eyes seductively raked her nakedness.

Genny tingled under his gaze, remembering his heated kisses of the night before, the way his hard body had felt pressed firmly to hers. Still, while pleased with their incomparable intimacy, she could not deny that she longed for the love Tristen seemed ever to withhold from her. Worsening her plight was that, with each day, her own love for him deepened and intensified.

"I shall await you in the bailey," said Tristen when he finished dressing. "Do not be long," he commanded, then swooped down to capture her mouth in a swift but searing kiss.

"Aye, milord," replied Genny as he left the room.

She dressed quickly and ate hurriedly, feeling the beginnings of a fragile hope. Seldom before had Tristen requested her presence beside him other than in the marriage bed. Her heart soared with newfound anticipation.

Tristen chuckled at her as she fairly leaped down the castle steps into the courtyard. He helped her to mount before doing so himself.

"Where are we going?" she asked again.

"There is something I want to show you. Besides, I think my men would appreciate a day in which they do not have to traipse behind you."

Tristen laughed as Genny flashed him a wry look.

They rode away from the keep, traveling much farther than Genny had ventured since her arrival at Ravenswood. A radiant sun warmed them as their ride continued well into the late morning.

Genny had begun to think they would never reach their destination, if indeed they had one, when at last they stopped by a small brook, where Tristen allowed the horses to drink. Taking Genny's hand, he led her up a slope to higher ground. Once they reached the top of the hill, Genny sucked in her breath at the view of a shining, crystal-blue lake gleaming amid vibrant green trees.

" 'Tis beautiful," she murmured in awe.

" 'Tis my favorite spot. I come here every chance I get. Every time I see it I am speechless, for each time, like you, it seems to become more beautiful still.''

Genny blushed deeply at his words. ''This must be the loveliest place on earth,'' she said almost reverently.

''It is now,'' Tristen replied. Taking her face between his hands, he kissed her tenderly. Then, releasing her, he smiled broadly. ''Stay here. I will return shortly.''

Genny stood admiring the magnificent view, and soon Tristen returned, bearing a blanket and staggering under the weight of an enormous basket.

''Tilly made sure we had plenty of food for our outing. I could barely carry the thing up here,'' he proclaimed of the bulging basket.

Genny giggled at the sight.

''Come, wench, do not stand there laughing while your lord grows weak from hunger,'' he commanded as he put the basket down and laid out the blanket.

Together they set out the feast Tilly had prepared for them, complete with meat, cheeses, hard bread, and fruit. After eating their fill, they sat drinking in the quiet serenity of the hilltop setting.

As they lounged, Genny was once again taken by the devastating handsomeness of her husband. The past several days had only confirmed for her what she already knew. She loved this man. Not once since the night he had tenderly initiated her into lovemaking had they fought, and she reveled in the feeling of contentment that had, at last, settled over her. But would it possibly prove enduring? How could she be sure, when all else about her was so unclear? For instance, how could Tristen stir such powerful passions in her if he, for his part, felt nothing but lust? Perhaps, she thought hopefully, he was beginning to accept her, and the situation into which they had been thrust. She wished fervently that this idyllic interlude could continue forever, but instinct told her it would be short-lived, turning to ashes when the flame of desire burned out.

Tristen lay back and closed his eyes, puzzling over Genny's power. Her soft lips yielded to his yet seemed to command him. Nightly he entered the velvety warmth of her womanhood, yet he was not so much master as mastered when she eagerly engulfed him and held him within her. He never tired of bedding her, and secretly he wondered if he ever would. Although he delighted in her body, Tristen knew that the woman sitting next to him would be the last woman in the world he would have chosen to love. For not only did she inspire his passions, she could equally ignite his anger and drive him to distraction.

He frowned. It was just as well, he reflected, that he was leaving in the morning. He had clearly been spending far too much time in her seductive presence.

Genny glanced up to see his expression. "Is something amiss?" she asked.

"Alexander and I will be leaving in the morning," he said simply.

Genny's heart sank. Though she had just

surmised that their peaceful time would come to an end, she had not known it would be this soon. "Where will you go?" she asked faintly.

"King Edward has need of me in Wales."

"Will you be gone long?"

"As long as it takes to bring the Welsh under Edward's control."

The silence that followed was broken only by the faint cries of birds high in the towering trees.

"Then I shall pray for a swift victory," Genny finally said softly.

"Edward would have it no other way," Tristen replied.

"And what King Edward desires shall be. Who better than us to know?" added Genny quietly.

Tristen studied her profile. The bright sunlight touched her hair, making it shimmer like a curtain of polished gold. He silently assessed her form, amazed anew to consider the strength and stamina contained in that petite body. For the first time in his life, he suddenly found himself reluctant to go into battle, and that realization unnerved him.

"Come here," he said as he reached out and caught Genny's hand in his.

Genny made no attempt to retrieve her hand. She felt the blood surge from her rapidly beating heart to her fingertips where he touched them. She watched him remove a small cloth sack from the basket and place it in her hand. She looked up at him questioningly.

'' 'Tis a gift for you,'' he explained.

Opening the small sack, Genny was delighted as the smell of lavender coiled through the air.

''I sent to Montburough for the herbs and flowers. Your Maggie was most gracious in her assistance. She sent explicit instructions for the preparation, insisting you would bathe in nothing else.''

Tears clouded Genny's eyes as she gazed at her husband. This simple gift meant more to her than any she had ever received. ''Thank you,'' she whispered.

In one swift motion he pulled her close to him. He lifted her chin, and his lips slowly descended to meet hers. Genny returned his kiss with reckless abandon, but abruptly he drew away and buried his face in her hair.

''Genny, I beg you, do not shame me while I am gone.'' Although his words were whispered, there was a fierceness to his plea. He crushed her more tightly to him as his lips reclaimed hers once more, this time brutal, demanding, committing an act of raw possession.

Though she wanted to protest that she was ever and always his, wanted to argue away his lingering doubts, she recognized that beneath his closed, almost ferocious expression lay an aching vulnerability he could not or would not admit to. He needed to know her body and soul belonged solely to him. And though his means might be primitive, his kisses punishing, Genny felt a tiny hope burgeon in her heart.

She willingly helped him strip away her garments, feeling the warm breeze brush her naked skin as he rid himself of his own clothing before lowering himself atop her.

His lips moved down her neck, and she surrendered herself fully to him, upthrusting her breasts and parting her thighs at the pressure of his. He fondled one small globe, teethed its pink nipple, rousing her impossibly quickly, impossibly deeply.

Genny struggled for breath as his hands moved over her everywhere. Her body writhed as he sought the moist folds of her womanhood, expertly kneading the hidden bud that instantly swelled to the touch of his fingers. She moaned aloud as hungry desire surged through her. Now as frantic as he, she ran her hands over his massive shoulders, raked her nails down the length of his spine. Her frenzied touch caused him to lose whatever control he might still have possessed, and as he slid up her body, his hardness thrust impatiently against her belly.

"Genny, Genny," he murmured breathlessly, "be you innocent or cunning, I know not. I know only that I desire you as I have desired no other woman." And entered her in one swift thrust.

As he moved within her, Genny cried out, meeting each stroke with a force all her own. Passion spiraled them higher and higher, till they soared to an awesome, shuddering ecstasy together.

As Tristen began to roll off her, she pulled him back, not willing to release him yet. She lovingly smoothed back a damp lock of hair from his temple, letting her fingers glide over his sweat-slick skin.

"I shall pray daily for your swift return," she said quietly.

Tristen edged gently off her, gathering her next to him, silently stroking her shoulders and hair until he lulled her into sleep, trustingly curled against him, his gift clutched tightly in her hand.

Chapter 30

Genny awoke to find herself alone in bed. Tristen had once again left without saying good-bye. They had, however, loved and pleasured each other well into the early-morning hours, until exhaustion overtook them, and no doubt he had been loath to wake her. Feeling well satisfied yet wistful, Genny dressed and went down to the hall, her appetite healthy after the long, passionate night with her husband.

Elizabeth fairly leaped to greet her when she entered the hall. "Genny, I have been so eager to talk with you," she said, aglow with excitement as Genny seated herself at the table.

"You are looking especially cheerful today, Elizabeth," Genny remarked fondly.

" 'Twas a wonderful night," said Elizabeth, blushing. After having been separated for months due to her pregnancy and the birth of their babe, she and Christopher had enjoyed a wondrous night of rediscovery.

"And you wished to speak with me?" asked Genny.

"Genny, I would like you to teach me how to handle arms."

Genny nearly choked on her cider. "What?"

"I would like to learn to be able to defend myself. I so admire your courage and skills."

"Christopher would not thank me for teaching you skills the Sinclair men find unsuitable for a lady," said Genny, reflecting on her own husband's displeasure at her proficiency with weapons.

"Genny, I assure you, Christopher would have no objection to my learning how to defend myself. Does he not admire your abilities?" Elizabeth questioned.

"Perhaps, but admiring my abilities does not necessarily mean that he condones the activity for a woman—or that he would wish his wife to pursue it," Genny asserted reasonably.

"He joins you in your practice. How could he object to your tutelage of me?" Elizabeth argued with conviction. "But if you will not instruct me, I suppose I shall have to teach myself," she said with an enormous sigh, as if her friend would truly allow her to risk potential harm to herself. "Do you think I should begin with the sword? Or would the longbow be a better choice?"

"Enough," cried Genny through her laughter at the obvious manipulative tactic. "I concede. But in the interest of safety, yours and mine, we will start with a simple lesson. When the men have finished at the practice fields, we shall begin."

"Oh, thank you, Genny! You will not regret this," Elizabeth pledged excitedly.

"I hope you are right, Elizabeth," Genny said with a smile. "I can only abide the ire of one Sinclair man at a time."

At midday Genny, knowing that the men would have completed their exercises, arrived at the practice fields as planned, only to discover that Elizabeth was already there. She was stumbling around in the middle of the field battling some unseen foe, brandishing a large sword that appeared to have more control of her than she of it.

"Elizabeth."

At the sound of Genny's voice, Elizabeth abruptly spun around. Due to the weight of the heavy sword, she could not control its arcing descent, and it embedded its sharp point in the ground.

"Perhaps you should learn to walk before you attempt to run," Genny suggested, grinning as she pulled the unwieldy weapon free. "Where did you get this sword?"

"'Tis Christopher's," Elizabeth informed her. "He is very proud of it. It was a gift from his father."

"Sweet Jesu," muttered Genny.

"Don't worry, he never uses it. It serves only as decoration. Most of the time it simply hangs above the mantel in our chambers," declared Elizabeth guilelessly.

"Still, perhaps we should start with something a bit . . . smaller," Genny suggested.

Over the following days Genny attempted to teach Elizabeth how to throw a dagger, and she often wondered if anyone noticed the numerous gouges appearing well outside the intended boundaries marked on the targets. Nonetheless, she developed a new admiration for Elizabeth, noting that her lack of natural ability was more than compensated for by her perseverance.

By the beginning of the second week Elizabeth was despairing that she would ever acquire any accuracy with the small weapon.

"You will if you but keep your eyes open when you throw the dagger," Genny admonished.

"But then I would see how deplorably inaccurate I am," Elizabeth wailed.

"Elizabeth," Genny pointed out wryly, "it may just improve your accuracy to see where you are throwing."

"Do you really think anything will help?" asked Elizabeth.

"Indeed. Now try again, only keep your eyes on the target this time," Genny directed.

Elizabeth stepped up to the line they had drawn in the dirt. Focusing on her intended mark, she hurled the dagger exactly as Genny had taught her, this time keeping her gaze firmly affixed to the target.

The small blade embedded itself just inside the outermost boundary. Elizabeth could not have been more excited had it landed dead center.

"I did it!" she shouted in triumph, jumping up and down.

"Aye, you did," injected Christopher, who had for some time been silently observing the two women. "However, the men-at-arms need not worry just yet."

"Oh, Christopher, do not spoil my victory. I have worked hard to conquer this piece of wood," she said, gesturing toward the target.

Christopher stepped up to it and ran his fingers over the dozens of gouges the wood had recently accumulated. "I can see it has been a hard-fought battle."

"Are you proud of me?" asked Elizabeth spiritedly.

"Aye," replied Christopher. "I am always proud of you," he added as he kissed the tip of her nose. "But I would recommend a bit more practice, darling. So if you will excuse me, I shall leave you and your instructor"—he nodded at Genny—"to your lessons," he said before he quitted the field.

Genny was surprised by Christopher's ready acceptance of Elizabeth's pursuit of weaponry. How unlike his older brother, who had angrily denounced his wife's participation in the same activities. Indeed, in the weeks following Christopher's discovery of them, Elizabeth progressed rapidly in her apprenticeship, as if newly inspired by her spouse's love.

Genny kept herself busy during Tristen's absence not only with instruction to Elizabeth but also by tending to the newly birthed foals at the stables. Nonetheless, as the weeks wore on, though she could not fault her husband's obligation to the crown, she grew impatient for his return to Ravenswood and her.

Genny looked out wistfully at the beautiful summer morning, raising her face to the warm sunshine. After Mary helped her dress, she dismissed her and sent a message to one of the guards that she would be visiting the village today. Tristen had left strict orders that she was not to leave the castle without an escort. Indeed, he preferred she did not leave at all. However, even he evidently realized the futility of that wish.

An hour later she was galloping away from the castle and toward the village, flanked on either side by one of Tristen's most trusted guards, both of whom were among those he had left behind to protect Ravenswood. The wind blowing on her face and the strong, rippling muscles of the horse beneath her renewed her vigor, and so engrossed in pleasant thoughts was she that she neither saw nor heard the other riders till the guards beside her were engaged in fighting. She saw in horror that her guards were badly outnumbered, and, unsheathing her dagger from beneath her skirt, she, too, began to fight. But in only moments the guards lay lifeless and bloody upon the ground, and two men were restraining her, taking away her dagger.

Anger and fear warred within her as she continued to struggle. Then she heard a barked command issued in a familiar voice coming from behind her. ''Bring her here!''

Snatched from Apollo's back, Genny was led
to stand beside the man's horse. Not wanting
him to sense her fear, she looked boldly up at
the man. "What is the meaning of this outrage?" she demanded, hoping her voice
evinced strength and conviction. "What do you
want with me, Thomas?"

"You, Lady Genevieve, are going to give me
what I have long waited patiently for." He
gazed down smugly from his lofty perch and
pronounced with evident self-satisfaction, "You
will give me the Earl of Ravenswood."

"What!" she exclaimed in perplexity and dismay. "What nonsense do you speak of? What
purpose will this abduction serve?"

He did not deign to reply to her queries.
"Take her," he commanded one of his men.
"It's your life if she escapes."

With Apollo tethered behind them, Genny
was forced to ride in front of one of the men
on his horse, her hands kept bound behind
her. They traveled at a punishing pace for two
days, stopping only to eat, sleep, and take care
of personal needs. Even then she was not allowed any privacy. At night her arms remained
bound, her upper body securely lashed by another rope around the trunk of a tree to prevent
her escape.

Genny had worn herself out demanding explanations, only to recognize that Thomas had
no intention of explaining his actions until they
had arrived at their destination. By the third day
she was exhausted and dirty, feeling light-
headed as she continued to ride in front of one

of the men on his horse. Her head bobbed lightly as she nodded in and out of sleep. Finally she opened her eyes, blinking to clear her vision when she espied Aldred Keep. Her heart beat loudly in her ears while they drew closer. Her mind reeled in confusion. Of all places for Thomas to take her, why would he choose Aldred Keep? What had happened to Aunt Beatrice and Philip?

"Take her to the tower room," Genny heard Thomas command, and she was half pushed, half dragged up the long winding staircase.

Dazed with weariness, confusion, and desperation, Genny did little more than glance bleakly around the small room before laying her tired, dirty body down upon the hard mattress. But her last thoughts before sleep claimed her were not of her plight, but of her husband. She prayed, as she had every night since his departure for Wales, for his safety, adding to her petitions only that she, too, might remain alive long enough to greet him upon his return.

Tristen sat staring into the campfire while the men, having finished their meal, were tending to the horses. The lone rabbit remaining on the spit was his, and he sat leisurely relishing the meal.

The campaign had been more than successful, and King Edward now had control over the Welsh. Reflecting upon the adventure's duration, Tristen was glad to see it coming to an end. He did not mind admitting that he was

eager to return to Ravenswood and Genny. He
missed her laughter, her warm, receptive body,
and even her heated quarrels with him.

Had anyone told him just scant months ago
that he would have such an attachment to any
woman, he would have vehemently refuted the
possibility. Yet Genny had never been far from
his thoughts.

However, Kathryn's treachery also seemed
ever on his mind the longer he was away from
Genny. Would he return to find this wife, too,
had played him false? He knew now that Genny
had been an innocent before he first took her,
but he was painfully aware that virginity
brought to a marriage bed did not assure fidel-
ity throughout that marriage. Kathryn, too, had
been innocent when they'd married, but in his
absence she'd wasted little time in procuring
substitutes to feed her carnal desires.

He could not bear the thought of any other
man touching Genny, being the recipient of the
passions he had aroused in her. He reflected
that never before had he had a woman whose
sensual enthusiasm so equaled his own. Although Genny had been tentative at first, it had
taken little time before she began eagerly initi-
ating their lovemaking. She was a woman of
unusual intensity in all things, and while that
was pleasing when it suited his own physical
hungers, her penchant for impulsive behavior
made him worry at what she might do in his
absence.

The fire crackled and smoked under the drip-
pings from the spit, and Tristen leaned forward

to adjust the skewer over the flame. As he did so, he heard a sudden commotion behind him.

The first moments of the attack were filled with blinding confusion and deafening noise, but Tristen focused on rallying his men to gain the upper hand. The advantage of the men mounted to those in the camp was great, and the attack had come as a surprise, but the aggressors were not prepared for the fierceness or expertise of Tristen's battle-seasoned warriors.

The clanging of swords and the screams of wounded men filled the air, and the vagabond horde began dispersing when it became evident that their shabby weaponry and meager skills were no match for those of the superior warriors they confronted.

With a swift glance Tristen made sure his men had matters well under control. Then, mounting Demon, he took off in pursuit of one of the men who, from his shouted commands, appeared to be the leader of the brigands.

When the man turned his horse sharply and headed into the woods, Tristen swiftly urged Demon into a gallop. As the chase continued into the dense woods, Tristen was forced to slow Demon's pace. He feared he had lost the man until he heard the hooves of the other horse not far in front of him. Spurring Demon on, he broke into a small clearing, where he spotted his armor-clad assailant sitting erect in his saddle, poised as though he had been awaiting Tristen's arrival.

Then everything happened at once. Tristen found himself surrounded by other riders, arrows whizzing at him from all directions. Greatly outnumbered, and with only his sword to defend himself, Tristen attempted to cut a path out of the snare into which he had been lured. Hacking mercilessly with the expertise his years of battle had honed, he felled several of his assailants and nearly broke through their undisciplined ranks. Then he felt the sharp blade of a sword pierce his side.

As he fell to the ground, he cursed his carelessness at having been led into what he now knew had been a well-laid trap. He struggled to his knees, blood covering the hand and forearm pressed tightly to his wound. Lifting his head, he stared up at the face of his assailant, who was slowly removing his helmet.

"Thomas," he spat, attempting to stand.

"An interesting exercise in humility, wouldn't you say, *milord?*" sneered Thomas. "Yours," he added. Menacing laughter rent the air while darkness and pain overtook Tristen.

Chapter 31

G enny restlessly paced the confines of the small tower room she had occupied for days. The only person with whom she had contact was one of Thomas's disreputable brutes. Twice a day he brought food to her and removed the chamber pot, much to Genny's embarrassment, returning it emptied and gathering the remains of her barely touched meals.

She was engulfed in weariness and despair. Her tired nerves throbbed with apprehension. Sighing wearily, she lay down on the hard pallet, her exhausted body succumbing to fitful sleep.

Sometime later she awoke to someone shaking her shoulder. As she blinked rapidly to clear her vision, her eyes came to rest on the face of her cousin.

"Philip! Oh, Philip! I am so glad you have come for me. We must get word to Lord Tristen that . . ."

Her speech trailed off when she noticed Philip's bland expression. He made no move to comfort or warn her, and she felt the room begin to spin at the confusing implications. Were Philip and Thomas somehow in collusion? How could that be? Taking a deep, steadying breath, she slowly sat upright on the bed.

"Philip?" she questioned in disbelief, "are you . . . are you somehow involved in this?" When he offered no argument, she whispered, "Why, Philip? Why have you done this?"

"For you, Genny," he said with sincerity.

After his mother had informed him of the abusive treatment Kathryn had undergone at the hands of Tristen Sinclair, he had immediately understood why they must take action. Although initially he had opposed the idea of taking Genny against her will, his mother had eventually persuaded him that Genny's safety could only be guaranteed through removing her from the earl's domain.

"For me! You and Thomas kill my guards and capture me, and you claim it was for me? Pray, forgive me, Philip, if I do not understand," she said bitterly.

"Genny, I am sorry that your guards were killed, but Thomas only did what was necessary."

"Killing two of my husband's men was not necessary. None of this was necessary!" said Genny adamantly.

"But it was, Genny. When I learned of Lord Tristen's attempts to kill you, I could not allow you to spend another day at Ravenswood."

"Kill me? My husband would never harm me! Who told you this lie?"

"Thomas came here most distressed by your husband's ill treatment of you."

"The man lies, Philip. It was *he* who tried to harm me."

"And who told you this? Your husband, perhaps? Genny, I know that you have been through much these past few days. We will have plenty of time to discuss this later. For the time being, I will have water and some fresh clothes brought to you."

"I do not want to waste time bathing, Philip. I want to go home!" Genny insisted, her green eyes flaming in anger.

"Genny, please believe me, your welfare is my only concern. I won't allow anyone to harm you." With that declaration, he left the room.

Genny heard the resounding thud as the door was barred from the outside. Soon thereafter, as promised, two guards arrived with bathwater and clean clothing. Deciding that stubbornness would serve no immediate purpose, Genny availed herself of the water to bathe. Once she had dressed in the clean clothes, she reluctantly admitted to herself that she felt somewhat physically restored. However, her spirits remained low as the weak sunlight of early evening filtered through the lone high window into the dismal room.

The grating sound of the bar sliding back from the door alerted her to yet another visitor. The surly guard and a companion entered, carrying a small table between them. They had scarcely set the table down when other men arrived, their arms laden with food and drink.

Genny watched her scruffy wardens, wondering why they were laying out this expansive meal but not wishing to engage any of them in conversation.

"Lady Genny," said Thomas, who now entered the room and dismissed the men.

Genny stiffened at the sight of him.

"You look lovely," he said, seizing her hand and placing a kiss on the back of it.

His touch sent a shiver through Genny's body.

"Come join me," he said, gesturing at the table.

"I am not hungry, Thomas," she declared, snatching her hand from his grasp.

"I find that hard to believe. You have barely eaten for days."

"Captivity tends to rob me of my appetite," she replied caustically as she glared at him.

"I suppose this useless anger is to be expected." He sighed and held out a chair for her. "Do sit, milady. We have much to discuss."

"I do not wish to sit."

"Wine?" Thomas asked, ignoring her reply. Filling a goblet, he pushed it across the table toward her. "I dare say I could use some."

"The only thing *I* could use is an explanation," replied Genny, leaving the goblet untouched. "Beginning with the reason you have repeatedly tried to harm me."

"I had hoped you would wait till we had shared an amicable meal."

"My husband will see that you pay for this, Thomas. He will come for me."

"That is exactly what I plan on. And rest assured, milady, I will be ready for his arrival." Genny watched in silence as he poured himself another drink. "However, we have some time before we need be concerned. The earl has met with a, shall we say, mishap." Thomas sneered at the audible gasp that escaped Genny's lips.

"What do you mean? What has happened to him?" she asked in a choked voice.

"Your dear husband has taken a very nasty sword cut. Suffice it to say that we have some time together before he will arrive."

"Dear God, no!" Genny moaned in anguished disbelief.

"Aye. But I promise you will see him one more time. Right before he dies."

"You bastard! You fool! You will never defeat the Earl of Ravenswood!"

Genny saw the muscle in his jaw tense. Barely holding his temper in check, Thomas grabbed her shoulders tightly. His next words were as cold as ice.

"I shall. And then, when you have served my purpose, I will do with you whatever I please," he said, running his cold fingers over her soft throat.

"Never," she vowed emphatically. "Philip will never allow you to harm me."

"Philip?" Thomas laughed. "Your precious Philip listens only to his mother. And dear Beatrice listens to me."

Genny's heart sank. If Aunt Beatrice had aligned herself with Thomas, it was true that

Philip would be of no help. He would never cross his mother.

"What have I done to provoke this, Thomas?" she asked, her voice barely above a whisper. She gazed into the depths of Thomas's insolent brown eyes, attempting to comprehend his deranged scheme.

"My reasons are my own. I will reveal them in due time," he answered, reaching up and clamping her chin between his thumb and forefinger.

Repulsed by his touch, Genny attempted to jerk her head free of his hold.

Bringing his face close to hers, Thomas continued softly. "You still don't understand, do you?" he asked mockingly as he ran a finger along her jaw. "I alone control your fate. You would do well to remember that, *Countess*."

Summoning the guard, he left her to contemplate his words.

Tristen looked to be on the threshold of death. Alexander had hastened him to Ravenswood and carried him into his chamber, but his fever was raging and he remained incoherent.

It had taken the men more than a day after the attack to reach Ravenswood. When they had first been set upon, they had not had time to reason on the assault, only to defend themselves. However, it had soon become apparent to Alexander that the target was Tristen himself. Before he could stop his friend, Tristen had headed off in pursuit of the fleeing attackers. By the time Alexander and the men had tracked him to a clearing, he was gravely wounded, lying motionless in a pool of his own blood. Alexander regretted that none of the wounded villains had lived to disclose the purpose of their assault. He had brought back six of their own men dead, and now he watched helplessly as his dearest friend lay fighting for life.

Lady Eleanor and Matilda had tended to Tristen's wound as best they could while fretfully awaiting Thisbe's arrival. Lady Eleanor now raised her eyes as Elizabeth ushered in the old woman.

Thisbe's white, wiry hair sprang wildly around her deeply wrinkled face, but a deep warmth emanated from her eyes as they lingered on Tristen, who lay thrashing feverishly on the bed. She bent to examine the gaping wound in his side. It was oozing with infection.

"The flesh needs to be seared and the wound packed," she pronounced. "One of you men bring me a poker, and then I will need you to hold him down," she commanded in her crackling voice. "I am an old woman. He be too strong for the likes of me."

Alexander gently ushered a tearful Lady Eleanor and Elizabeth from the room as Christopher heated the poker in the fire.

Thisbe then took the red-hot poker, instructing Alexander to lean across the lower half of Tristen's body, Christopher to hold down his brother's shoulders.

As Thisbe touched the hot poker to the edge of the gaping wound, Tristen's piercing scream echoed throughout the castle as the smell of burning flesh permeated the room. Though the earl did not truly awaken, Alexander and Christopher had to fight to control his thrashing limbs.

Finally Thisbe finished treating and bandaging the wound.

"Will he live?" Christopher asked the old woman as she began gathering her herbs and medicines.

"He be strong. It will take time, but he will heal." She glanced first at Christopher, and then at Alexander. "He needs to be strong to bring back his lady."

Alexander's eyes narrowed. "What know you of Lady Genny's disappearance?" he asked with suspicion.

"I know that she lives," she replied.

"How know you this, old woman?" demanded Christopher. "Reveal your source!"

"I would have felt it here," she replied, placing a gnarled hand to her chest. "And so would he," she added, shifting her gaze to Tristen.

Without another word, Thisbe finished gathering her things and left.

Chapter 32

$\backsim \mathcal{OO} \frown$

Genny walked to the window of the chamber and pulled back the tapestries, allowing the afternoon sun to filter into the room. Some days ago Philip had had her moved to a chamber adjacent to his own. Although the conditions were better, she was still a prisoner, trapped behind a locked door with one of Thomas's guards standing outside. Philip visited daily but refused to give any credence to Genny's accusations of Thomas. Of her aunt Beatrice, Genny had seen nothing.

At the sound of riders Genny's heart beat faster, as it did every time someone approached. Each time she let herself believe it was Tristen come to rescue her, but each time she was disappointed. Thomas had told her that Tristen knew not yet where she was, but she had steadfastly refused to believe it. Now, however, as the days wore on and summer ushered in intolerably hot weather, she was forced to admit that her hopes of rescue were ill-founded.

Over the weeks of her captivity Thomas had become increasingly abusive. During his fre-

quent visits he would stroke her hair or fondle
her cheek while he spoke soft, cruel words de-
scribing the torture Tristen would endure before his death. Genny knew he took pleasure
in taunting her in this manner and she attempted to deprive him of satisfaction by sub-
duing her revulsion at his touch. But yesterday,
as if wisening to her game, he had gone further, boldly clasping her to his chest and fon-
dling her breasts. Genny had become so
nauseated that after he'd left she ran to the
chamber pot and emptied her stomach. And
now she feared that he might go further still to
intimidate her with his perverse form of amusement.

With concern she placed her hand to her ever
so slightly rounded stomach. She now knew
what she had only suspected before Thomas
had carried her away. She was with child. She
breathed deeply, aware that all too soon her
condition would no longer be her secret, and
the thought dismayed her. She must find a way
to escape before that time came.

"Ah, Genny, you are a vision of loveliness
standing there in the sunlight."

Genny turned to look at Philip, who had just
entered the chamber. She stared at him coldly,
offering no smile, no thanks for his praise. Hatred and disgust were all that emanated from
her wary green eyes. Remaining silent, she
pointedly pulled the tapestry closed against the
hot sun.

"Genny, must you always be so cold to me?"
Philip asked as he laid a hand on her shoulder.

Genny moved away from his reach. "You have not the right to touch me," she replied through tightly clenched teeth, eyeing him with utter and complete contempt.

"Ah, yes, often these many weeks you have reminded me of your husband. But I would not worry, Genny. Thomas assures me he will not be a problem to us much longer."

"What are you saying?" she asked anxiously. "Answer me, Philip! What do you plan to do?"

"Whatever is done to your husband will be only what he deserves, my dear."

"By whose precepts, Philip? Yours? Thomas's?" she demanded in a shrill voice. "What right have you to judge my husband? What has he done to you, Philip?"

"He took you away from me and any chance I had of obtaining Montburough," he said in anger. "But more than that, he harmed you and Kathryn. For that," he added bitterly, clenching his fists, "he will forfeit his life."

"Philip, you cannot! I beg you, do not harm him," she pleaded.

"It is the only way, my dear. I cannot allow you to stay with the beast. He will only hurt you as he did Kathryn."

"He did not harm Kathryn," she declared with quiet but desperate firmness, trying, as she had repeatedly over the past weeks, to convince him of the truth of his sister's situation. Now, as then, he simply glowered at what he considered the vile lies she had heard from the untrustworthy Sinclairs. "I love him, Philip," she attempted desperately when her cousin remained unmoved.

"And I love you," he said, moving closer to her. "All that I do is because of my love for you."

"Love! You do not know the meaning of the word. If you did, you could not do this evil," Genny cried.

Philip paced in agitation. Stopping in front of her, he raised her chin with his hand until her eyes met his. "You will grow to love me," he declared. Releasing her, he turned to leave but stopped at the doorway. "Genny, there will come a time when you will thank me." With those words, he took his leave.

Genny stood deathly still. Her first reaction was to weep, but tears would offer neither comfort nor help. Fighting the nausea that threatened to overtake her, she breathed deeply, trying to think. She had to free herself somehow, and she had to save her husband.

Lord Tristen Sinclair led the way, his banner unfurling softly in the wind. He was followed by Alexander and all but the smattering of knights and men-at-arms left behind to guard Ravenswood.

Tristen had wavered for several days between life and death, calling out for Genny in his fevered state. When he had finally regained his senses, Alexander gravely informed him of Lady Genny's abduction. Knowing that Tristen would not remain abed long enough to fully recover from his injury, Christopher had left posthaste for London to apprise the king of the situation and prepare him for Tristen's petition to wage a private campaign against Thomas. The well-intentioned strategy had won them only a few precious days before Tristen, weak and still fighting infection, demanded they ride for London.

Alexander reined in beside Tristen as they crested a hill overlooking London. "We should rest, my friend," he urged, observing that Tristen's face was pale and pinched.

"I do not wish to take the time," Tristen murmured.

"Aye, but you can scarce afford to provoke Edward's wrath by storming the throne in a lather. My friend," he pointed out, "Edward arranged your marriage. I am sure he will give you leave to use force, if necessary, to find Genny. Do not fret so."

When Tristen spoke, his voice was low and laced with emotion. "God help me, Alexander . . . I love her."

"At long last." Alexander smiled. "I thought never to hear you say the words."

"Truly, I had never supposed I would say them. Now it is my desire to be able to say those words to my wife."

Tristen had admitted to the feelings in his heart when he awakened days ago to the news that Genny had been abducted. To never again look upon her beautiful face, to never hear the soft caress of her voice, was an agony he had realized he could not endure.

To acknowledge these feelings was an entirely new experience for him, and it was heady. He had not thought to love again, and certainly not with this intensity. The horror that now ate at him was that his awakening might have come too late. He would move heaven and earth in order to bring Genny back to his side. And, regardless of the power she would then wield over him, he swore a sacred oath to tell her of his devotion to her and to never be the cause of another unhappy moment in her life. But had his stubbornness in the face of their marriage cost them both their happiness forever? he goaded himself.

Now, however, was not the time to indulge in remorse. Now was the time to steel himself for the matter at hand—to approach Edward with the situation and request authorization for his convoy to pursue Genny's captors. He was not accustomed to requesting anything from anyone, and it rankled to thus delay. But he knew what was needed, and he must not let pride stand in his way. His recent endeavor on the king's behalf and his long years of loyal service to the crown would surely entitle him to a bit of leeway when it came to a personal pursuit—and he would not hesitate to remind Edward of his acts if the situation warranted it. If need be, he was prepared to make monetary concessions to the crown, if that would sway the royal decision.

The familiar stench of London wafted up to greet them, assaulting their senses as they approached Westminster Palace. Tristen had chosen a route that would allow them to avoid the market district and thus hasten their arrival. If all went well, the king would see him and hear his appeal without delay.

Upon entering the gates of the palace, Tristen obtained shelter and provisions for his men and animals. With that responsibility discharged, he went in search of Christopher, finding him in the inner ward.

"Ah, my brother, you look weary from your journey," said Christopher in greeting, noting Tristen's haggard appearance.

"I am well. What news have you for me?" Tristen asked impatiently, brushing aside his brother's concern for his health.

"You have an audience with Edward in three days," Christopher reported.

"Three days! I cannot wait that long. I must see him now!" Tristen shouted.

"But it is arranged, Tristen. Edward is holding court for the southern region now. It will be weeks yet before he has finished with the scheduled audiences. It is due only to your good standing that you will be allowed to see him so quickly."

Christopher was visibly agitated. He understood his brother's anxiety over the wait, but was also well acquainted with the king's disposition. It would be foolhardy for Tristen to defy Edward's ruling that no one might seek personal vengeance without royal sanction.

"Tristen, it is the best we dare to hope for. Come, let me accompany you to your quarters."

Aware of Tristen's fragile temperament at this

time, Christopher chose to wait till his brother was rested and in a better frame of mind before disclosing the information that his inquiries had uncovered.

Chapter 33

Tristen sat soaking in a tub of hot water, feeling achy and exhausted, willing the heat to soothe away the soreness in his side. His thoughts wandered back to the last time he had been here at the castle—when his marriage had been decreed. What changes that decree had wrought in his life. He had lost his freedom, lost his equilibrium, lost the iron clad control that had seen him through so many battles. Indeed, he had nearly lost his mind. What had he gained?

Genny. She had turned his life upside down, leaving him raw and vulnerable. He smiled, remembering the last time he had seen her, lying asleep in his bed with nothing but her golden tresses about her small, exquisite form. That morning he had ached to make love to her one last time before leaving, but he had known it would be a mistake. Once in her arms, he would have found it impossible to leave.

It had not occurred to him then that he had already fallen in love with his wife. The realization had come slowly, and now that he had

faced that truth, he had also to face the fact that
it might be too late. He might never see her
again, never hold her, never be able to tell her
of his love.

Despair washed over him, causing his head
to droop, his body to bow down at the ache in
his heart that felt like a death blow.

How could he have denied Genny and himself a chance for happiness because of his experience with Kathryn? That he had wasted a
moment of the precious time he had with
Genny, punishing her for the actions of another
woman, was reprehensible. Even the anger he
had nurtured over the years for Kathryn's betrayal of their love paled in comparison to his
feelings for Genny. He now realized that what
he had felt for Kathryn had been a shallow, carnal attraction. Many men had desired her, and
Tristen, in his youthful arrogance, had taken
pride in his ability to acquire one so sought after.

When Kathryn died he had isolated himself
in his rage, but his anger was out of hatred and
contempt, not love or sorrow at losing her. She
had played him the fool, and he had fallen. He
had sworn in his haughty, prideful outrage
never to love a woman again, never to allow
himself to be that vulnerable again.

Now he was cognizant that he had done
Genny a great injustice to have compared her
in any way with Kathryn. What he felt for
Genny was far deeper than mere physical attraction. It was a feeling so intense, he knew

that losing her now would be like ripping his heart from his chest to leave only emptiness.

Stepping from the bathing tub, he dressed hurriedly to meet Christopher and Alexander in the hall to sup, suddenly anxious to know if Christopher, while waiting in London, had learned anything new that might help in the campaign to reclaim Genny.

The banquet was lavish, the lords and ladies dressed elaborately for the evening's meal and festivities, but all this was lost on the men seated at the table with Tristen.

"It may be that I have uncovered information that will shed some light on Thomas's motives," Christopher was saying.

"Well, go on! What are you waiting for?" Tristen demanded urgently.

"I discovered that Thomas used to be in attendance here at court as a young squire in service to His Majesty."

"I was aware of this. The crown has given me many squires over the years in reward for my loyalty," Tristen snapped, impatient for more useful news.

"Well, this particular squire sought to associate with the nobility, and it is rumored that he spent much time in the company of Kathryn Aldred."

At the mention of Kathryn's name, Tristen's face twisted with anger. How many times must she be brought back to life to torment him?

"After your marriage to Kathryn, he campaigned diligently to be sent to Ravenswood." Leaning closer to Tristen, Christopher lowered his voice. "It is rumored that they were lovers."

Tristen blanched as his meal began to rise in his stomach.

"What has any of this to do with Lady Genny?" asked Alexander pointedly.

"That I cannot know," Christopher answered honestly.

"It matters not why he does what he does," Tristen stated, an ominous note in his voice. "I will kill him for what he has done to Genny."

"Do not be foolish, my friend," Alexander interjected.

"I was foolish to have come here. We've wasted enough time. I am going to find my wife," he declared in restless anger, rising to his feet.

Alexander placed a restraining hand upon Tristen's forearm. "If you think to circumvent Edward's directive, you will be severely punished, and well you know it."

Tristen looked down into Alexander's eyes. "Then so be it."

Robert Burnell entered the king's private chambers, clearing his throat nervously. "He is here, sire."

"Have him brought in," King Edward commanded curtly, seating himself.

"You sent for me, sire?" asked Tristen sarcastically, eyeing the armed guards at his sides.

"You may leave us," Edward commanded the guards. When the door had closed behind them, he turned back to Tristen. "I have received some distressing news concerning you. I had thought perhaps you might put my mind to rest," Edward said.

"Sire," Tristen began in a determined voice, "I can only speak the truth to you. I came seeking an audience with you concerning my wife. Lady Genny has been abducted. I was informed that it would be days before I could speak with you on the matter."

Edward raised a hand to silence him. "I have been apprised of the situation concerning your wife, and I am most distressed by the turn of events."

"Then I am sure, sire, you are aware that I must leave at once, for I have lost much time already."

"It appears to me that you take much upon yourself, Sinclair!" the king reprimanded. "How dare you attempt to gainsay me in my own court?" he bellowed. "Did you think to leave as a traitor to this crown, following your own edicts?"

"Nay, sire. I am a loyal subject to you, as was my father before me," Tristen replied.

"It bodes well for you that I am aware of that," Edward said, his voice somewhat softening. "It is not often wise for a man of battle to let his heart rule his mind. And yet I have been informed that you have taken your wife to heart. Is this true?" he asked, his eyes fixed intently on his unruly subject.

Tristen stood rigid and still. "Aye, sire, it is true."

The silence became deafening as Edward rose to stand.

"Good," he finally proclaimed, much to Tristen's amazement. "I had heard rumors that your love was hard won. The queen will be most pleased."

"I was not at first as loving a husband as I should have been," Tristen replied, guiltily lowering his head. "She deserves better."

"What is hard won is more dearly cherished," Edward replied. "However, we have first to find your wife and bring her home."

"You mean to grant my petition?" Tristen questioned in surprise.

"Aye. I have not a deaf ear to your pleas. I merely sought to give myself more time."

"I do not understand."

"Do you think I know not what goes on within these walls? I know who took your wife. What I do not know is where he has delivered her, for most assuredly even Thomas is too intelligent to kill her. Indeed, I would venture it is really your life Thomas wants."

"I must find him and make him take me to Genny!" Tristen replied, clenching his fists at his sides.

"Oh, I quite agree. That is why your men are readied." Edward laughed at the surprised look on Tristen's face. "I was prepared to grant favor upon your pursuit on the morrow. However, Tristen, your impetuous behavior has hastened my approval."

Tristen smiled fleetingly, thinking how amused Genny would be to find *him*, not her, smarting under an accusation of impetuousness.

Placing his hands upon Tristen's shoulders, Edward gazed into his eyes. "I, too, am loyal to my subjects. Never doubt that, and never—I repeat, never—try to usurp my authority again. Now be gone with you, and when you have reunited with your lady, I command you to bring her here, where I and my Eleanor may meet this woman who has tamed one of my fiercest warriors."

Chapter 34

All the men felt the tension as they camped for the night. Their recent journeying had been grueling. In Lord Tristen's pursuit of his wife they had traveled long days to London, only to turn around and head now in the direction whence they had come. No one questioned the forced march—not openly, in any event—but the subtle exchanges of eye contact and nods amongst the men let each know what the other was thinking. Lord Tristen was obsessed with finding Lady Genny. Although many had begun to question whether she was still alive, none had voiced doubt, and they truly hoped that their fears were unfounded. Ravenswood would never be the same for any of them without Lady Genny.

The glow from the campfire lit Tristen's haggard features as Christopher observed him in silence. Tristen's posture told more of his mental and physical state than anything he had said since they had made camp for the night. He sat hunched over on a low stool, his hands firmly grasping the tankard of ale he had yet to sample. Angry and in pain, he had silently but effectively isolated himself from unwanted, if well-meant, attention.

He sat reflecting on his predicament. Would that Thomas possessed enough honor to challenge him directly. Tristen would gladly give his own life to protect Genny.

For him even to have imagined a calling greater than duty to those subjects under his stewardship at Ravenswood would have, at one time, been impossible. Now all motives paled beside his devotion to the woman he loved. He knew he would relentlessly pursue his course until he found Genny and punished the man responsible for her abduction.

The calm night was more unsettling than soothing to Tristen as he sat steeped in regret. His many years of fighting—and winning—offered no help in this, his most important pursuit.

All the time with Genny he had wasted, fighting her and doubting her. Never had he known such a love as this, which could send him to heaven one moment and crush the soul out of him the next.

Their lovemaking transcended the physical. Each time they came together was more intense than the last, transporting him beyond the realm of reality. He loved her, he knew that. What he could not say with certainty was exactly when he had fallen in love with her. Perhaps it had happened the first time he had ever laid eyes on her, dancing wildly atop the table in the knights' hall. Or perhaps it was when he had watched her willing life into Sarah's silent babe.

Lord, what if he were never to see her again? At the odious thought, Tristen threw back his head, raising a clenched fist high as he let forth with a fierce and furious roar.

"I imagine that did you good, but the rest of the men might find it hard to sleep tonight after such a start," said Christopher from beside him.

"Why has he taken her, Christopher? And why, when it comes to Genny, can I no longer think clearly?" Tristen groaned in an anguished voice.

"I knew from the first moment I met Genny that she would cause your heart to betray you. Did I tell you of the time your wife felled me to the floor and placed a dagger at my throat?" Christopher laughed at the look of confusion that crossed Tristen's face. "It's true, although I am abashed to admit it, even to you. Your wife's gentle demeanor can be very deceiving."

"How well I know that," replied Tristen, thinking of the night she had pulled a dagger on him in their bed. "That, however, does not explain why Genny threatened your life."

"Suffice it to say that she does not like to be caught unawares. I'm afraid I did not announce my presence soon enough, and before I could say anything, I found myself staring up at her as she straddled my chest with a dagger at my throat."

Picturing his brother in this most compromising position finally brought a light laugh to Tristen's lips.

"I did not find the humor in the situation till I was assured that my throat was to remain intact. Although I will admit your wife is quite a beauty in her bed robe," Christopher added mischievously, laughing openly at Tristen's jealous scowl.

"Relax, Brother. Albeit my Elizabeth is at times too acquiescent, I could not handle a woman with the ardor Genny possesses. I leave that to you." Clasping his brother's shoulder as he raised himself, he added, "We will get her back. I do not intend to watch you languish for the rest of your days without her."

With that Christopher left Tristen to his private demons and the quiet of the night.

Chapter 35

L ady Eleanor sat with Elizabeth in the formal receiving room, realizing she had a very important decision to make. The young stranger who had just arrived from Aldred Keep and told them of Genny's captivity there stood facing them, obviously exhausted from his journey.

"By whose authority have you come to us with this message?" queried Lady Eleanor.

"I came of my own accord, milady."

"Why?"

"She is held prisoner, milady. I could not prevent it, though I could not condone it either. I escaped with my life and came here to inform the earl," the young man asserted.

"The earl will require proof. Have you any?" questioned Lady Eleanor.

"Nay, milady. I know only what I saw with my own eyes."

Although not entirely convinced of the stranger's virtue, Lady Eleanor suspected that there was some validity to his story and decided her only course of action was to have the message delivered to her son.

"We thank you for taking such a risk," Lady Eleanor said and then summoned servants to see to the man's comfort.

Once they were alone, Elizabeth drew herself up and addressed Lady Eleanor. "We need to get word to Tristen and Christopher immediately."

"I agree. There is no time to lose."

"I will have Edmund ready the horses, and I will take only two men. We are shorthanded as it is, and I dare not leave you and the children any less well attended," Elizabeth said with conviction.

"What foolishness is this, Daughter?" Lady Eleanor exclaimed.

In her advanced years Lady Eleanor thought she had seen and heard everything and was well beyond shock, but she had just learned otherwise, and from the last place in the world that she would have expected. This faithful and loyal daughter-in-law, who had always been exceedingly timid and demure, was now suggesting a most daring, and clearly unacceptable, proposal.

"I will not hear of it, Elizabeth!"

"Then what would you propose?" Elizabeth asked, her chin thrust out at a defiant angle. "It is all too obvious that we know not whom we can trust, and this information is too important to trust to anyone else. I will ride tonight," she said, rising. "I hope that one of Genny's riding costumes will fit me," she added with an impish grin.

"My dear, you would do well to remember

that you are not Genny," Lady Eleanor asserted in a final effort to dissuade Elizabeth from
her madness.

"I know who and what I am, Lady Eleanor.
And if there is one thing I have learned from
Genny, it is that one must never back down in
the face of adversity."

The finality in Elizabeth's voice did not afford
an opportunity for retort. As Elizabeth left to
don a riding habit, Lady Eleanor raised a silent
prayer for all her children.

Taking two men with her, Elizabeth set out
to find her husband and Tristen. Christopher
had sent a message just yesterday informing her
of their whereabouts, so she knew in what general direction to travel.

Although her intentions were good, all too
soon she realized how unused she was to riding
for hours. However, sheer determination overrode physical discomfort, and she pressed on
through the night, stopping only to rest the
mounts.

Shock was inadequate to describe the look on
their faces as Christopher and Tristen watched
Elizabeth, flanked on each side by a guard, ride
into their small encampment. Her brown tresses
hung to her waist in snarls, but her skin, even
beneath the dust of the road, was glowing from
a combination of exertion and excitement.

Tristen instantly recognized the outfit she
wore as one of Genny's. Not many women
owned the riding attire his wife did. It was tight
on Elizabeth but molded her figure attractively.

He could see that his brother, too, approved of the picture she presented. He himself had never seen Elizabeth look more alluring.

It was he who regained his composure first. "Elizabeth, what are you doing here?" Tristen demanded.

"I have come with word of Genny!" she exclaimed as she started to dismount.

She was not prepared for the weakness that overtook her as her foot touched the ground; her weary legs gave way.

Christopher instantly rushed to his wife's side and gathered her up in his arms. "You came here yourself?" he asked in alarm as he held her tightly. "Are you a fool? We have already lost one of the Sinclair women. Did you wish to be next?"

"I am not a fool!" Elizabeth replied angrily as she wrenched herself from her husband's possessive hold. She strode over to Tristen. "A messenger came to us yesterday from Aldred Keep. He claimed that Genny is being held there."

"Aldred Keep?" Tristen repeated in surprise.

"Aye."

"I don't understand. Why would Thomas take her there?"

"I don't know," Elizabeth said in frustration and despair. Tears began to stream down her cheeks as all the emotions that had been pent up since Genny's abduction overtook her. "That is all we were told," she finished, helplessly weeping.

Christopher moved to comfort his wife while a silent Tristen walked away.

"Oh, Christopher, I wanted to be strong for you and Tristen. I wanted you to be proud of me. I wanted to help Genny," Elizabeth sobbed into her husband's chest.

"You are strong, love. Never did I think to see you as you look today."

Wiping her eyes with her hands, she gazed up at him.

"Never would I have thought you possessed such courage, such fire."

"Truly?"

"Truly," he replied, lowering his lips to hers.

"Have the men mount. We leave immediately," commanded Tristen, his voice intruding upon the intimate moment.

Elizabeth took hold of Tristen's large, callused hands as she looked into his tormented eyes. "All will be well—I know it. Genny is strong, and you are strong. You will get her back."

Her compassion touched Tristen's heart, and he fought to control the emotions that made his hands tremble and his voice falter. "Thank you, Elizabeth. You risked much to come here."

"How could I not? I love Genny. We all love her, Tristen."

"Aye, we do," he replied as he gathered strength and comfort from his sister-in-law's embrace.

"You will go with the guards to escort your wife home," commanded Tristen, looking at Christopher over Elizabeth's head.

"Nay! I will not go!" she exclaimed, backing away from Tristen's arms.

"It is dangerous. You should not have come even this far," said Tristen.

"But I did come, and I will not leave till Genny is safe," she replied, her voice filled with determination.

"Elizabeth," said Christopher, turning her to face him, "Tristen is right. It is far too dangerous. I will not risk having you hurt."

"You would not say such things if you were talking to Genny. Well, I refuse to be coddled, by you or your overbearing, condescending, pigheaded brother."

Christopher was sure he caught a glint of amusement in Tristen's eyes when he looked over at him.

"Very well," Christopher conceded, "we will trail behind and await word in the woods. However, if you disobey me once, just once, I will send you home," he warned in a stern voice.

"Thank you, milord," Elizabeth replied agreeably, smiling sweetly at her husband in triumph.

"And when we get home, I think I shall have to watch just how much time you spend with your sister-in-law. Your bold attitude of late leaves much to be desired." Turning on his heel, he stalked away, ignoring Tristen's laughter, which pealed through the night.

Chapter 36

Genny lay in her bed contemplating her dilemma, trying to devise a means of escape, something she had done ceaselessly since Thomas had brought her to Aldred Keep. Exhausted from the fruitless efforts, she placed a hand on her slightly rounded abdomen and fell into a fitful sleep.

Late in the night a small noise at her door awakened her. Slowly she turned her head toward the door, sickened with fear that it was Thomas.

"Genny, wake up," came a whisper in a familiar voice.

In the muted flicker of a single candle, she beheld the face of her former nursemaid.

"Maggie!" she exclaimed, and she hugged the woman fiercely.

"Shh!" urged the woman. "You must come with me now, before they know I'm here."

"How did you find me?" Genny asked as she quickly rose and began to dress. "How did you get in?"

"When your husband sent word to us at

Montburough that you had been seized, I immediately suspected Beatrice Aldred might be behind the despicable deed. Your father was not convinced that my suspicions were accurate, but he agreed to send an envoy to Aldred Keep to inquire whether any within these walls had information regarding your whereabouts. I insisted upon accompanying the envoy, and your father reluctantly consented. Our polite inquiries were rebuffed summarily, as I knew they would be, but I returned here alone. I kept myself well hidden, knowing your aunt would not take notice of a lowly servant, until I could find out where they kept you. But we can talk later. We must leave now."

"Maggie, you should not have endangered yourself this way," Genny said with deep concern.

Maggie placed her hands on Genny's cheeks. "I would do anything for you, child," she said, briefly hugging her tightly. "Now hurry!"

Genny nodded her consent. She must think of the life she now carried—Tristen's babe and Montburough's rightful heir.

As they stole quietly out the chamber door, Genny chose not to ask how the guard came to lie still and lifeless on the floor. Silently they made their way down the back stairs through the oldest part of the keep, which they hoped would be deserted.

Thomas raised himself from the bed. He was fast becoming bored with the attentions of Beatrice. Tonight had gone much as the past few weeks had. She lacked not only youthful beauty but also the inventiveness of many of the women with whom he had lain. In the darkness he sneered at her in disgust. Even the castle wenches were preferable. At least they knew how to please a man, or worked hard trying. This one only thought she did. Her daughter had been far more stimulating.

However, Thomas now knew that in sleeping with him, Kathryn had only been availing herself of a willing bed partner, just as he was with Beatrice. At the time, though, he had loved the earl's wife above all else and had thought she felt the same. But when he had declared his devotion, she had made it abundantly clear, with her derisive laughter and cruel remarks, that she had no intention of jeopardizing her status as the Countess of Ravenswood for his pitiable sake. It had haunted him for years that Kathryn had so casually rejected him.

"You're still awake?" asked Beatrice. "I would think you'd be quite tired," she said, running her palms up his chest. "Perhaps I can help you relax."

"Nay," Thomas said, pushing her hands away.

Beatrice pouted. "Do not be vexed with me. Not when everything we have planned for is finally coming to pass. I would imagine by now our 'messenger' has done exactly as we instructed. Surely Lord Tristen will not be able to resist our trap. He will soon be ours."

"Do not underestimate the man," Thomas warned.

"I don't underestimate him. I do, however, know who he is up against," she said, pressing her naked breasts to his chest.

Thomas again pushed her away. He rose from the bed and crossed the chamber to stand before the window. The moonlight streamed into the room as he stood surveying the grounds in silence. Idly scanning the surrounding terrain, he caught a flicker of movement. As he focused his gaze, he observed two women creep silently into the night. He turned and saw that Beatrice was also staring out the window.

"We must stop them! We cannot let that bitch get away," she snarled, then rapidly began to gather up some clothes. "I'll get Philip. You go after them." Beatrice emitted a startled gasp as the clothing was ripped from her hands.

"You won't be telling that pathetic, sniveling excuse for a man you call a son anything!" Thomas taunted as he threw her garments to the floor.

Beatrice looked into his cold, ruthless eyes. She had seen the ugly, unpredictable side of him before, but she was not afraid of this young knave. Obviously he had never dealt with a woman such as she.

"You wanted her for yourself, didn't you?" Her thin lips curled in disgust.

"Perhaps, but not for the reasons you are thinking," Thomas sneered as he dressed. "Your jealousy is really quite insipid. You served your purpose while I was here. You and several others, when I needed to wash the taste of you off me." He laughed as she narrowed her eyes in outrage. He then proceeded to strap on his sword.

Beatrice's mistake was in taking too much time, giving too much thought. As she raised the dagger to his back, he deftly unsheathed his sword while quickly pivoting. The dagger fell to the floor as Beatrice, wide-eyed with astonishment, grabbed at the sharp blade imbedded deep within her abdomen. The edges of the sword sliced into her palms and fingers. Blood flowed freely down her naked legs.

Slowly Thomas withdrew the sword, and her body slumped to the floor. With callous indifference he wiped the blade clean on her bed sheets and did not even glance behind him before departing the chamber.

After saddling his mount himself, Thomas quit Aldred Keep, leaving behind his small band of men, none of whom were yet aware of Beatrice's death or his stealthy departure. Heading in the direction he had seen the two women take, he proceeded to search for them as morning dawned over the woods. Much to his disappointment, he had yet to track down his quarry when he spotted Sinclair's banner headed toward Aldred Keep. Carefully concealed while the company passed, he assured himself that the women were not part of the procession. Then he intensified his efforts to find them.

Tristen led the procession in silence, grim determination on his face. As his men surrounded the keep, he was surprised no alarm rang forth to herald their presence, nor did the draw-bridge rise. Aldred either did not know or did not care that he was under attack. The few guards in the courtyard were easily disarmed, as were the men guarding the hall.

Cautiously, sword drawn, Tristen, followed by Alexander and several of his men-at-arms, made his way up the stairs. Hearing an eerie wailing, they followed the sound to a chamber at the end of the hall, unprepared for the sight that greeted them.

Philip sat on the floor in a pool of blood, cradling his mother's naked, lifeless body in his arms, rocking back and forth as he wailed uncontrollably.

Tristen could almost pity the sight if not for the fact that this pathetic man had played some part in abducting his wife. "Aldred! Where is my wife?" he demanded, while leveling his sword to the hollow of Philip's throat.

"You are too late," Philip moaned. "Genny is gone, and so is Thomas."

"I should kill you now, Aldred," Tristen growled.

Alexander stepped forward, moving Tristen's sword from Philip's throat.

"Now is not the time. There would be no honor."

Nodding terse agreement, Tristen summoned two of his men. "Bury the woman, and lock him up till I have time to deal with him," he commanded, gazing in revulsion as Philip sat stroking his mother's brow.

Leaving behind a few of his men to guard the

keep till his return, Tristen set out with the remainder to find Genny.

Genny paused to rest, settling herself on a large, smooth rock. The late-morning sun was unmercifully hot, and she and Maggie had traveled without stopping since leaving the keep in the wee hours of the morning.

Removing her slippers to rub her sore feet, she almost regretted that Maggie was with her. For if Thomas were to catch them, Maggie would forfeit her life for having helped her former mistress escape.

The soft nicker of a horse startled Genny to her feet.

"Well, well, look what I've found in the woods."

Genny paled as she looked up into Thomas's pock-marked face.

Thomas smiled at her distress. "You do not look at all well, milady," he said calmly as he dismounted, holding a rope in his hands.

Genny stood motionless. Although she might be able to get away, she would not leave Maggie. "Please do not take us back," she said simply.

"I have no intention of returning you to Aldred Keep," he said. "I do not wish to meet with your husband just yet."

Genny felt a short-lived rush of relief as his words penetrated her fear. Tristen was still alive! And he had finally come to rescue her.

Only now she was not at Aldred Keep, she thought with despair.

Thomas was obviously enjoying her horror and gleefully added, "I did, however, lessen his number of foes by one. Dear, sweet Beatrice has met with an untimely demise." He threw back his head in laughter as Genny gasped at his words. "Now come, my dear, you were not really all that fond of your aunt. I know she was not overly tolerant of you."

Genny's head was spinning. Aunt Beatrice, dead? True, they had never shared any closeness, but still the news of her death was unnerving.

Moving closer to her, the rope clenched tightly in one hand, Thomas grabbed Genny's wrist with the other. Reaching up with her free hand, she swiftly clawed three long slashes into his face with her nails. He instantly backhanded her, sending her head snapping at the force of the blow.

Maggie, who had been frozen in fear, set upon Thomas, hitting and kicking. He swiftly lashed out, sending her sprawling to the ground.

"You bastard!" screamed Genny.

"As much as I would like to continue our most enlightening conversation, we really must move on, *Countess*."

His ominous sneering caused Genny's heart to beat faster within her chest.

"Where are you taking us?" she demanded in a voice stronger than even she thought possible under the circumstances.

"It is of no concern to you."

"It most certainly is. I will not move from this

place," she declared. "You cannot possibly imagine that we will willingly go anywhere with you."

"I had expected you to defy me. It is the reason I am letting her live . . . for the time being," he said, inclining his head toward Maggie, who was struggling to her feet. "I am well aware of your less-than-compliant disposition."

Thomas quickly secured the rope around the older woman, then bound Genny to her, allowing only enough rope between them to permit walking.

Genny's stomach knotted with helpless fury and fear. "Why do you want to harm me?" she asked in a voice soft with bewilderment.

Thomas slowly moved closer to look her full in the eyes. "At one time I would have died for you. But you foolishly sealed your own fate when you so callously rejected me. Perhaps you would care to remind me again that you are the *Countess of Ravenswood*," he spat as he tightened the rope that bound her to Maggie.

Genny struggled, but her efforts were futile.

"I was content to let the past die until you came to Ravenswood. But you are just like her. Why could you not be content with my love? We were so happy together," he said, his voice trailing off strangely as he seemed to gaze not at but through her.

"Thomas, we were never together," protested Genny.

"Nay! Do not deny what we had, Kathryn!" Genny stumbled backward. The ferocity of his impassioned words was chilling. Worse, icy fear twisted within her as she realized that in his mind he had confused her with another.

"I have always loved you, Kathryn," Thomas said, moving slowly toward Genny. "There was a time when you said you loved me, too." Placing his cold hands on her throat, his thumbs gently traced the lines of her jaw. Then, as his vivid recollection of Kathryn's love blurred with her renunciation of that love, his fingers began to tighten around Genny's throat.

"How could you discard our love so easily?" he raged, squeezing harder.

Genny grabbed frantically at the large hands that were cutting off her breath. "Thomas," she gasped. "I'm not Kathryn!"

"I know who you are!" he said sharply, abruptly releasing her. "You are the *Countess of Ravenswood*," he snarled.

As Genny fought for breath, she tried to collect her thoughts. His confusion was alarming, his hostility terrifying. Genny could not imagine how Thomas had contained so much rage and pain for all these years. She knew only that something had unleashed his fury, and he had lost what must have been his fragile grip on reality.

"You are the countess," Thomas hissed again, "and your husband is the earl. And he will yet reap the rewards of his arrogance." His voice had lost its eerie, distant tone. His sanity, at least partially, had returned. But when he continued, his words were full of rage.

"Kathryn's fear of the earl caused her to rid

herself of our unborn child. The potion she took
killed her. For years I ignored his guilt, but
when he turned you against me, too, I knew I
must act. The mighty earl will soon endure the
agony of seeing what he loves suffer and die
before his very eyes, just as I watched my Kathryn die. Her death was slow and painful, and I
was unable to do anything to stop it. So, too,
will yours be. My only regret is that your husband will not live long enough afterward to
fully discover the depths of that agony. For he,
too, shall forfeit his life," spat Thomas as he
again fiercely tightened the rope that bound her
to Maggie.

"Nay, do not do this!"

Mounting his horse, Thomas threw back his
head in laughter. "Though it pleases me to see
you beg, you waste your breath." He leaned
down and brought his face close to hers. "I intend to show no mercy. You both must die."

"Nay! You have me. Can you not be content?"

His eyes raked her contemptuously. His
mouth curved into a sneer. "Content? He was
not satisfied till Kathryn was dead, and I will
not be *content* until he suffers the same torment
I have. Vengeance is mine!" Thomas pronounced with conviction as he gave a wrenching jerk to the rope, setting them in motion. He
was anxious to find a secure haven from which
he could exact his revenge.

Tristen and Alexander rode in taut silence,
uncertain and tense. Throughout the morning

Tristen had been splitting his men off into small groups, sending them searching in different directions. Now only he and Alexander remained. Despite all their efforts, Tristen was frantic with the fear that he might be too late to help Genny. He knew now that he could not live without her. Indeed, in the past, even when he had tried to cut her off from his life, she had remained foremost in his thoughts, and now it was ever so.

Alexander noted that Tristen rode with his hand pressed tightly to his injured side. His face was drawn, and beads of perspiration glistened on his forehead at the immense effort he exerted to stay in the saddle. Although no words passed between them, Alexander could guess at the mental and physical agonies his friend must be experiencing. And, tired himself after traveling for days at a grueling pace, he could only imagine what damage Tristen's demands were exacting on his already weakened body. His hope was that his friend would have the strength to face whatever awaited them at the end of their journey.

Chapter 37

Under the intense heat of the midday sun, Genny fought back another wave of nausea, but her stomach resisted all her efforts.

"Maggie, I am unwell." She barely had time to grit out the words between clenched teeth before falling to her knees to vomit.

Maggie pulled hard on the rope to alert Thomas to the situation.

Impatiently halting the horse, Thomas watched as the old woman knelt beside Genny and held her hair away from her face while she heaved uncontrollably. When Genny finally stopped retching, Thomas dismounted and grabbed her arm, dragging her to her feet. His eyes narrowed as he studied her pale face.

"What makes you sick?"

"I have not eaten since yesterday," she replied weakly, her stomach still churning.

"We move on," he commanded harshly.

"Nay, my lady is sick! She must rest," Maggie cried out, placing a protective arm on Genny's shoulder.

Thomas raised his hand as if to strike Maggie,

whose face was already bruised and swollen from the blow he had inflicted earlier.

"I am better now," Genny asserted quickly.

They proceeded in silence as Genny feebly tried to keep pace with Thomas, not wishing to cause him to vent any more of his anger on Maggie. Soon they approached a stream, and Thomas dismounted.

"Wash. You stink," he told Genny as he tied the rope that bound the two women's wrists securely to a tree whose branches extended over the water.

The cool water felt good as Genny splashed it onto her face and neck. When she finished bathing as best she could, she sat down, taking in deep breaths of the fresh air.

Maggie sat studying her before she moved closer, making sure Thomas, who had remained at a distance while Genny washed, was not within hearing.

"How far along are you, child?" she whispered.

She should have known Maggie would deduce the truth. She never missed anything. But Genny looked up fearfully in Thomas's direction, aware that her condition, in the face of his earlier revelation, could be of dangerous significance to him. She was relieved to see from his unchanged demeanor that he had not overheard Maggie.

"Did you think I couldn't tell? I've been with you since you were a babe. I would know if a hair was out of place," Maggie said in a hushed voice.

"Oh, Maggie," Genny breathed as she fought for control of her emotions, "I was not certain till I had been at Aldred Keep for some weeks. I fear that Tristen may never know of our child."

Maggie had no chance to respond as Thomas moved within hearing.

"Be done. We move on," he commanded.

Genny rose to her feet. And suddenly the waves of despair within her swelled into a towering wave of anger.

"You are mad!" she spat defiantly, her green eyes colliding with Thomas's vengeful black stare.

Outraged by her charge, Thomas struck her full force with the back of his hand. Genny slumped to the ground, blood trickling from the corner of her mouth.

"Nay!" shouted Maggie, stepping between the two to shield Genny.

Thomas laughed derisively before ordering, "Rouse her. We move on!"

Once revived, Genny managed, with Maggie's help, to walk for a considerable distance. However, in her exhausted state she had difficulty maintaining the relentless pace. Stumbling, she slipped to the hard ground.

"Get up!" growled Thomas as he yanked violently on the rope, causing it to cut deeper into Genny's wrists.

"I cannot go on," she replied weakly.

"Have mercy," pleaded Maggie. "She is unwell."

"I thought you were of a stronger constitution, *Countess*," he said, sneering down at her.

"I need but a few moments rest."

Staring into Genny's damp and ashen face, Thomas felt his anger falter momentarily. Even in her sickly state, she was a beauty, small and fragile. He dismounted, impatiently pushed Maggie aside, and untied Genny's wrists. He hesitated at the sight of the open wounds caused by the coarse rope.

"You will ride with me."

Genny had expected his touch to be rough, and, although it was not gentle, it was not with brutality that he lifted her and placed her in front of him on the large horse.

They resumed their pace as they rode in silence, Thomas holding tightly to Genny's waist, with Maggie trailing behind. Genny stiffened when Thomas pulled her closer to him, his hand brushing the underside of her breast. She felt his warm breath upon her neck as his lips snuggled next to her earlobe.

"It has been so long since we rode together," he whispered suggestively. "I have missed holding you, Kathryn." His hand moved up to cover her breast fully.

Repulsed by his touch, Genny shuddered. "Thomas!" she said harshly in an attempt to recall him to the present.

"Always you were so passionate for me," he said before placing his wet lips to her neck.

"Thomas! Stop!" she begged frantically while struggling to free herself from his grasp.

"I suggest you sit still, Lady Genny. 'Tis a

long fall to the ground,'' Thomas said, moving his hand back to her waist.

Although relieved that he had released her, Genny sat rigidly upright on the horse, trying to maintain some distance between herself and Thomas. Were it not for the present circumstances, she could almost feel pity for the man at the way Kathryn's cruel rejection and ultimate death had caused him to become so wildly embittered and blinded with vengeance.

Sadness flooded her as she thought of Tristen and how he, too, had been hurt by her cousin's betrayal. Kathryn, it seemed, had inflicted much pain and misery in her short life. Genny's heart ached for Tristen, knowing that the wounds he had sustained in the past had prevented him from returning the fathomless love she had for him.

For she now knew she had always loved him, and that was why she had withstood his temper, endured his false accusations, and welcomed his passion. During her marriage to this aloof and often insolent man, even through the moments of acute despair, her heart had recognized the love her mind had refused to acknowledge.

Her musings now brought her full circle. If she was ever to be with Tristen again, she must get free. The time had come for her to thwart Thomas's scheme . . . or die trying.

Chapter 38

It was nearing dusk when they entered a small clearing in the woods through which they had been traveling. Thomas, having some time ago noticed that his mount had developed a slight limp, halted his steed. He lowered Genny to her feet, then ordered the women to sit upon the ground while he assessed the extent of the animal's injury.

Settling awkwardly on the soft green grass, Genny turned her attention to Maggie, whose appearance was drawn and haggard from the punishment and pace they had been forced to endure. Leaning toward Maggie to comfort her, she halted as her palm scraped across the rough bark of a thick branch that lay in the tall grass.

Instinctively she curled her fingers around the object, keeping her eyes on Thomas, who was using his dagger to dislodge the stone that had made his animal lame. She cautiously pried the branch loose from the earth and tested it as best she could for strength, pleased to discover that it was reasonably sturdy and rather long.

Raising herself to her knees, maintaining her

grasp on the limb, Genny cast Maggie a conspiratorial glance, careful to keep the branch hidden behind her. Gradually she rose to her feet, hoping to cover the distance that separated her from Thomas without detection.

Becoming aware of the movement behind him, Thomas released his hold on the horse's hoof and turned toward the women, but he was unprepared for the sharp blow to his forearm, which caused the dagger to fall from his fingers.

In rapid succession Genny quickly claimed possession of the dagger and discarded the sturdy branch that had served to disarm Thomas. Brandishing the weapon bravely, she brought it up with deadly intent.

Thomas, however, dodged the attack expertly, avoiding contact with the sharp blade. He backed away and unsheathed his sword from his waist. An evil glint glimmered in his eyes as he advanced toward Genny, sword outstretched.

Maggie released a shrill, terrifying scream of horror and, fearing for Genny's life, angled her body between them just as Thomas lunged forward. The sharp blade of the sword pierced the fleshy part of Maggie's side.

Horrified at the injury to her beloved nursemaid, Genny faced her foe, determined to vanquish the ruthless fiend with only the small dagger and steadfast determination.

A scream permeated the silence of the woods through which Tristen and Alexander rode. After a startled glance at each other, they began racing through the dense forest.

As they entered the clearing, Tristen's heart lodged in his throat. Before him stood his wife, her eyes blazing as she held Thomas and his long sword at bay with only a small dagger.

"Kill me now, bastard! I'll not give you a chance to murder my husband," shouted Genny, her expression wild and fierce as she backed away from Thomas's raised sword.

"I won't kill you now, but you'll wish you were dead. I want you alive enough for him to see you suffer," snarled Thomas as he advanced upon her. "Perhaps you will even plead for mercy before you die."

Both Genny and Thomas were momentarily taken aback when the deep, familiar voice echoed loud and clear through the glen. "Prepare to meet your death, Thomas!"

Turning to confront the intruder, Thomas carelessly exposed his back to Genny. She lunged with the dagger, and this time her attack found its target.

Thomas howled in pain as the dagger sank into his left shoulder. Outraged, he spun back around, bringing his left arm full force against Genny's head, sending her sprawling to the ground.

Tristen's anger became a scalding fury when he saw Genny slump to the grass. Every muscle in his body was tense with rage as he advanced on the man.

The two opponents circled each other, both well aware of the other's skills in battle. Thomas lunged for Tristen's ribs on the right side, but Tristen swung hard with his sword, meeting his opponent's blade side-on. The force of the impact almost disarmed Thomas.

Furious, Thomas threw all his weight into his next thrust, attempting to obtain the upper hand. Tristen found his opening in the careless lunge and, bringing his sword up swiftly, cut a deep wound in Thomas's sword arm from elbow to shoulder. Thomas reeled away, staggering in pain.

Tristen's heart beat heavily in his chest. His breathing was ragged, and his wounded side throbbed from the exertion of the fight.

Thomas recovered quickly. Turning back, he once more faced his opponent, blood running profusely down his injured arm onto his sword. His strength was ebbing, but he noticed that Sinclair, too, appeared to be weakening. His mouth quirked in a sardonic smile as he observed Sinclair's labored breathing. It was obvious from the effort it took to wield his sword that the man was not yet recovered from the injury Thomas had dealt him weeks ago. Thomas had presumed aright that the earl would not have the patience to let himself heal before he attempted to locate his wife. But, aware that Sinclair's weakened condition alone would not assure him victory, Thomas sought to bait him into a making a mistake.

"Fool! You would fight for a whore? All your women moan for me!"

"Liar," Tristen answered, unperturbed. And he swiftly turned the taunt against Thomas.

"Though you would only be familiar with the grunts of a slut after having lain with Kathryn."

Blinded with rage, Thomas lunged. Raising his sword, Tristen took the thrust on the end of his blade, causing Thomas to lose his balance and tumble to the ground. Before Tristen could press his advantage, however, Thomas's feet snaked around Tristen's ankles and sent the earl toppling down beside him.

Tristen felt excruciating pain and then warm blood soaking his tunic as Thomas's sword pierced his barely healed side.

Retracting his sword with a vigorous jerk, Thomas raised himself above Sinclair and, hoisting his weapon high above his head, prepared to deliver one last, deadly blow.

Darkness threatened to envelop Tristen as he struggled to rise. The rapid loss of blood had drained his stamina and with blurry vision he saw Thomas standing over him, bloody sword poised to strike him a fatal blow.

Genny and Alexander had observed the battle helplessly while attempting to stanch the flow of blood from Maggie's wound. But now, noting Tristen's disadvantage, Alexander quickly rose to his feet, his hand on the hilt of his sword.

But Genny had already rushed forward to retrieve Tristen's fallen sword, and, heaving it high above her head, faltering only slightly under its weight, she brought it down on the back of Thomas's skull. The sickening sound of ripping flesh and splintering bone was followed by a moment of absolute silence and arrested activity before Thomas's body fell to the hard-packed ground, where convulsions continued to rack his mangled form.

The sword slowly slipped from Genny's hands to the ground, its overwhelming weight and size now an impossible burden. She began to shake uncontrollably, and Alexander moved swiftly to gather her into his arms.

Such was the setting as Christopher and Elizabeth rode into the clearing. Quickly, both dismounted.

"Sweet Jesu!" exclaimed Christopher as he looked at Thomas's distorted form lying in a pool of blood that was rapidly soaking the earth beneath him.

Elizabeth gently took a trembling Genny from Alexander.

"It's all right now, Genny. He is dead," she murmured in soothing tones.

Genny stood frozen in horror, unable to take her eyes from the mesmerizing sight of the now inert body of the man who had spent years nurturing hatred for her husband, who had just now nearly killed him. Dear Lord, Tristen had to live! Released from her daze, Genny dropped to his side, her heart pounding at the sight of his apparently lifeless body.

"Tristen!" she breathed. Kneeling beside him, she gathered him into her arms, openly weeping.

Tristen's eyelids fluttered as he felt the warm tears fall on his cheek. "Genny . . ." he rasped.

"Oh, Tristen, I feared he would kill you," she cried.

Christopher glanced at the prone body of Thomas and back to his brother. "You are a lucky man, Tristen. That is a most remarkable wife you have," he said in a voice filled with admiration.

Tristen looked full into Genny's tear-streaked face.

"I love you," he declared softly before slipping into darkness.

Chapter 39

Tristen survived, and after returning to Ravenswood, Genny spent all her time and energy in the constant care of him. She never left his bedside, save to check on Maggie, who was healing nicely in another chamber.

For days, through his raging fever, Tristen thrashed restlessly, calling her name over and over as Genny attempted to calm him with soothing words of reassurance.

When at last Tristen awoke, it was to the sight of Genny sleeping, slumped forward in the chair beside him. Slowly he reached out and stroked the golden hair that streamed down her shoulders. Genny raised her head at the soft touch, and tears of relief welled in her eyes and spilled down her pale cheeks.

"Genny . . ." he said, his parched throat closing upon further words.

Genny quickly poured him a goblet of fresh water and, holding his head, brought the drink to his lips. Tristen drank heartily before leaning back to rest against the pillow.

"Genny, my love, I have caused you many tears during our short marriage. I am so sorry." His rasping voice, barely a throaty whisper, was full of contrition. His callused fingers tenderly brushed away a tear that trailed down her cheek. His gaze, as soft as a caress, traveled over her face and searched her eyes.

Genny reached up and laced her fingers with his, holding them against her cheek.

"Oh, Tristen, these are tears of joy. I have been so worried," she said, her voice low and trembling.

"I promise I shall never again be the cause of an unhappy moment in your life," he pledged solemnly.

"I will not hold you to that, husband," Genny murmured, half laughing, half crying as she recalled their numerous arguments.

"My word is my oath," he declared. "Do you doubt my veracity?"

Amused that he was so easily provoked, Genny baited him a trifle.

"Does this mean, milord, that you no longer object to my dancing with other men, or riding Apollo astride, or practicing the longbow, or—"

"Enough," cried Tristen in feigned horror. "Perhaps, milady, I should reconsider spending my life with such an unmanageable woman."

"Nay, milord. If you will consider overlooking my eccentricities, I shall consider overlooking your overbearing, arrogant, domineering manner."

"You forgot 'insensitive' and 'stubborn,' my heart." A glint of amusement shone in his eyes.

"Oh, nay, milord. I merely summarized, in deference to your weakened state," she countered, an incipient smile trembling on her lips.

Tristen silently gazed at Genny. Her twinkling green eyes were full of life, and their unquenchable warmth compelled him to relinquish his heart to her.

"Genny," he said, his voice hoarse with emotion, "despite my foolish determination to prevent it, you released me from the agony of the past the night you danced into my life."

Genny smiled, remembering his enraged astonishment at discovering it was his wife who danced on the tabletop in the knights' hall. Her gaze fell guiltily to the faint scar on his forearm from the wound she had inflicted with her dagger that night, then traveled up his arm to the bandage that was wrapped around his massive, muscular chest. Fear, stark and vivid, glittered in her eyes.

"I nearly lost you, my love," she said in a voice choked with tears.

Tristen's fingers, still entwined with hers, tightened reassuringly.

At her words *my love*, his heart swelled with a feeling he had never thought to experience. Perhaps he had not completely damaged their chance for the kind of loving union he now longed to share with her.

"Genny, that is the first time you have ever said *love* to me," he noted tentatively.

Genny did not respond immediately. Could

Tristen possibly have the same need to hear the words of love that she longed for?

"Tristen—" she began.

"Nay, Genny," he interrupted, placing his fingers gently on her lips. "Please, let me speak." He gathered his considerable courage to place his heart, his very life, in her hands to either reject or embrace.

"Genny, my sweet Genny, I love you," he said thickly. "If it takes the rest of my life, I will do all within my power to make you believe that, and I will pray to someday win your love in return."

"Oh, Tristen," murmured Genny, "I already love you. Till the end of time I will love you. And then I will love you more."

Mindful of his injuries, Genny moved carefully into Tristen's embrace, sighing contentedly as his mouth moved over hers, devouring its softness.

Ending the kiss, Tristen looked deeply into her eyes. "Genny," he said huskily, "I once vowed something very foolish. I told you that you would never truly be my wife. I was wrong. You are not only my wife, you are my life. And from this day forward, we will begin anew."

Genny's eyes sparkled with promise and quiet joy as she studied her husband's handsome visage. Then silently, in affirmation, she placed her hand in his.

Chapter 40

At last the priest closed his prayer book and stood silent, bowing his head. Genny walked forward to stand beside the open grave. There were tears in her eyes, and she felt a genuine, wrenching sorrow.

Scattering the symbolic first handful of earth over the coffin, she bade her final farewell to her once-beloved cousin.

Philip, in his remorse, had chosen to take his own life. In the letter he'd left behind, he had begged Genny's forgiveness for his part in her abduction. Genny's mourning and prayers were not for the Philip who had yielded to his mother's ruthless plot to claim Montburough, but for the Philip who would ever live in her childhood memories. And it was in memory of that Philip that she had had his body brought to Ravenswood for burial, that his final resting place might be nearby her.

When the priest murmured the final words, Genny stepped back into the shelter of Tristen's arm. Though still pale and weak, he had insisted on escorting her this day.

"Perhaps Aldred has at last found peace," he now said comfortingly to his pale and tearful wife. After a moment he offered her his arm. With the priest trailing behind them, they began walking back to Ravenswood.

Genny sensed Tristen's fatigue as they climbed the steps to their chambers, and she insisted he lie down and rest. Moments later she slipped into bed beside him. Comforted by the steady rise and fall of his chest as he slept, she soon joined him in slumber.

Sometime later she opened her eyes to find Tristen sitting up in bed and gazing at her.

"What are you doing?" she asked, smiling up at him.

"Watching you sleep," he replied softly while running his fingers through her silky hair.

Genny savored his touch. She had not afforded herself the luxury of sharing his bed since his injury, resisting his insistence that having her lie next to him would hasten his recovery.

Now he leaned down and kissed her, his mouth warm and hungry. Wrapping her arms around his neck, she pulled him to her as her body shivered with anticipation.

"Tristen, your wound," she protested through her ragged breathing.

"What wound?" he asked, nibbling his way down her throat.

Genny gasped as he fixed his mouth over one nipple through her light gown. His hand traveled up her thigh, and he swiftly pulled the gown off over her head. The fire caught hold of them as his fingers feverishly moved over her body, stopping as one large hand splayed across her abdomen.

When he paused, Genny opened her eyes and met her husband's questioning gaze. She held her breath.

"Oh, Genny," he breathed. "Oh, my God . . . a baby?"

She nodded.

"But . . . how?"

"The same way it has happened since the beginning of time," she replied as she lightly traced his lips with her finger. "Are you happy?"

"Happy? Oh, Genny!" He buried his face in her hair as tears of elation overwhelmed him. Raising his head, he asked with excitement, "When, love? When?"

"December, I think."

"Jesu, why did you wait so long to tell me?" he demanded.

Genny laughed openly at his indignation.

"Husband, we have only been reunited for a little while. With so much going on, I have hardly had time."

"Do you think it will be a boy or a girl?" Tristen asked, running his hand over her belly again.

"Do you have a preference?"

"Nay, love. Besides, I am sure we will have many babes—boys *and* girls," he hinted as he captured her lips once again in a proud, possessive kiss.

His ardor was surprisingly, touchingly, restrained, but Genny had been denied too long. Her desire for him overrode all else. Her thoughts fragmented as her hands and lips began a hungry search of his body. He groaned at her fervent ministrations and rolled carefully atop her, pressing her beneath him. Genny trembled as his manhood brushed her thighs.

"Oh, please, Tristen," she pleaded. "It has been so long." Her voice quavered with barely checked passion as he slowly moved his hips.

"Ah, Genny love, I burn for you," he rasped.

"Let me feel your fire, then," she challenged. Her body arched toward him, and gently, mindful of his child deep within her, he slowly eased into her, the heat of her moist womanhood threatening his self-control.

Genny moved her hips, wanting more. Wordlessly, she pleaded, clutching at him with her hands, showering his neck and face with fevered kisses. When she grasped his flanks to urge him deeper, it was finally his undoing. With a strangled groan he slid completely within her, filling her. She shuddered and held him tightly, and, in exquisite harmony, they began to move in a rhythm as old as time.

Tristen's ardor soared as he realized he was loving not only his wife but also the mother of his child. He worshiped her with his every thrust, raising her to the pinnacle of desire as he whispered her name over and over. They fused in a hot blaze of splendor that seared away all their past doubts and fears, crying out their devotion to each other in love's passionate surrender.

Epilogue

"Relax, love," Tristen murmured into Genny's ear as he watched her slender hands clutching nervously at her gown. Genny smiled weakly in response as they entered the private chamber.

King Edward and Queen Eleanor sat in silence as they observed the small family being escorted into the room.

No wonder this knight had fallen so hard, reflected the king. Lady Genevieve was indeed a beautiful woman. Small but exquisite, she held herself proudly.

"Your Majesties," Tristen said, addressing the royal couple. "May I present my wife, Lady Genevieve." His eyes gleamed with pride.

Genny curtsied most proficiently despite her wobbly legs.

Edward stood and offered his hand to Lady Genevieve. "Rise, my dear. We have eagerly waited to receive you," declared the king earnestly.

"I apologize, sire, for our delay. However,

many unforeseen events prevented our travel," Genny offered.

At those words a large wail burst forth from the squirming bundle Tristen held. Queen Eleanor offered her arms, and Tristen gently laid his son into them.

"And I assume this is one of those 'unforeseen events' that could not wait," the queen said, gazing at the babe.

"Aye, Your Majesty," said Genny, blushing.

"Stephen Christopher Alexander Sinclair. Our firstborn," proclaimed Tristen proudly.

"My goodness, such a large name for one so small," said the queen, laughing.

"Dear Lady Genevieve," said the king, patting her hand, "I do so hope this means that you hold no ill will toward me for the choice of your husband."

"Nay, sire. I am very content," replied Genny, gazing lovingly at Tristen.

"Good, and I am glad to hear your father is doing well. Lord Richard has long been a loyal servant to the crown."

"He sends his highest regards, sire."

"And I to him," Edward countered as the child Queen Eleanor held cooed softly in her arms. "He must be very proud of you, my dear. I hear your courage would rival that of many of my knights."

Genny shifted nervously at his proclamation.

"I think, however, that it would be wise to keep your husband at Ravenswood, close to you, nonetheless."

"Sire?" questioned Tristen, unsure of Edward's intent.

"Sinclair, I am not dismissing you. I am merely giving you an opportunity to spend more time with your lovely bride and son. That does not mean I will not call on you if the need arises, but I think you would be, shall we say, more content to preserve and protect those at Ravenswood."

Edward smiled broadly, delighted with the outcome of this union, both for the throne and for the couple before him.

"Thank you, sire!" exclaimed Genny while her husband stood in mute surprise. "We are indeed grateful."

Queen Eleanor smiled warmly as the couple gazed tenderly, lovingly, excitedly, at each other. "It is fit," she declared, "that two who are so strong, so courageous, and at times so impetuous should produce such a babe."

At the pair's perplexed glance, she raised the child above her skirt. "I fear young Stephen has soaked the royal gown," she said, her musical laughter echoing through the chamber as the king's loyal knight blushed deep scarlet and his wife quickly reached for the babe.